W9-AAE-511

dying for dana

dying
for
dana

jim patton

A Tom Doherty Associates Book *New York*

DYING FOR DANA

Copyright © 2003 by Jim Patton

This book is printed on acid-free paper.

A Forge Book
Published by Tom Doherty Associates, LLC
175 Fifth Avenue
New York, NY 10010

www.tor.com

Forge® is a registered trademark of Tom Doherty Associates, LLC.

Library of Congress Cataloging-in-Publication Data
Patton, Jim, 1953–
    Dying for Dana / Jim Patton.—1st ed.
        p. cm.
    "A Tom Doherty Associates book."
    ISBN 0-765-30649-2 (acid-free paper)
    1. Public prosecutors—Fiction. 2. Victims of violent crimes—Fiction. 3. Portland
(Or.)—Fiction. 4. Robbery—Fiction. I. Title.

PS3566.A8256D95 2003
813'.6—dc21

                                                                    2003054183

First Edition: November 2003

Printed in the United States of America

0 9 8 7 6 5 4 3 2 1

For Mom—inspiration and role model, conscience and support. You're the most.

acknowledgments

All my gratitude to Philip Spitzer, class act, for perseverance above and beyond the call.

Bottomless thanks to Jim McIntyre—dude, DA *supremo* and the brains behind this creation—for the bottomless wit and wisdom, and for paying all the bar tabs a starving *artiste* couldn't pay.

My life to Elisa, of course, for whom no words suffice.

part one

saturday night, may 12

"Enough of this damn smoke and noise," Roop says, even though it's only a few minutes past eleven. "Let's go out to my house. A little pool, a little single-malt, Classic Sports Network on the big-screen, dancing girls . . ."

"Sounds good to me," Highwire says.

Not to Max. "I'll pass. I'll stick here."

"Aw, come on," Highwire says. "You not glad to see me? Now that I'm not a baller anymore, I'm nobody?"

"It's not that. And give me a little credit—it was never about you being a pro ballplayer."

"Come on, then," Roop says. "What, you got a curfew? Or you just getting too old to party?"

Roop owns the bar, the Veritable Quandary, an upscale spot in downtown Portland, a favorite of lawyers and TV people and moneymen. It's a few blocks from the courthouse and Max started dropping in after work during his second divorce. Dropping in and staying for hours—drowning his sorrow, halfheartedly scoping out women. Roop still poured drinks back then and Max sat at the bar and they talked or didn't, depending on Max's state. Roop always knew when to talk, when to listen, and when to steer clear altogether. A friendship happened.

It's been years now. Max still spends too much time at the Quandary. Roop doesn't tend bar anymore but he's here most nights, circulating, keeping an eye on his staff. Doing his legendary Lothario thing with the women.

Saturday nights he usually stays until closing, so he can take the cash receipts home and stash them in his floor safe until the Monday-morning deposit, but tonight Highwire Harris showed up for the first time in a while and Roop's ready to take off.

"Don't wanna hang with a TV personality?" he asks Max, meaning Highwire. "Before the network snags him and he forgets us Portland pipsqueaks?"

"Sheeeeit." Highwire's smiling. He likes hearing it, likes thinking his playoff analysis on Channel 2 could lead to the big-time, but he probably knows better. If he's watched tapes of himself—stuttering, stammering, misusing words—he's got to. A pretty face and the fact that you played pro ball will get you on TV in your hometown, but that's about all.

"I'm just not up for it," Max says. "I'll have another drink and head home."

"We don't amuse you? You'd rather stay here and pule?" *Pyool.* Roop loves using it. "He's still puling, Highwire."

"Puling. Uh-huh."

"Over the great Paige Prescott. What do you think?"

"Man, I don't know. Guess it's his own business. But I do hate seein' my man down like this, yeah."

"Well, I keep telling him she's just another chick. Some good qualities, great legs, but she's got her *foibles,* as one of my honeys used to say, just like everyone else. Just 'cause she did the dumping doesn't mean *he's* got the problem, right? Maybe it's her. Good-looking as she is, she's never made it work with anyone either."

Max groans. "Look, I came down here to have a drink, not to get into all this."

"Hey, I'm sorry. I'm on your side, only reason I'm saying what I'm saying. I'm just saying you need to quit dwelling on it, quit *thinking* so much. Take it from me, there's a lot to be said for being shallow."

It works for Roop. In his early thirties he fell into the perfect situation, for him, after years tending bar at the Shake, *Rose City Review*'s Bartender of the Year seven years in a row: got some well-heeled friends to help him buy the VQ, turned it into a downtown institution, bought out his partners and moved out from behind the bar to be simply lord and master of the place, hanging out in his linen pants and cashmere sweaters, holding court, picking and choosing women for brief, superficial romances, the only kind he's ever wanted. He skis in the winter, takes his boat up and down the Willamette and the Columbia in summer, takes nice vacations in all seasons. His version of the good life, and not a bad version.

He says, "I just mean you need to get over this, Maxwell. Get another babe and forget Prescott."

"It'll happen. Or not. Either way."

"I told you who to call. You still got her number?"

"Yeah, but I'm not in a hurry. I'll probably see her in here sometime."

"Babe like that won't be on the market long."

Highwire: "Who y'all talking about?"

"Blonde I was with last month," Roop says. "Dana. Maxie noticed her a while back and asked me about her . . . when he was still with Prescott, so what does that tell you? Tells me he knows a tasty morsel when he sees it."

"If she's so tasty," Max says, "why'd you drop her?"

"You gotta ask? They get serious, I move on. No reflection on her. Anyway"—to Highwire—"she's free since about a week ago. I told her I've got a friend she might like and it turned out she's noticed our boy, too. Knew who he was when I said the name. Knows he's the big DA."

Highwire: "So, man, what you waitin' on?"

Max: "Look, why don't you guys just go have a good time, leave me here to pule in peace?"

# # #

He's not just puling about Paige (not only), he's thinking about the long trail of failed relationships. Charming guy, people say, funny and smart and all; and no, getting together with women has never been a problem. Staying with them is the problem. Sometimes he's the dumper, but more often dumped. And they always say the same things. Basically, that they wind up getting too much "Max Faxx" and too little Max Travis.

Max Faxx. From the Sergeant Friday line on *Dragnet*, long ago: *Just the facts, ma'am.* McGowan came up with it the year Max took over Violent Crimes and made a name as the so-called prosecutor's prosecutor—trying and winning seven murder cases in nine months, including two that looked next to unwinnable going in. Max Faxx, mythical DA: cracking cases on the slightest evidence, swaying judges in trial, befuddling defense attorneys, reducing juries to tears, leaping tall buildings in a single bound. Name in the paper, face on TV.

Great. What does it get him?

I'm sorry, Max. You're a great guy, very talented, born to do what you do; the DA's office is lucky to have you, victims' families are lucky you're working on behalf of their loved ones. But being with you isn't easy.

When you've got a trial going on you're preoccupied, you're irritable. Even when you're not, you're always busy. Even when you're not at work your mind is there. The pagers, the cell phones, calls at all hours. I need more of you and I don't see it happening.

He used to think he could change, but apparently not. Friends speculate that maybe deep down he doesn't really want to: doesn't want to be tied down with one person, so he keeps the pedal to the metal at work, knowing he'll eventually be cut loose again.

He doesn't necessarily agree. Once upon a time, maybe, but he's past forty now and the thought of getting old alone appeals only to the Roops of the world, who are few.

Paige didn't shed any light in their last conversation. Same stuff he's heard before, and when he asked "What else? There's got to be something else about me," she said there didn't have to be anything else, the Max Faxx manifestations were plenty and she was simply looking out for herself, looking for something more.

That was a jolt, losing someone he'd come to believe was the one. Maybe he *is* puling.

He flags his waiter and orders another Max Blaster, the power-house combo of Rumplemintz and Jaegermeister that Roop con-cocted on one of those long nights years ago.

# # #

He should have gone with Roop and Highwire.

No, he should have gone home.

Somewhere. Anywhere. Instead he grabbed the Max Travis Memorial Barstool and now he's flirting ridiculously with a dim-bulb blonde who bumped him a few minutes ago, spilled part of his drink and, used the opportunity to introduce herself—Rhonda, a perfect Rhonda—and hasn't stopped yakking and shoving her tits in his face since. Too much makeup, too much perfume. Proud to let him know she works at Snap!, the pseudo-hip ad agency that does the inane Beauregard Auto Group spots, among others. Yak-yak-yak about TV shows he's never heard of, about the endless rain, about blind-drunk Channel 8 anchor Mark Pusman, draped all over a woman at the other end of the bar. Leaning in close to make herself heard over the din, her perfume stinging his nostrils. Is he going to see the Dalai Lama at Pioneer Square tomorrow? She is; she's looking for more inner peace, isn't everyone? She considers herself a very spiritual person even though she's living in this fast-paced, superficial, material world. . . .

Max is ready to bail, get home, go to bed. He cracks a couple jokes so as not to seem rude, but Lord, her laugh! Laugh? It's a bray, a whinny, a bleat! He's got to get out.

Maybe she senses it, because she thrusts her tits at him again and says she's good at reading people and he seems like a man who knows what he wants. Like *her*, is what she means.

Take her up on it? Have tawdry sex that probably won't be very good anyway, then have to deal with the aftermath? Forget it. Go home.

But she's leaning in. "What do *you* do?"

"Me? I'm, uh, a cowboy."

"What, in Portland? No way. Where, out toward the coast? But those aren't cowboys out there, are they? They're what, logging guys? Logmen?"

"Loggers."

"Right. But hey, you can be a cowboy if you want."

"All right. And I've gotta saddle up, missy, and get back to the bunkhouse." Looking for Louie behind the bar, ready to pay up and leave.

She leans close again. "Cowboy? You like to ride 'em, cowboy?"

Max nearly bursts out laughing. "Darlin', I got roundup in the mornin', I gotta get my shut-eye. You'll pardon me this time, won't you, ma'am?"

"Cowboy doesn't like a buckin' bronco? Don't like a rootin'-tootin' ride?"

At the very moment he's about to reach for his pager and pretend he's got a call, it beeps for real.

And everything changes. As soon as he sees Stormin' Norman's number he knows it's serious, probably murder; there's no other reason the assistant DA calls Max, the VCU boss, at this time of night, Saturday night. Someone's life is changed out there in Multnomah County somewhere, maybe a lot of lives are, and like Clark Kent turning into Superman, loser-at-love Max Travis becomes super-prosecutor Max Faxx, man on a mission.

He slides through the crowd and out to the sidewalk for some quiet, punching in Norman's number.

"You rang?"

"I rang," Norman says. "A shooting, most likely a murder by now. I know you're in court Monday so I called Witty, he's on his way. But I thought you might want to go too."

"Yeah? Why? If Witty's on it I'll just get along home. I've had a couple, anyway."

"You at the VQ?"

" 'Course."

"See Roop?"

"He was here before."

"But he left," Stormin' says, as if he'd been here himself and seen Roop walk out.

"What's up? Yeah, he left a while ago with Highwire Harris."

"What's up is that Harris is at St. Vincent's ER with part of his face blown off, probably dead by now. It happened at Roop's house."

"*What?*"

# # #

The upscale Raleigh Hills neighborhood, normally so serene, is buzzing at midnight. Yellow crime-scene tape is strung around Roop's front yard. Patrol cars in the driveway, detectives' bland Chevys on the street, the lab techs' state cars, vans from three TV stations. Neighbors milling around under the streetlights in pajamas, bathrobes, sweats, and the uniform cops advising them there's nothing to see so they might as well go home.

Max swings into the driveway next door, crosses the soggy lawn, hops over the tape, flashes his ID at the youthful cop at the door and walks into the house he knows so well.

The action is upstairs. Voices. People on the landing outside the game room. He takes the carpeted steps two at a time, booziness gone now, adrenaline pumping. At the top he bumps into Bob Peterson, detective and pal.

"You too?" Peterson says. "Witty's already here. Upstairs. It happened up there." Third floor, which was an attic until Roop spent fifty grand turning the front end into an office, the back into a guest suite.

"How's Harris?"

"Alive when they took him out of here. In surgery at St. V's now. We don't know."

"What the hell happened?"

"Home invasion, according to Roop. They're all the rage, right?"

Right. Breaking into unoccupied homes is too risky these days, with ever-evolving high-tech security—better to ring the doorbell when someone's home, stick a gun in their face, and make your demand. You're not supposed to shoot. You're not supposed to have to.

On up to the third floor. In the office Roop's standing with Charlie Witty while the lead detectives, Koontz and Berm, coordinate the crime-lab crew, ID techs, photographer, videographer. There's a huge bloodstain on the Oriental rug near the streetside wall and a spatter on the ceiling where it slopes down low.

Max asks Roop, "You all right?"

"Considering what it could be, yeah."

"What the hell happened?"

"Two jokers wanted money." Roop's shaken. Mr. Cool, always, but clearly working at it right now. "We were down there shooting pool, having a glass. Someone rang the bell and I went down. Figured you'd changed your mind and come out after all. But it's these two jokers wearing masks, waving guns, pushing me back. The one had a witch mask on, said he knew I had a safe and they wanted the money. The other one, big guy with a Donald Duck mask on, looked up and saw Highwire on the landing and went bonzo. Screaming at him to get the hell downstairs, *move* it. Highwire came down and the guy kept harassing him, nigger this and nigger that, fucking lunatic. I brought 'em up here, right to the safe, but this lunatic kept screaming at Highwire, nigger this and that, something about Highwire and white women, I don't know. Waving his piece all over. I got down and got into the safe, with this other guy jabbing *his* piece in my back. I got the money into the bag they brought and they were about to tie us up. My guy told me to get on my belly and put my hands behind me—meanwhile he's screaming at the lunatic to cool it, cool it, cool it, but the lunatic's just cussing Highwire. Then . . . Man, I couldn't believe it. First word Highwire said the whole time: 'What's your trouble, mister? You're gettin' what you came for,' something like that." Roop's eyes swing to the bloodstain on the rug.

"I can't believe it. That's all he said, and this maniac *lost* it. 'What's my *trouble?*'—and then this blast. I mean a blast. I don't think my guy could believe it either, the one starting to tie me up. He's screaming 'What the hell? What the *hell?*' Then they took off and I looked over and I couldn't believe it, blood everywhere and Highwire lying there with his face a mess like you've never seen. . . ."

# # #

Downstairs later, feathers get ruffled. Roop refuses to give the detectives the names of everyone who might know he's got a safe in the house.

"It wasn't anyone I know who did this. What, you don't know anything at all from this whole scene? These bunglers didn't leave a single trace?"

"Nothing yet," Koontz tells him. "People are still out interviewing your neighbors. One lady, Mrs. Gibadlo, thinks she might've heard a car taking off—but that's all, and she was half-asleep and doesn't even know what time it would've been."

"Well, that's great. Excellent."

"So there's nowhere to start except with the people who know you have a home safe."

"I'm telling you, none of them would've done this." Roop looks to Max for support.

Max can't give him more than a shrug. "Bill, listen. We can't be sure none of them would do it. You can't be sure one of them didn't at least share information with someone *they* know, intentionally or by accident. We gotta start somewhere."

"Look, I heard their voices and they weren't anyone I know. And I'll be damned if I'll put people through police interrogations when I know good and well they can't help."

Koontz: "You'd rather kiss off the money? What'd you say it was, thirty thousand? And how about Harris? He's your friend, but you won't help us out?"

"If I thought—"

"Bill," Max says, "you're wasting time. They'll get the names. Witty'll drag you in with a grand-jury subpoena and you'll have to talk."

"Grand jury?"

"I'd drag you in too. Look, save everyone the trouble. Give 'em a list. Meanwhile, you guys can start with me," Max tells Koontz. "I know about the safe."

# # #

Jack Nitzl, moron of the year. Whatever made him think to do this? And with a crazy like Nicky Bortolotti!

Nicky *shoots* the guy! The guy didn't do a thing but Nicky blew him away!

As if that weren't bad enough, Dana saw them leaving. The last thing Jack expected. Supposedly she wasn't even seeing the guy anymore, Roop, but they came flying out of the house, across the front yard—the street dark, dead, so it seemed, but the instant before Jack started down the hill he noticed some movement to the left, fifty, sixty feet away, someone on the sidewalk, under the streetlight, coming this way . . . Dana!

They tore down the hill toward the Jetta Nicky had stolen for the occasion. In the car they pulled off the masks and Jack stuffed them in a garbage bag while Nicky wiped the bloody gun on the front of his sweatshirt. They yanked the gloves off, threw them in the bag, then Nicky wriggled out of the sweatshirt . . . glancing down at his prized jean jacket and saying how smart he'd been to put the sweatshirt on over it, otherwise he'd have to get rid of it.

Jack wondered if Nicky had seen Dana. Pretty sure he hadn't, or he'd have blown her away too.

"Sonofabitch," the fool kept muttering, "black sonofabitch . . ." And then exploded when Jack asked why the hell he shot the guy. "Sonofabitch deserves what he gets if he's dumb enough to yap when I got the gun!" Slammed the car into gear and screeched out from the curb, probably waking up everyone within a mile. "Anybody smarts off to me that way's gonna wish they didn't! This jungle bunny especially!"

"He didn't smart off! How cranked-up *are* you, man? I said none of that meth tonight!"

Nicky swerving back to the curb then, slamming to a stop, turning and grabbing Jack's throat with one of his gnarly grease-monkey hands: "Eat me, Jack! No jungle bunny gonna mouth off to me like that! Asking me my *problem!*" Then screeching off again, leaving rubber.

Losing it again as they crossed the Hawthorne Bridge a few minutes later. Jack asked him for his gun, meaning to fling it into the Willamette along with the trash bag. Nicky ignored him. "Come *on,* we've gotta ditch it," Jack snapped—and suddenly the fool turned and screamed at him to back off, he was keeping the gun, he'd get rid of it later, it couldn't be traced to him anyway, he won it on a bet. . . .

#

One-ten A.M. now. Almost thirty thousand dollars on Jack's kitchen table, stacks of smoothed-out tens, twenties, fifties, hundreds. And Nicky wants his share. Wants it right now, and gets hot when Jack suggests he take part of it now and pick up the rest some other time.

"I'll take it *all* now, Jackpot. Mine's mine, you just take care'a your own."

Jack doesn't want to argue, not when Nicky's tweaking on methamphetamine. They say the stuff's guaranteed to make anyone violent, and look what happened already. But he doesn't like the idea of this nutcase loose with ten grand, either. He'll go spreading it around like his hero Edward G. Robinson did in his beloved *Little Caesar*, draw all kinds of attention.

Christ, this *Little Caesar* fixation of his! Jack caught the show on AMC one night and couldn't believe it. A million movies, a million guys to model yourself on, and Nicky's stuck on this cartoon character from what, 1930? A thug from the sticks who goes to the big town, takes over the underworld . . . then *loses everything and winds up dead because he's got the sense of a potted plant!* Nicky must have fallen asleep early, because all he got out of it was Robinson's slicked-back hair and swagger and tough talk out of the side of his mouth. He doesn't realize that Rico—Little Caesar—made it to the top by being shrewd, careful, not just cold-blooded. He'll go blowing money on booze and meth, never mind that Rico was so careful he wouldn't even drink a glass of Champagne at a banquet the gang held in his honor. He'll shoot his mouth off to impress this whore he's infatuated with, never mind that Rico considered women risky business. He'll probably brag to his meth-freak buddies about shooting Highwire Harris, retired basketball pro, the pride of Portland.

"Listen to me," Jack says. "We know what your cut is—ten grand almost, let's call it ten even. I'm not trying to rip you off, all right? But please just take part of it now and get the rest later. Please." Trying to be nice, wary of the madness in the fool's eyes and his gun lying on the table within easy reach. "We've gotta be cool now. Lay low. Don't go spreading money around, don't do anything different. Go to work, do what we always do. Understand? Cops're gonna be all over this—we gotta be cool and let it pass. Trust me, all right?"

Fat chance. Even as he speaks, Nicky grabs the stack of hundreds and starts counting: *Two for you, one for me, two for you . . .*

Jack tries again: "Man, just take part of it now, please! A couple grand—"

"A couple? Look, I didn't help you out so's you could turn around and hold back my cut."

Help out? He thinks he helped out? By killing someone?

Jack was out of his mind to set it in motion. In forty-two years he's never been in a fistfight, much less fooled around with guns, but Dana lets on about her boyfriend having a safe with a bunch of cash in it and he hatches this plan, and needs someone who can help him pull it off. . . .

He was out of his mind.

Scared to death, anyway. Definitely that, after the Russians drove by the car lot Thursday afternoon with guns blazing, shattering the plate-glass office window and putting holes in three Beamers and a Lexus. He was scared enough to play dumb when the cops showed up ten minutes later with Vlasitch and two of his boys in handcuffs. "Never seen 'em before," Jack said, feeling the Vlasitch evil eye on him. "No idea why they'd come around here shooting." "Well, they did," the cop said. "An individual across the street called in and ID'd their vehicle. We stopped 'em and they gave us this '*Nyet, nyet,* no understand' act, but the artillery was under the seat, still warm." "Sorry," Jack said, "I don't know 'em." But Friday morning he was outside sweeping up glass when Vlasitch came by with his nose out of joint, like it was Jack's fault the cops had taken them downtown and charged them with unlawful possession of weapons, unlawful use, attempted assault. Jack asked what the hell was wrong with him anyway, shooting up the lot over a piddly eight grand Jack owed him. *We've been doing business for how long? . . . but all of a sudden you think I'd try to stiff you?*

As if you could reason with Vlasitch. Even without drugs the guy's crazier than Nicky, and a stone killer. Everyone knows he blew up the guy over in Vancouver last year, even though the cops still can't hang it on him. The Russians made sure the word got around.

Vlasitch didn't want to kill Jack, of course, he just wanted what Jack owed him for four stolen cars. But with these lunatics, who knows for sure? Jack was scared enough to think of ripping off this Roop, this bar owner Dana dated for a while—who, she'd mentioned, had a safe in his house with considerable cash in it.

Nicky wasn't sure about helping when Jack called him yesterday, but by this morning he'd changed his mind.

So here they are, with a local celebrity probably dead and Nicky blathering about how he helped out. "You ain't holding back nothing'a mine, Jacko. I got lotsa fun I'm gonna have. This hot number I told you about, freaky as a frog with a mustache . . ."

"Great. Do a lotta dope, get crazy, get blabby, get people asking questions or calling the cops so *they* come asking questions. Beautiful."

Nicky keeps dividing the cash, doesn't even look up. "Things'll be cool, my man. We had the masks on, they can't ID us, and we had the gloves on so there's no prints. What's your sweat?" *Two for you, one for me . . .*

"I'm just saying—asking—let me hold on to some of that for you. You're gonna—"

"Gonna *what?*" Abruptly on his feet, the wild look in his eyes. "Listen here, mother! I did my bit, now I want my hit! You hear me?"

Jack's up too, scared to death of the freak. Nutcase! Thinks he's not only a badass but also a brain, a sex machine, a charmer, all things to all people; doesn't have a clue that he's 100 percent small-time, nothing but a brain-dead welder and chop-shop artist, doper, loser. Has no idea he smells like cat piss all the time, the chemicals in the meth seeping out his pores—how cool is that? A joke, with his slicked-back Little Caesar hair and lowlife goatee and pumped-up muscles going soft now as the meth takes over his life; with the Kmart suits for his dates with waitresses and grocery clerks and this hooker; with his ridiculous—

This! His ridiculous Edward G. Robinson tough-guy riffs! "You hear me, Jacko? You don't wanna fool with me! If you're lookin' for trouble, I got plenty'a that!"

"Easy . . ."

"Easy? You wanna hold back my cut and you're telling me to take it easy? How 'bout *this* for taking it easy?"—and grabs his gun off the table, levels it at Jack, turns and points it at the kitchen window, finally raises it overhead and *boom!* blows a hole in the ceiling! And *boom!* another, and *boom!*

Finally standing there in the smoke with the gun dangling at his side, grinning crazily at Jack.

sunday, may 13

"Unbelievable," Roop's saying. "What Highwire gets for being in the wrong place at the wrong time."

Max says, "For being the wrong color, it sounded like."

Seven A.M. After spending all night at Roop's place with the detectives, they're sitting on Max's front porch with a couple of stiff Bloody Marys, looking out at the Willamette, the West Hills on the other side, downtown Portland in the distance.

"I was sure it was you at the door," Roop says. "I knew Dana had left her sweater but I didn't think she was coming back for it, as awkward as things were when she was there."

Dana. The angelic-looking blonde, the babe. Roop explained it to the detectives several times during the night: how he and Highwire left the Quandary, drove out to the house, started shooting pool and drinking single-malt, and a few minutes later the doorbell rang. Roop expected Max but it was Dana Waverleigh, saying she was on her way home from somewhere and thought she'd drop by—this a few days after Roop explained to her that it was nothing personal, nothing against her, but he never stayed with any woman very long, their fling was over. He thought she understood, but here she was at his door. He invited her in and took her on up to the game room, hoping she'd realize she was interrupting. That's what happened: they kept on shooting pool, not paying much attention to her, and after a few minutes she got the message and said she'd better get going. Roop walked her downstairs, said good night, and walked back upstairs wondering if she was one of those who was going to make it difficult. Back upstairs he realized she'd left her sweater lying on the wing chair by the windows. When the bell rang again a few minutes later he thought maybe she'd realized it too and come back, but more likely it was Max.

It turned out to be the two goons wearing masks, waving guns.

"Unbelievable." Roop shakes his head and takes a long slug of his drink. "I'd been telling Highwire, not five minutes earlier, that he's one of the chosen ones. You know? He keeps fretting about what happens now that he's thirty-two and his career's over. I'm telling him, 'Look, it's perfect, even the way things ended. You get your championship ring, then wreck your knee in the next training camp and it's over just like that, when you're still pretty much in your prime. Sure it's too bad, but it's better than getting old and no one wanting you anymore. And this way everyone feels bad for you, all that.' And look, he comes back to town and everyone's proud of him, everyone's sad for him, the whole thing. It's only been a few months but he's already done the Cadillac spots, the Nordstrom shirt ads, and now he's doing hoops commentary on radio and TV both. I told him, 'Man, you'll always be taken care of in Puddletown.'"

They look at each other. No need to say it: Highwire got taken care of, all right.

# # #

Nicky left Jack's house last night with only half his money, like Jack wanted, because he felt a little bad about shooting up the kitchen ceiling. What the hell. He'll go get the rest whenever he wants.

He came straight out to Nicky's Body. His favorite place, the body shop up against the woods at the end of Johnson Creek Road, out of the way. He loves it here among the shells of cars, his works-in-progress, with the familiar smells of oil and paint and the rest, his Salvation Army easy chair in the corner with the stack of *Hustlers* on the floor. He laid out a fat line on a magazine, hoovered it, slapped the Sudden Death CD in the box and picked up his acetylene torch. His favorite time to work, middle of the night.

Thinking *Goddamn Jack.*

Things are different now. Jack doesn't understand that it's been a while since he was such a big deal to Nicky.

Not like when they met a few years back. Nicky was always impressed by people who got by on smarts, and hell, anyone would be impressed by that one scam Jack ran.

They were drinking beer and playing pinball at the Hideaway one Saturday afternoon when Jack poked him and said check out the TV up in the corner. The local news was showing a bunch of U-Hauls and vans and station wagons parked in front of some house, a bunch of people in the yard, curious neighbors looking on. Yeah, so what? Jack, with a big smile, said to keep watching. And Nicky caught on as the reporter explained that a "flimflam man" had rented the house under a fake name a few weeks earlier, then turned around and rented it to six different people as if he owned it, collecting first and last months' rent and deposits and telling everyone they could move in on this particular Saturday. And they all showed up with their U-Hauls that morning, only to find out they'd been hosed. The real owner, the lady who rented the house to Jack in the first place, came on and said the flimflammer had seemed so normal she never suspected anything.

Fourteen K all at once, Jack said with a sly smile. It was the slick-est thing Nicky'd ever heard of. No wonder the guy could make a living without getting his hands dirty.

But ever since, it's like Jack's the smart one and Nicky's a cluck. At least that's how it feels, even though Executive Motors wouldn't amount to squat without Nicky turning stolen cars into something Jack can sell. Those are the ones he gets fat on, not the legitimate ones with the piddly 30 percent markup. Jack even admits he needs Nicky. Calls him "a true ar-teest."

But Nicky's never asked for his fair share. Two or three grand a shot wasn't bad—break down the cars Vlasitch brings in, use the parts as needed, give Jack something untraceable to sell—plus he liked hanging out with Jack, trying to figure out ways they could score.

But the hell with it. If Jack's so cool, so smart, he wouldn't have gotten his tit in a wringer with Vlasitch, he wouldn't have needed to rob this dude Roop, and they wouldn't be in the spot they're in now. But he did get in trouble, and came to Nicky to bail him out, and they go and score thirty grand—but all he does afterward is bust on Nicky for shooting Harris. Well, forget that. He's lucky Nicky didn't shoot holes in something besides his ceiling a while ago.

Then again: *Chill, big guy.* They've had a pretty good thing going. Be nice to keep it going, if this little problem doesn't blow up.

No reason it should. They had the masks and gloves on and there was no one around. No way anybody can touch them.

#

By noon, going strong again on another fat line, he feels like calling Candy. See what the whore thinks about her black stud now.

He can still see her at Ringside last Sunday night, foxy thing with her fine jugs resting on the edge of the table, wearing that thick red lipstick he'd chew right off her face if she'd kiss.

The whore.

His plan that night was to ask her to *quit* whoring and be with him, even marry him. He can't stand knowing other guys are getting off on her sweet stuff. But before he could say anything, *she* announced she was quitting. Not the strip-club dancing or the lingerie modeling, but at least the escort service. Yes! But before he could get his hopes up she said she's going to keep doing what she's doing, she's just cutting out the middleman. She's built up a clientele, working for Blondes Galore and X-Citement and finally Experience Heaven; from now on she's having them page her directly, that's all, leave the service out of it.

She said she made up her mind after she got arrested a few nights earlier. "It was a sting. This guy I'd seen a couple times wanted a three-way and I brought my friend Rusty along, this hot redhead. As soon as we got our clothes off the vice cops came busting in. No big deal—my first bust, probation's the worst that'll happen. This time. But next time, who knows? That's why I quit the service. But then I realized I don't need them anyway. Independent is the way to go if you can."

She gave him her everything-happens-for-a-reason spiel. Big thinker. Like the time she told him there's no doubt God gave her looks and a body so she could earn money to go to college, take advantage of her brains. Nicky thought, Maybe you got the body to make a living with because you didn't get brains at all.

Not that it matters. What matters is that she's a drop-dead, to-die-for babe, likes to get druggy and have fun, his kind of girl. What matters is that he gets wiggy thinking about her being with anyone else.

She acted shocked at Ringside when he asked her why she didn't just quit the life—whoring, stripping, kinky-underwear modeling, all of it—and be with him. "Why *would* I? I don't want to quit. Any of it."

Now, as the crystal kicks in, the whole exchange comes back.

Him asking, "You *like* dancing at these clubs? With all these losers spanking their monkeys under the table?"

"I do. It's good money, and when you dance like I dance it's a workout, too. Exercise."

"But you go to the gym every day!"

She just gave him that little smile. "What can I tell you? Maybe I do like turning 'em on, I don't know. I do know I like the money."

"*I* can support you, and you turn *me* on, and I know you like the way I do you. Seems like it, or else you sure fake it good."

The look on her face then pissed him off royally. Like she was being patient, giving him a chance to settle down—making him feel like a kid, really. Finally she said, "Look, Nicky, I like you a lot. But I don't want to give up everything else I'm doing, not now. Even if I did, how could you afford me?"

"I'll afford you, don't sweat that. I'm doing all right and I can make more if I want. You can take it easy, go to community college or the massage-therapy school if you want to. What's wrong with that? Am I too old for you, is that it?" Thirty-five, but he knows he looks younger.

She said it wasn't that.

"You don't want to be with a guy that runs a body shop?"

"It's not that."

"Then what?"

"I've told you."

"What? That you wanna keep modeling kinky undies and doing pole dances for pervs and putting out for every loser that can pay? That's why?" He was getting crazy, remembering her getting out of the white stretch limo in front of McCormick & Schmicks a few days earlier with this Highwire Harris, the basketball player. He'd been having a few beers in the Tank when the limo pulled up across Third and the two of them got out, all dressed up, laughing and having a good old time. Nicky recognized Harris from TV. He saw them go inside, then reappear at a booth in the big front window, and he stayed at the Tank another two hours, drinking and getting steamed watching them have cocktails and dinner and dessert and laugh and laugh. He knew the black bastard wouldn't have to pay to get what he wanted afterward.

"It's none of your business what I do," she said, "or who I do it with."

He couldn't help it, he blurted it out: "Why Highwire Harris, though?"

Big mistake. "How do you . . . ? Are you *following me?*"

He stammered, then finally managed to say he just happened to be at the Tank one day and saw them getting out of a limo, that's all, he never followed her.

"Well, it was only dinner," she said. Then she got huffy again, saying it wasn't any of his business anyway. Saying maybe she should just go home.

"Or go do that spade some more," Nicky snapped.

Big, *big* mistake. She started to get up and he grabbed her wrist, apologizing. She sat down again, telling him she had a life and she was going to do whatever she wanted without asking permission from him or anyone else. She wasn't in love with Harris but—

"With anyone?" he asked. "You in love with anyone?" he asked.

She gave him a tired look and told him to lighten up, give her a break. He knew that if he hadn't had money and crystal meth in his pocket she would have walked out, the whore.

"No one?"

She definitely got mad then. She stared at him. "All right, you really want to know?"

"Yeah, I do. Why you think I'm asking?"

"Okay, if you say so. Am I in love? Well, I don't know what to call it, but there *is* someone in my life and . . . Whatever I'm in, I'm in it with a woman."

Stopping him cold.

They got through it somehow, and went on and partied that night—drinks after dinner, then crystal and sex at the motel—but it was all different for him. He couldn't kid himself that he was getting anywhere with her. She might have lied about being involved with a woman—a way of getting him off her case—but there was also the washed-up basketball jock and his money. She likes the money.

That was Sunday night, a week ago. Jack called on Friday, with a way Nicky could make some cash quick. Saturday morning—only yesterday!—Nicky called him back saying okay.

Then they were there, inside the Roop dude's front door, and Nicky spotted that spade Harris at the top of the stairs. Then . . . Who knows what the hell happened, or how it happened exactly?

Only a few hours ago, wow.

He wonders what the whore will have to say now, if she's heard Chocolate got his head blown off.

monday, may 14

"Bizarre," Max says, in his living room, holding up the Monday-morning *Oregonian* to Roop. Dominating the front page, under the headline MESSAGE OF PEACE FOR ALL, is a full-color aerial photo of the throng overflowing Pioneer Square yesterday, some twelve thousand people downtown to hear the Dalai Lama. "World peace must develop from inner peace," he told them. "Peace is not just the mere absence of violence. Peace is a manifestation of human compassion." By the end of the twentieth century, he said, wasn't everyone on earth fed up with violence?

At the bottom of the page, in the little space remaining, there's the beginning of another story: TERENCE "HIGHWIRE" HARRIS CRITICAL AFTER ROBBERY, SHOOTING.

Roop points the remote at the TV and runs through the channels again. Due to Highwire's middling fame the case has made the news on *Today* and *Good Morning America,* and leads off all the local reports. "Investigators say they still have no solid leads. . . ."

Max heads downtown a few minutes before eight thinking

about mortality, as you so often do when you work in law enforcement. *No one,* the saying goes, *ever wakes up in the morning thinking "I'm going to be murdered today."* Or robbed, raped, assaulted, shot. Maybe the occasional dealer or gangbanger, but that's it. Highwire certainly wasn't thinking any such thing at the VQ Saturday night. Now he's lying in the ICU, unconscious, hooked up to tubes and machines and monitors. While the world keeps turning. While Max drives out of his neighborhood feeling intensely alive, as you so often do. Rainy Portland morning, the lawns electric green against the dark sky, all kinds of shocking colors jumping out at him: rhododendrons, azaleas, dogwood, magnolia, rose of Sharon, lilac, flowering fruit trees. You go weeks without noticing, then suddenly you notice *everything,* grateful you're here to notice at all.

Thinking about dirtbags wearing masks, waving guns . . .

He'll take it out on Harry Fletcher in the sentencing hearing today. He's not feeling great after being up all weekend and drinking with Roop most of yesterday, but he's so pumped up on outrage and adrenaline he should sail right through.

# # #

In court, cracking on Fletcher, he's thinking not only of LaWanda House, the hooker Fletcher murdered, but of Roop and Highwire and all the victims all these years; thinking not only about Fletcher but about all the victimizers, the sociopaths and psychopaths and assorted monsters. He tears into Fletcher, the old scumbag, and takes his shots at Henke, too, the kind of well-dressed sleaze who gives defense attorneys a bad name. (Thinking of Paige, who redeems them.) This is what the job is all about, this is the fun—a sort of fun, anyway: getting to slam people who do terrible things to others. Over the years you sacrifice friendships, marriages, your nervous system; you often wish you were a farmer, a Blockbuster clerk, anything but this—but in the end, as Paige said when she urged him to go back to work after New Year's, this is what you do, this is who you are. Max Faxx.

". . . Even after getting a verdict that can only be considered favorable to the defendant, Your Honor—manslaughter instead of murder—the defendant and counsel will sink to the most shameless depths. . . . The state asks the court to impose the maximum sentence."

# # #

When it's over, when Fletcher's been shackled and taken out and Max has said what he can to the survivors and answered the *Oregonian*'s questions, he heads straight up to the VCU and into Charlie Witty's office for the latest on Highwire and the investigation. There's no good news.

He calls Roop's cell phone, not sure if he stayed at the house all day or went back to his own place after a cleaning service took care of the mess from Saturday night.

He's at the Quandary. "Went home for a while but didn't want to stay, frankly. I'll hang here and maybe be ready to face it tonight. You coming by?"

"Believe it. Have a Blaster ready at five after five."

A few minutes later they're sitting on bar stools, Max with a Blaster and Roop with 101-proof Wild Turkey. Max tells him there are no breaks in the case yet. "The shell casing we found doesn't match anything in the computer. No prints because of the gloves. The detectives are reinterviewing your neighbors but it doesn't look like anything new's coming out. They've been on their computers looking at anyone who's on parole or probation for home invasions. And they're working the list you gave 'em, but nothing helpful yet."

"They won't *get* anything helpful from those people. I kept telling you."

"They have to try."

"Sure they do. Well, how's Highwire?"

"Still in the coma. They don't know if he'll make it or not. If he does, he'll never look like Highwire again. Might not look much like a human being."

Roop staring off . . .

Which is when Dana Waverleigh walks in. The great-looking blonde Roop broke up with recently, the one he thinks Max should make a move on. She's with a woman Max saw her with once before—another hairstylist, he recalls Roop saying, a colleague.

He's a little surprised she's here, considering Roop dropped her just a week or two ago. Maybe she's not giving up so easily, or maybe she simply likes the Quandary and doesn't have a problem with Roop, a master at letting women down gently.

Definitely a babe. Max remembers the first time he saw her, out on the Quandary patio on a bright afternoon last fall; he kept sneaking glances past Paige . . . .

They're coming this way. She looks distressed. She's heard about Highwire, obviously.

"Bill, what *happened?* What's going on?"

Roop hits the Wild Turkey, shuddering as it goes down, then sits there shaking his head.

"Bill? Are you all right?"

"Not exactly."

"What about Highwire?"

"He's not so good. He *might* live."

She turns to Max. "Hi. You'd know, wouldn't you? You're a DA? Have they . . . Do they know who did it?"

Sky blue eyes, impossibly blue. Sweet little voice, a coo . . .

"No one knows much," Max says.

"I've been sick since I heard," she tells Roop, freeing Max to study her. The thick blond hair, translucent skin, gloss on her lips.

Roop asks if detectives have talked to her yet. "They wanted names of everyone I've ever met, just about. I told 'em we dated for a while and that you dropped by the other night."

"They came to the salon today."

"Sorry. I didn't want to put people through it but they insisted."

"It's fine. I wish I could've helped."

"I wish someone could."

"Well, hopefully someone will. Wow"—turning to her friend. "We'd better sit down and order something. Bill, I'm so sorry. For whatever you lost, and mostly for Highwire. Will you tell him I'm praying for him? I mean, when you can?"

"I will. Oh, and I've got your sweater in back, you left it the other night. I'll catch up with you in a few minutes."

When the women are gone, heading for the next room, Max says, "You sure it's over between you two?"

"I'm sure. She's all yours."

"Hmmm. That'd be wild. I've never had a ten before."

# # #

Roop went to return the sweater, then shifted into his circulating, schmoozing mode, leaving Max at the end of the bar pondering his disastrous romantic history yet again.

He could never get anywhere with this babe. Couldn't make it last, anyway.

That job is more important to you than anything or anyone. It's great for everyone except a woman who wants to love you, who wants to be loved.

He's still swimming in it when the babe and her friend reappear—coming this way, heading out.

She's looking at him.

She's coming over!

She's here. . . .

With all the noise she's got to lean close, like Rhonda did Saturday night, but this is altogether different. No troweled-on makeup, no heavy perfume making his eyes water, strictly a turn-on. "Nice to see you again," she says. They've never talked before today, but she's admitting she's noticed him.

"You too. Ever so briefly."

Clever!

Yet she's still here, still so close he's getting a whiff of shampoo. Max almost believes something's happening—that is, not only on his end. Well, take a chance!

"Gotta leave?" he asks.

She smiles, and says she was planning to but doesn't *have* to, her kids are with their dad tonight. Max says "Well . . ." a sort of invitation, and she says okay, she'll go say good-bye to her friend Whitney waiting by the door. A minute later she's back, and the guy on the next stool happens to get up to leave, and she hops up and here they are. Max thinking, If she were any better looking there'd be a holiday for her.

# # #

Candy can't believe it, about Highwire.

Tonight more than ever she's glad she's dancing. She needs to be busy, and she wouldn't feel right about having sex.

No sex in a week, since Nicky hurt her. He pouted at Ringside after she told him she likes her life the way it is, he got sarcastic after she mentioned June (a woman, egad!) and at the motel later he pounded away like she was an inflatable doll, not a person. She was sore for three days.

What he doesn't understand is that she wouldn't have changed her life for Highwire, either (not that Highwire ever asked her to). June might be a different matter, but she and June are a thousand miles from that point.

So why not keep doing what she's doing? Dancing, for instance (Nicky calls it stripping). She likes the exercise, and it's nice to feel wanted, desired. But it's the money too. Money is independence. What happens if you give up everything for a man and then one day he gets mad about something and calls you a whore and throws you out?

Some nights you make as much money dancing as you could make turning tricks, especially when you've got a following, guys who ask you for your schedule and show up wherever you're working. Club 205, the Acropolis, Girls Girls Girls—the same faces every night, losers with some kind of fantasy that you're going to suddenly find them irresistible and offer them a little taste of heaven for no charge. Something like that.

Nothing to it. She puts on a good show, gives them a smile, says a few dirty words when she's at the edge of the stage, and they lay down their fives and tens and even twenties . . . which she tries to hide from the other girls, who collect mostly singles and consider a five or ten the nearest thing to a marriage proposal.

Even tonight, a Monday, she makes out fine. Nine till eleven at the Acropolis, then over to Girls Girls Girls for the late shift, and she'll pull in as much as she'd make turning tricks, without the body odors and sad stories.

# # #

Nicky!

She's on center stage, 1:00 A.M., thrusting to Marvin Gaye's "Keep Gettin' It On," when he appears at the back of the room. Just standing there trying to look cool in his jean jacket, staring at her until she makes eye contact. Same thing he did at the Acropolis two hours ago.

When a front table comes open he walks up, sits down, and gives her a wink. She can tell he's whipped out on meth: eyes bugging, sweat on his forehead. She doesn't know what to think—why he came to the Acropolis but never approached, why he shows up here and does. What's up? What does she do? He probably wants to get together, but after last time she's not sure she ever wants to be alone with him again.

She feels better when the set ends and he puts down not a five or a ten or even a twenty, but a fifty. He's still there when she comes back for the closing set. When she goes to the edge of the stage and gives him a crotch shot he puts a fingertip to the side of his nose like he's snorting, letting her know he's got some stuff and he wants to party when she gets through.

She's been getting into it too much, but she's tempted.

He knows she is. He jerks his thumb toward the back door, meaning he'll be out in his truck afterward.

Sure enough, he's waiting in his jacked-up pride and joy when she walks out twenty minutes later. When she comes around to the window, he says, "Feel like a bite?" even though he's way cranked-up and probably doesn't have any appetite. A gentleman, thinking of her. "Hotcake House?"

She ignores the disconcerting eyes for now. She's hungry, and hey, he likes her. Claims he loves her. Go have a bite, get a room, do some meth, screw, go home with cash and some product—he always gives her some at the end. "Hotcakes," she says.

He grins. "Sliders." He thought it was so funny the night she referred to the greasy eggs that way.

"Mud in a cup," she says. The coffee.

"LSD trip." The way you feel in Hotcake House late at night, with all the weirdos.

"See you there," she says, and walks to her car.

Forty-five minutes later, after pancakes and sliders (coffee only for Nicky), she's ready for a line. She follows him to the Caravan Motel and waits in her car, doing arithmetic, while he checks in. A hundred bucks to suck him, one-fifty for a jump, some meth to take home—not a bad way to finish off the night.

She follows him to the usual upstairs room. Only a minute or so behind him, but when she walks in he's already got his jacket and shirt off and he's laying out lines on the tabletop. She gives him a smile and a grope.

"Little wildcat," he mutters, still working the powder. He likes to call her that, "little wildcat," what Edward G. Robinson called Lauren Bacall in *Key Largo*. He was amazed she recognized it the first time he said it, but she'd rented some Bacall movies after an old retired contractor, said she reminded him of her—"sexy as hell, and the same throaty voice."

In bed after the first line he's all over her, breathing heavy, and it's not long before he whispers, "Just put your lips together and blow." The famous Bacall line she told *him* about, which he loved.

She throws the covers back and gives him a little mouth action, then finishes him with her hand. He usually sulks over the fact she won't take him all the way with her mouth, but not tonight. It's like he's trying to be nice, after last time.

# # #

She shouldn't have done the second line, but she always needs something after they screw. Nicky's like a kid, wanting her to carry on like a porn star—whoop and moan, rave about his tool—and when it's over she needs booze, crank, weed, whatever's on hand. Usually it's crank.

And now she's flying. *Flying.* And he looks ridiculous sitting there, tipped back in the chair. She's only known him a few months but the decline is striking. He's still got some muscle, but speed freaks don't eat, and he's lost twenty pounds at least. He twitches and sweats and grinds his teeth. And that smell! If *she's* ever that far gone she can forget about business, no one will want her.

Thinking how pathetic he is, she's reminded of his ridiculous crush on the anchorwoman. And can't help teasing him. "How's Pam? Have you met her yet? Pam, Pamela, whatever you call her."

He just stares at her, eyes glazed.

One night a few weeks ago, out of their minds, they started talking about famous people they'd like to sleep with and Nicky said Cameron Diaz, Winona Ryder, and Pamela Gramm. Pamela who? The fox who does the weekend news on Channel 2, he said, with the reddish hair and pointy chin. Candy knew who he meant and couldn't believe he had the hots for such a prissy thing. But he went on and on about her. About her name: how the coanchor and weatherman and sports guy all call her Pam in their small-talk—*Big story today, Pam*—but she introduces herself as Pamela—*Hello, I'm Pamela Gramm*—because "Pam Gramm" would sound like a joke, right? He wondered how she felt when the guy proposed, knowing she'd be "Pam Gramm" the rest of her life. Maybe the ring convinced her to go ahead, he said, biggest damn diamond he's ever seen. The way she shows that sucker off, keeping her left hand up on the anchor desk all the time . . . On and on. Candy pictured him jerking off during the five o'clock news and again at eleven, Saturdays and Sundays.

"Still haven't called her?" She can't help it.

"Not yet," he says, a little slurry, and flops down on the bed again, closes his eyes.

"Probably just as well. She's not your type."

"You don't think so?"

"She's a prim-and-proper talking head. Prissy. That tight little mouth, my God, like she's been sucking on a lemon. Which is all she sucks on, I'm sure."

A grunt. Eyes still closed.

"And not very smart. All she does is read the news, but she doesn't even know words. I heard her talking about a consortium once—you know, a con-sor-shum?—and she kept saying con-*sort*-e-um, like you're supposed to pronounce it the way it looks."

"Boy oh boy." His eyes come open. "Like *you're* smarter than she is? A news reporter?"

"She's a news*reader*. You think they have to be smart? The most popular one in town, the dweeb on Channel 6, went from weatherman to anchorman overnight—what does that tell you?"

"Answer my question. You think you're smarter than Pamela Gramm? You didn't even finish high school, right?"

"I know words. I master five new words every week, including how to pronounce 'em."

"Aren't you hot." Closing his eyes again, like there's no point in trying to get through to her.

"I'm just saying I know some words. Not every word in the dictionary, but most of the ones a newsreader should know. Hey, I'm sure she's nice, she's even kinda cute in a prissy way. But not your type. She probably lives someplace like Happy Valley, her and Mr. Gramm. He sells hospital supplies or something. They probably screw once a month, strictly missionary. She doesn't go down on him and she wouldn't go down on you."

"Not like you, huh?"

"Ex*cuse* me?"

His eyes laze open. "I said, 'Not like you, huh?' She wouldn't go down on me like you do?" The eyes close again and he mutters, "Not that it's much, what you do."

"Listen, you prick—"

"But forget it. Enough about her. I wanna hear about you and this girlfriend you told me about. What can she do for you that I can't do?"

Asshole. Ignorant asshole.

"I'm sure I can't explain. Not so you'd understand."

tuesday, may 15

All day long Max is thinking about her. *Dana.* Still tingling from last night.

He can't wait till five. She's at the salon till six, but he'll walk down to the VQ and have a drink with Roop and just enjoy being alive again. The last few weeks haven't been fun.

Last night was amazing. After she joined him at the bar he bought her a glass of wine and they talked for a half hour or so. By then the eye contact was almost like sex. They stopped to pick up Mexican food on the way to Max's house, but they never got around to eating.

Naked in the backyard hot tub with her, under the blooming apple tree, he couldn't get over what a babe she was, angelic and sexy all at once. When he finally said so she said no, no, no, she's never felt attractive. "I've never forgotten when I waitressed for a while, this man saying, 'How about sending the good-looking one over here to get my order?' Those things stay with you."

"Please. The guy was nuts, or blind, or teasing you. What did the other one look like?"

"Big boobs, big butt, big hair. What men want, right?"

"Arrested-development types, yeah. I rest my case."

He could hardly believe he had her there naked. This fast, this easy, he was in for a little taste of heaven. He wondered if she'd ever done it in a tub. That whole weightless thing—it wasn't always graceful, but it was fun.

He drifted toward her. Kissed her. Her little nibbly kiss—tentative, tender—finally turning deep, passionate, popping a boner on him that felt like it might displace half the water in the tub. He held her hands and drifted back to the bench he'd come from, bringing her with him, bringing her up on his lap crossways, on top of his monster rod. She felt it—how could she not? He wanted her to reach for it, hoist herself up on it, do something; he didn't want to be forward.

But she sort of tensed up instead, didn't do anything but press her face against his neck and put a few kisses there. So as not to have to look at him? Was she sorry she'd come, or that she'd gotten undressed, anyway?

When his cock finally calmed down she raised her face, gave him a quick kiss and drifted away, smiling again as if that awkward bit had never happened. Asking how long he'd been renting the house, how often he used the tub . . . Peculiar.

It got more peculiar still. He invited her to spend the night and she said yes, she'd like to. And a little later they went upstairs and got in bed and touched, clutched, kissed, and his thigh pressed between her legs and she gripped him and he knew she'd climb aboard any minute, or ease over on her back and pull him aboard. . . .

Except she didn't. She let go of him and stopped riding his leg and got all prim. What the hell?

"I'm sorry," she said finally. "I don't know, I probably shouldn't have come over, not tonight. I wanted to be with you but . . . I don't know, I can't do it the first night, it doesn't feel right. . . . I'm sorry."

What could he say?

"Another time?" she said.

"Sure."

"If you still want to."

He didn't say anything. Not sure, right then, what he was getting into here.

"Max?"

"Yeah."

"You're mad."

"No."

"Are you sure?"

Was he *sure*? He didn't mean it at all, but what was he supposed to say?

And it got more peculiar *still*.

They lay there quiet, awkward—disconnected, although she kept her head on his shoulder to pretend things weren't *too* weird. A few minutes passed.

What a bust, and he didn't have a clue. Chicks, Jesus.

But then she stirred, a tentative hand moving across his chest. Caressing him. His belly. And whoa, going down to his poker again, as Max lay there wondering what the hell. She'd already said she didn't feel right about doing anything, first night and all.

Then—talk about a shock—*she* was down there, not just her hand. Zounds.

Wowie, Howie.

But why this? Why now?

Worry about it later, fool.

But he never did. A few minutes later he drifted off to sleep smiling, his head filled with cheese like "This is the first day of the rest of your life," and in the middle of the night she rolled into his arms and reached down and got him ready and took him for a ride—*whoa!*—and he wasn't about to dwell on why she'd been weird at first. It was endearing somehow, looking back.

All day today, he's been reliving it all. Dying for more.

# # #

He loves the way she dresses. A quirky style. Many styles. He remembers seeing her at the Quandary in corduroy pants and a blouse with a vest over it, cute as could be. Another time she reminded him of Jane Fonda in *Klute,* long ago, with a long wraparound skirt over some high, tight boots. Another time, one of the first springlike days, she was Earth Mother in one of those vintage granny dresses and sandals. Yesterday she was wearing pants again and a white blouse with a narrow man's tie, a look he's always liked.

Showing up at the Quandary today she's snappy, not to mention sexy, in a navy blue blouse, white pants, and navy open-toe shoes. None of which registers right away, though, because he's fixated on the luminous face, the smile, the eyes.

"I didn't get a lot of work done today," he says once she's up on the bar stool next to him. "Couldn't get you out of my mind."

"I've been thinking about you too, Max."

"I wondered how you'd look when I saw you again. If you'd have the same look in your eyes as when you left the house this morning."

"And?"

"Hard to believe, but yes."

When their drinks arrive he asks if she'd rather sit here or go find a table.

Doesn't matter, she says, she's just glad to be with him.

"Tell you the truth," Max says, "I'd rather not stay too long, no matter where we sit. I can't see you tomorrow night, I teach a class on trial testimony for cops, so I want all the private time I can get tonight."

"That's what I want. Thursday I get my daughters back from their dad and I won't have much free time till they go back to him on Monday. Let's make the most of tonight."

wednesday, may 16

Nicky's in the Willamette U. library in Salem, an hour south of Portland, remembering the first time he saw Pamela Gramm. She was standing on a freeway overpass during Channel 2's all-day blizzard coverage two years ago, rosy-cheeked, a ball cap low on her forehead, wind whipping her hair. Nicky stayed in front of the TV all day, waiting for her occasional reports. . . .

Someone tap-taps on his shoulder. "Sir? Excuse me? These annuals are university property."

He looks up into the face of a little old lady.

Busted. The Exacto knife in his hand, the old Willamette yearbooks on the table. The pictures he's already cut out are in the manila envelope, but this old biddy probably saw him stash them.

But Nicky's tired of people messing with him. He gives her a hard look and doesn't say anything. See what she's gonna do.

"University property, sir."

"So what?"

"You can't do this."

"So what?"

Gertie doesn't have an answer. Looks back over her shoulder toward an old security guard gimping this way, about as scary as Barney Fife. Nicky grabs his envelope and stands up, towering over the hag, waiting to see what the old man's got to say.

He never heard from Channel 2 after he wrote them a letter asking for information on Pamela, a PR handout or something, but last week the *Oregonian* TV columnist mentioned that she went to college at Willamette and this morning Nicky decided to drive down. Someone in the main office told him he'd find yearbooks in the library, and when he got here the homo at the desk pointed him this way. Nicky didn't know exactly what years Pamela attended, but she looks about thirty now and he did the arithmetic and started looking. Finally found her, Pam *Pinney,* in a picture of "Media Mavens," and cut out the picture and looked for more.

"This man is defacing university property," Gertie tells Pops. Pops gives Nicky the once-over and Nicky gives him the look: Rico staring down Little Arnie Lorch after the meeting with Diamond Pete Montana. *Yeah? You got something to say?*

"Wh-what's going on, sir?" Pops's voice is shaky.

"Just looking at these books. But I'm leaving now." Standing up. *You gonna stop me?*

"He's cutting them up," Gertie says. "Cutting things out and putting them in that envelope."

Nicky ignores her. *What about it, Pops?* The old fart doesn't even have a gun, just a flashlight hanging from his belt. A walkie-talkie in one hand, but he's not calling for backup.

The geezers look at each other.

"I'm outta here," Nicky says, and walks off. He listens for action behind him, maybe Pops calling for help on his walkie-talkie, but nothing. A moment later he's outside, crossing the grass to the parking lot. With five or six Pamela pictures, and that's all that counts.

Except that people think they can mess with him, think he's some kind of a chump.

Bad idea. Reminds him of Rico warning Vittori, *Bad business to mess with me, Sam, One guy tried that—once.*

What he's been thinking the last few days is that it was bad business for Jack to promise him only a third of whatever Roop had in his safe. Jack talked like the job would be a breeze, but he never would have gone over there without Nicky, wouldn't have gotten a dime.

Bad business for Jack to give him a hard time afterward about shooting Chocolate, and about how he'll probably blow everything by throwing money around and talking too much. If Jack's the smart one, why'd Nicky have to bail him out in the first place?

And there's the fact that Nicky does all the work on these cars that *Jack* makes the money on. Jack goes to a wrecking yard, picks up a totaled Beamer for chump change, pays Vlasitch two or three grand for a stolen one, gives Nicky two or three to rebuild the wreck ("a true ar-teest") and then sells it off his lot for fifteen or more.

Well, Jack can go stroke himself. Let him find another ar-*teest* if he won't do what's right.

But right now Nicky just wants his other five grand from Saturday night—and five on top of that to make it a split, now that he's thought about it.

# # #

Not knowing what time Candy will go out, he parks up the street from her northwest Portland duplex around five-thirty. He's driving a beater from the shop that she'd never recognize; he's wearing shades and his Harley-Davidson cap.

He waits.

At six he gets out his pipe and smokes two hits of crystal to break up the boredom.

BOING!!!!

Hard to sit still now, but he forces himself.

He sits waiting, thinking. Can't stop thinking about her being with a *woman*. Is it really true?

It's ten till seven when she finally comes out of the duplex, bitchin' in a tight black dress and a string of fake pearls. Off to meet someone, definitely.

She gets in her Tercel and he follows her downtown, careful to keep at least one car between them. She grabs a parking space on Washington between Fourth and Fifth. Nicky lucks into one a half block up, slouches down as she comes hurrying up the sidewalk, then gets out and follows. When she goes left on Broadway he's pretty sure she's heading for the Benson—fancy hotel, probably some rich pencil dick waiting for her.

Yeah, the Benson. Not the first time she's been there, either, from the way the doormen salute her. Don't they know what she is?

Nicky waits in the sandwich shop across the street. No appetite, but he orders half a tuna on wheat so they won't rag him about sitting here.

Is she with the woman?

Is there a woman at all, or was she trying to put him off?

If there is, they wouldn't meet at a hotel, would they? They'd be at Candy's duplex, or the girlfriend's place.

Girlfriend. He doesn't even want to think about it.

She comes out an hour later—an hour almost exactly, meaning she had someone on the clock. Meaning, probably not a girlfriend.

She's going back to her car. Nicky hustles back to his beater and waits for her to pull out, then follows her back up to Northwest. She's going home—but not to stay, not at eight-fifteen.

She comes out at nine-forty wearing a shiny red dress that's even tighter than the black one. She probably smoked some of the crystal he gave her last night, took a long bath, washed out her snatch for the next john—

Or the woman.

But no, another john. Johns get an hour, and back downtown she goes into the Heathman at ten and she's back out at five after eleven.

He can't stand it. It's not as bad as her being with a woman, but he feels like grabbing her anyway, shaking her, telling her the whoring's over, she's *his,* he'll earn all the money she needs and keep her happy with his tool. . . .

He follows her out of downtown. East this time, across the Hawthorne Bridge, and when she heads south on MLK he knows she's on her way to the Acropolis for the late shift. He wants to go watch her, then take her to the Caravan afterward, but no, she already suspects he follows her and if he shows up again she'll know. He could always tell her he called the place and they said she was working, but something tells him not to.

Just hang around and see where she goes afterward. Maybe that's when she goes to her girlfriend, if there is a girlfriend. Maybe she goes and spends the night.

With a carpetmuncher.

It can't be true.

# # #

What was she *thinking?*

She wasn't thinking at all—Dana—or she wouldn't be at the

Thirsty Parrot. Max is teaching his class, the girls are with Brian and she doesn't like being alone, but this was stupid. Jack knows she meets her girlfriends here most Wednesday nights. Not that she expected him to show up tonight—she thought he'd be hiding out, with the whole city talking about what happened—but she shouldn't have taken the chance.

She senses him before she sees him, and when she looks up he's there by the door, looking right at her, smiling like it's just another Wednesday night. She looks away, freaking inside. Pretends to rejoin the girl talk, but she knows he's spotted her.

She lets a minute or two pass, then asks Maggie if he's still there. No, he's gone and sat down at a table near the bar, his back to her like he's not the least bit worried she'll leave. Like he knows she'll come to him. She always has, and if she avoids him now he'll know she's scared, know she saw him and another man running out of Bill's house Saturday night—he'll know she recognized him, mask or not. He'll know she could be dangerous.

Finally she gets up—not quite steady—walks over and stops behind him. He knows she's there, of course. He looks up, smiling, and pulls out the chair on his right. She sits.

"What's up, babe?" He's so casual Dana half wonders if she was hallucinating the other night, if it wasn't him at all. "What's new?"

Casual, but his eyes are serious as can be. Looking right into her head, it feels like, seeing everything that's going on.

"Huh? How you been?"

She's afraid to say anything—certain her voice will sound as shaky as she feels—but afraid not to, too. "I'm okay."

"The girls?"

"Fine."

"You still at Hair on Burnside?"

"Still there . . ."

He asks about her parents, her sister. Whether she saw the Dalai Lama. What she's been up to, anything new and exciting? Fifteen minutes or so it goes on, she doesn't know how long, it feels like an hour. Cat-and-mouse: Jack not letting on that he was there Saturday night, Dana trying not to let on that *she* was. Still hoping that maybe he didn't see her coming down the sidewalk, or that he saw someone but couldn't tell it was her. It was one in the morning, there was some distance between them. . . .

But she knows better.

# # #

Yet she doesn't have the sense to say no when he asks her to come home with him. She makes a brief, feeble attempt: "I—I—can't, I started seeing someone—a guy," but he reminds her that's never stopped them. "Come on," he says, "I miss you," and she's afraid to say no.

But not only that. She's still praying that somehow she was mistaken the other night. She still can't believe Jack would do something like that. All these years, as far as she knew, he never owned a gun, never even talked about guns or robbery or anything like that.

And it's not only the fear and the crazy shred of hope that keep her from running out of the Parrot. She knows it's sick, sick, sick, but there's still some of the old attraction.

"Come on," he says. "You just *started* seeing someone? So what, then? You and I have twenty years' history."

"I—I can't. I'm serious about him, he's serious about me."

"You're always serious about 'em—and never serious at all, at the same time. So, who's this one?"

"A lawyer."

"Ah. Chasing the money and respectability again."

"Please, Jack. I'm not chasing anything."

"How long you been doing him, babe?"

"Not very long . . . Why do you have to say it that way, 'Doing him'?"

"Not long? But let me guess: you're thrillingly, cosmically in love already. Or you see a big house in the West Hills, anyway."

"That's not fair, Jack."

"True, though. Doctors, lawyers, Indian chiefs—you're always trying to soar with the eagles, hoping one of 'em will fly you away to a cushy lifestyle."

"That's not fair!"

"Don't get upset, babe. We're having a conversation, that's all."

"But you say those things even though you *know* it's not true. I left my marriage for you, not even a year ago, and it was no great lifestyle you were offering. I left a nice guy, a nice house, everything you say I'm after, and what did I get? You got what you *said* you always wanted—we got to be together—but then it wasn't even a month before you sent me away!"

"You *left*, babe. But—"

"You made me!"

"—but let's forget that. Look, keep your lawyer guy, do whatever you want, but come home with me tonight. You know I'll make you feel good. We'll pretend your dad's hanging around."

# # #

The whole twisted thing started twenty-two years ago: bad-boy Jack popping her cherry in the back of her father's old Malibu, right there in the driveway while her parents drank cheap scotch in the kitchen fifteen feet away. There would have been big trouble if they'd had any idea their fourteen-year-old virgin was giving it up to the eighteen-year-old "no-goodnik" they'd hated even before he was arrested for stealing cars.

The way her father talked about Jack, calling him no good, was exactly why she wanted to be with him. It always felt like the two of them against the world.

It never really changed. They grew up and time passed, years sometimes when they couldn't have located each other even if they'd thought to, but eventually they would connect and the thrill was always there. They'd end up necking and sooner or later going to bed, regardless of marriages and whatever else.

But that was all. Two or three hot sessions, some talk about how they were soul mates, but one or the other always let go, usually Jack, and months or years would pass before the next time.

Two years ago Dana married Henry Barris for his kindness and for what a dentist could provide, but after a few months she was bored stiff. Maybe she simply needed melodrama, as her sister said, but when Jack showed up last summer she didn't care about psychological theories. She was bored, Jack was free again, and she started seeing him. As soon as he told her go ahead, ditch the stick-in-the-mud, she told Henry it was over, and she and the girls left the estate on Council Crest for Jack's rundown two-bedroom in Southeast.

And just like that, Jack lost interest. He kept sleeping with the tramp who handled the books at the car lot. When Dana begged for it he'd tell her not now, maybe tomorrow, and get mad if she didn't drop it.

She cried and cried until she thought she was losing her mind. Finally she and the girls moved, for what seemed like the hundredth time. Into the big Lake Oswego house with her perfect sister Amy, squeaky-clean Josh, and their brilliant, straight-arrow kids, constant reminders of how she'd screwed up her life and was screwing up her daughters now. . . .

Yet tonight—despite the past, despite what she saw Saturday night, despite Max—she leaves the Thirsty Parrot with Jack, follows him to his house, and as soon as he shuts the front door behind them they're necking like old times. A few minutes later Jack pulls away long enough to go mix stiff gin and tonics, which they chug-a-lug to get ready for bed, like old times. Jack wants her now, she doesn't have to beg.

# # #

CLANG! *This greaseball's your true love? Lord help you.* Henry—last summer—in disbelief when she told him she was leaving.

CLANG! *Lose him, Dana. He's the type that'll only drag you down.* Her friend Cynthia, after meeting Jack years ago.

CLANG! CLANG! Voices torturing her. Not crazy, schizy voices (she prays), but things people have said over the years.

CLANG! *What are you DOING, Dana? Do you even have a clue?* Perfect, sensible sister Amy—many times, for many reasons.

And yet it pops out, as they lie there afterward: "Jack . . ."

"Yeah, babe?"

". . . Do you want me back?" She knows it's crazy, knows he came to the Parrot and invited her home only because he knows she saw them Saturday night, yet . . . "Jack?"

"Maybe. I might, babe."

"Or else I don't know what I'm doing here."

"But you're with this lawyer," he says.

"But . . . You know." *You know I'd be with you in a heartbeat if you wanted me, if you'd be good to me.* Tears in her eyes again. "What happened last year, Jack? We finally had our chance—"

"I was overwhelmed, I guess. I've told you this before."

"How could you d-*do* it? I gave up my marriage, everything, and as soon as I did you lost interest. You wouldn't even sleep with me. Why? Because you *had* me?"

Nothing.

But that had to be why. He got interested again a few weeks after she moved out, when she let him know she was dating a lumber broker, a man doing very well. She was glad for the chance to turn him down. Then she didn't see him again until he dropped by the salon last month. She was involved with Roop then, and Jack got interested a*gain.* Even she could see how sick it was. She turned him down again.

But made her terrible mistake in the process. *Why would I go with you now, Jack? This man's nice to me, and he could buy and sell you!* Trying to hurt him, but going too far: *The petty cash in his safe is probably more than you make in I-don't-know-how-long!*

# # #

She's been awake for a while by the time she rolls over and checks the digital clock on Jack's dresser, but it's still only 5:07 in the morning. Jack's been snoring all night but she barely slept at all, lying here berating herself for going to the Parrot last night, for coming here afterward, for the whole mess she's made of her life.

Yet maybe she's not in the spot she thought she was in. Jack never said anything about Saturday night. Maybe she *was* mistaken. Maybe it's fine.

When he finally wakes up she's even more hopeful. He's nice. He gets hard and she turns over the way he likes. Afterward he asks her to shower with him, and after they're dressed he tells her to relax, read the paper if she wants, he'll toast her a bagel. Who knows, maybe he did some thinking during the night and realized how much she means to him.

But of course that's it. A few minutes before nine they leave the house, he walks her to her car out front, and as she reaches to unlock the door he grabs her wrist and turns her toward him. Even before he says anything she knows the situation is exactly what she feared.

What he says is, "Listen to me, babe. We've been dancing around it but we both know what it is, don't we? We both know you were there Saturday night."

She's paralyzed.

And it's even worse than she feared. "We both know you were there and I'm telling you—hear me loud and clear, babe—if you say one word about it *ever*, to *anyone*, then you were not only there, you were *involved*. It was your idea in the first place. It was no accident, you letting me know this Roop had a safe in his house with a lot of cash. You didn't like getting dumped, plus you're always broke, you thought it'd be a nice score. You don't think that adds up? Say a *word* and you'll go down too, babe. You follow me?"

thursday, may 17

Dana looks a little drained, says she didn't sleep well last night, but Max is enchanted just the same.

They're walking in Grant Park at sunset, happy to be together again after missing last night. Holding hands like young lovers, which is exactly how it feels. Magical, is how it feels.

The future looks more hopeful than ever, now that he's met her daughters. He'd been edgy about it, his second marriage having exploded around stepfamily issues. He's got no doubts about him and Dana, but if you can't work it out with someone's kids you don't have a chance.

After his day in court, a pointless bail hearing for the three Larch Mountain killers, he worked in his office until she called saying she was leaving the salon, then drove straight to her apartment complex out near Rose City Golf Course. Her daughters were back from three nights with their father. Elizabeth was a pretty, bright, funny sophomore with a nice little touch of smart-ass. Emily was seven and charming: undersized but oddly mature, sort of a miniature grown-up, with a shiny, perfect face.

No surprise they were wonderful, of course, considering their mom.

It felt so good over there! The three of them so happy together, even in a cramped two-bedroom apartment, and Max so thrilled to be there with them. The only thing better would be time alone with Dana. Dana felt the same way, and after a trip for Subway sandwiches she told the girls she and Max were going for a walk while they did their homework and took their baths.

And now the not-so-young lovers stroll in the park on a spring evening that seems almost surreal to a man falling in love, a man who'd nearly given up on ever finding true love. Fiery orange sun dropping behind the West Hills in the distance, swirls of orange and blue and gray across the big sky; sweet, perfumy air, whiffs of earth and grass and lilac.

Teenagers throwing a baseball, kids throwing Frisbees, parents and toddlers on the swings and seesaws, people walking dogs. Idyllic. A few years ago Max sent a guy to death row for axing a girl and leaving her body in those bushes right over there, but it seems unreal now.

He realizes the Larch Mountain gang hasn't entered his mind since he walked out of the courtroom hours ago.

Paige hasn't entered his mind since Dana sat down with him at the VQ Monday night.

"Everything's changed," he says.

She doesn't understand.

"Thanks to you," he says.

She still doesn't get it. She's got no idea how special she is.

"You've changed everything. All right, I know it sounds stupid—

it's only what, our third night? But it feels like my life's going to be different from here on."

Finally she smiles, a little. "Mine too, maybe."

Tentative. Not exactly what he wanted, but hey, he's probably saying too much too soon, and she's told him she's gun-shy after her "failures" . . . Just ease off a little.

And besides—*Mine too,* she said. She's right there with him, even if she's a little gun-shy. He stops walking and turns her toward him, kisses her forehead, pulls her against him. He feels like doing a lot more, but at the same time, Lord, he'd be content to stand here holding her forever.

Which is when his blankety-blank pager beeps.

The job. The thing that cost him two marriages and how many girlfriends.

Nothing he can do. It's a Gresham Police Department number, meaning probably an MCT case. Aside from running the VCU he also coordinates Multnomah County's Major Crimes Team, an elite collection from the sheriff's office, Portland Police and state police that handles big cases outside the city limits.

"Sorry," he tells his love, pulling out his cellular, "but I've got to make a call."

She tells him it's fine, it's his job, giving him a sweet, serene look. Max remembers others saying the same thing at first.

Buckley answers the call, a Gresham detective, saying SERT has surrounded a house out in Troutdale. Some guy called 911 threatening to off himself, and when the cops showed up he pointed his shotgun at them instead. Buckley figures it will resolve itself without Max, but they had to let him know.

Go? He's never skipped anything like this. . . .

. . . but hey, Buckley's right, it'll resolve itself without him.

# # #

When they get back from the park the girls have taken baths, gotten into their PJs and settled in front of the TV in the living room. When Dana tells Emily it's bedtime, the little thing melts Max by asking him to read her a story. In the girls' room she snuggles into bed and Max sits in the chair and reads to her.

Afterward, back in the living room Elizabeth tells him and Dana about a boy at school who's got a crush on her.

What a feeling, being welcomed into their world.

When Liz goes to bed Dana pours wine, lights the fat pink candle on top of the TV, turns out the lights, and they take their shoes off and get cozy on the couch. Max feeling so good, sooooo good, he finds himself worrying about losing her.

Thinking about the MCT page earlier. What's happened to him before.

"I want you to know," he says, "you're going to come first. As much as possible. The worst thing about my job is that when you're in the thick of it there's not much time for anything but work—your whole personal life can get lost. But I'm going to fight it. I want this to work. Bad."

"Me too, Max. I'm sure you're busy a lot but it's all right. You're important, you've got an important job. I understand."

He's heard it before, of course. They sound different later.

Then again, he's never felt this way before. He can't remember ever blowing off a callout like the one tonight, even when his presence was optional. Changing could be easy.

". . . I think it's great, what you do," she's saying. "Do you like the job, even though your personal life gets lost sometimes?"

"Mostly. I could live without crime scenes, bodies, nightmares, sleazy defense attorneys, some juries—but you work with great people, it's always interesting, it's satisfying. Nothing more satisfying than putting away people who've done horrible things to others. Not that it brings a murder victim back to life or repairs any other damage."

"Mmmm." She's shaking her head. "I can't imagine."

He wants to kiss her, snuggle, but she's asking how he got into it. He tells the story he's told a hundred times, a thousand times:

Dad and two uncles were cops, he grew up with an interest in law enforcement—but he was such a clown in high school, he wasn't going anywhere. Joined the army, became an MP at Fort Bragg, trained dogs, decided law enforcement was definitely it. Majored in criminal justice in college, and somewhere along the way started thinking about becoming a lawyer instead of a cop. "Everyone wanted to change the world back then, and lawyers were gonna be the cutting edge of the sword that changed it. All I knew was I wanted to do criminal work instead of civil. The money's in civil stuff but the excitement's in criminal court, the sense that something's at stake. And coming from a law-enforcement background, it was probably natural that I'd become a prosecutor. Not a sure thing, 'cause I know defense is a big part of our system, but I was probably leaning that way all along and then . . . my first mock trial, I still remember it like yesterday, I knew what I was. I'd never felt so comfortable anywhere, doing anything. Even now, I'm still more comfortable in front of a jury than anywhere else."

A look on her face.

"Yeah? What?"

"Nothing. It's fun hearing you talk."

"I'd rather not, I'd rather go lie down, but you asked."

"I like hearing. We can go lie down if you want, but you have to finish what you were saying." Finishing her wine, setting the glass on the end table, taking his hand. "Deal?"

"Whatever gets me close to you."

She brings the big candle, careful not to spill the pool of wax, and they head to the bedroom. In the little hallway she nudges the door to the girls' room and they stand there looking in at the two in their beds, dead to the world, breathing deeply in the dark. Max overwhelmed—by the beautiful girls in their beds, by Dana, everything. Thinking he'll die if he loses this.

Whispering to her, in her bedroom a moment later, "Believe me . . . I've got this job, I get calls at all hours, I'm preoccupied sometimes, but believe me, the three of you are gonna come first."

On her bed, in her arms, the last thing he wants to do is talk about his career. Thankfully, she doesn't remind him that he promised.

# # #

"Max?"

"Hmm?"

"It's happening fast, isn't it?"

"For me it is."

"For me too. Is it too fast?"

"Meaning what?"

"I don't know. It's scary. I just thought maybe we should talk some more, before we're too involved."

"Talk about what?"

"Just some things . . . to let you decide if this is really something you want."

"It is."

"I believe you, but you should know some things anyway."

Max wondering, What?

"Like, did you know I've been married . . .?"

"Yeah, I realize you had a life before me."

". . . three times?"

Three times?

Three?

But what the hell, he's been there twice himself. Failed twice. He likes to think it doesn't make him hopeless.

"Max?"

"Forget it. I've had two divorces and some other flops. Sometimes things don't work out. All it means to me is that neither of us met the right person till now."

"I hope. I don't know. I just wanted to tell you. . . ."

"All right, you did. And I'm still sold." Kissing her forehead, stroking her cheek.

"Amazing," he says, "that other men let you get away. Listen. Whatever you've been through, whatever I've been through, none of it matters now. All that matters is that we found each other, right? And we like what we found."

"I do."

"Sometimes it happens fast. Sometimes people just know."

"I think so."

"You know the old thing about how every person is the sum of their experience, of everything they've seen and done and been through? Well, we are, too. Maybe you wouldn't be so perfect for me if your life had been different. Who knows?"

It's the right thing to say. It's what she needed to hear. She kisses him. . . .

Kisses him. Lord. Max is astonished, again, that there could be any insecurity in a woman like this. But then, divorces do something to you.

Three divorces? Hitting him a different way, suddenly. The old law-enforcement saw: *The best indicator of the future is the past.*

Moving too fast?

Step back a little?

But no no no no no. He's looked into those eyes, he's been with her, he's met her girls. When you know, you know.

# # #

"You crack me up," Max says when they've finally settled down from the fit of laughing.

Sex took some of the moon-June-spoon out of him, got them off the serious stuff—thank God—and something started them talking about the ways people kiss. He broke up when she described the Dental Probe: "You know, when their tongue is so far in your mouth they're exploring your molars, your tonsils." He asked her to demonstrate, and when she tried they both got silly. Then they got hysterical talking about Cow Kissing, Fish Mouth, Tongue-in-the-Ear and other turnoffs.

Then last night came back to her, and this morning—Jack—and she wondered if she was losing her mind. She's *laughing?*

And now Max gets serious again, tender, which makes her shaky. CLANG! *You don't have any trouble attracting men, but if they don't leave you pretty soon you always leave them. You like the excitement of the beginning, like a high school kid, but you don't have any idea how to turn it into a grown-up relationship. You run away. Why? You don't believe you deserve it? You run from anyone who's halfway normal and go find yourself some jerk or doper.* Perfect, good-sense Amy.

CLANG! *What are you* doing? *No idea, right? Careening from one disaster to the next with no idea what you're doing or why, and you're so afraid of being alone you won't take any time to sort it out! So afraid to get counseling, because of what you might find out, that you just keep making the same mistakes!*

CLANG! *Pretty sad, especially for your kids. Ever think about what it's doing to them, all the turmoil?*

Enough! She's got to shut off the tape, stay in the moment, don't think too much. . . .

She does want the turmoil to end! It's not her fault things haven't worked out. Brian turned out to be manic-depressive, Jesse was Goatman, Henry had all the personality of a dead battery.

CLANG! *Henry respects you, he's nice to you, so you leave him for someone who's always treated you like dirt? You leave another marriage for Jack Nitzl? Why? Because he treats you bad and you think that's what you deserve?*

She can't bear thinking about Jack. Why, why, why did she go home with him last night?

"Life sure looks different all of a sudden," Max is saying. . . .

It's too much. They think you're pretty or they like the sex so they think they're in love.

"For me too," she says—partly because she does like him, partly because it's in the script.

Not convincing? He looks disappointed, somehow.

"Max? I guess I have a hard time believing you feel the way you say. You're this important man, a knight on a white horse doing death penalties and all, and I do hair."

"Forget that. You're too modest. You're beautiful and sweet and smart and funny and all these things. You're perfect for me."

CLANG!

friday, may 18

Nicky Nutcase.

Roars into Jack's driveway in his jacked-up chrome-exhaust turbo diesel 4×4 with the supercab, the tires, roll bar, fog lights—looks like a 747 rolling in, and he's got Metallica or something screaming out of the sound system so loud you feel like you're in the middle of the San Francisco earthquake. Brain-dead motorhead, his wheels probably cost more than Jack's house.

Wild-eyed, wired, stinking of beer at two in the afternoon. Jack's heard meth makes people energized but not euphoric, not happy like good cocaine does, so these idiots drink or smoke dope along with it. The poor man's speedball.

The nutcase wants the rest of his money, is why he's here.

"The rest? What, you've already gone through that five thousand? What the—"

"Don't worry your little head about it, Jackpot."

"I've gotta worry. I'm in this too, remember?"

"I'm worried about getting my money, is what *I'm* worried about."

"What the hell're you doing, man? If you'd be cool this'll all probably go away, but you're asking for trouble if you keep spreading money around. Let me hold the rest a little longer. How 'bout you take a thousand and let me keep the rest for now?"

The badass eyes, Edward G. Robinson. "Look, I did the job, now that dough's mine." Talking the talk, playing the role. Reminding Jack how much of the *Little Caesar* character he's adopted: the slicked-back hair, tough-guy glares and gestures, tough talk in that cement-mixer voice.

"You've got it coming," Jack concedes. "But what did you do with what you took the other night?"

"Don't worry about it, I said."

"I just wonder. Because you should be okay moneywise, even without that dough. You do okay with the body shop, right?" Little fly-by-night joint, not even licensed anymore, but he gets business from dopers and kids and various losers who don't have insurance. "Between that and working with me . . . you make what, fifty grand a year, and declare almost nothing? No expenses except gas, acety-lene, Bondo, a few tools? How the hell're you so broke?"

"Funny you should ask, Jacko. 'Cause I been thinking, if we're gonna keep doing business on the rebuilt cars, I need to get my fair share."

"Oh? Which would be what?"

"More than it's been. You've told me yourself, you'd barely be makin' it without the profit you make on *our* cars. A couple of 'em a month add up for you, but it don't do much for me. I make two grand on a car, you make seven or eight or however much—that ain't right."

"I give you more than two for most of 'em."

"Three's the tops so far, and I know that was one you knew *you'd* clear ten on. I know you don't do me no favors."

"I'm taking the risk, having hot cars on my lot."

"I'm taking the risk of you turning me in to save your ass if you get busted."

Jack rolls his eyes. "You think I would?"

"Don't make me laugh. Anyway, that money's mine to do what I want with. Ain't nothing to worry about—I watch the news too, and they got nothing. And the spade ain't even dead."

"Great. So it's attempted murder instead of murder, along with armed robbery and whatever else."

Does the fool have any idea how dumb he is? Jack feels a little sorry for him sometimes, ever since Nicky's childhood friend from the cow town in eastern Washington passed through last year. They all had some drinks, and when Nicky went out to his mean machine to do some more meth the guy explained how he fell out of a tree when they were kids, landed on his head and had never been right since. There's a little part of his brain that makes him good with cars (the guy said he took one completely apart and put it back together for a junior high project), but otherwise it's hard to tell there's much left.

". . . they got nothing," Nicky's saying. "They're saying 'The investigation is narrowing to some items of physical evidence.' What the hell's that? They're also saying 'Detectives are seeking help from the public,' which means they ain't got shit."

Jack shaking his head. "I'm telling you, you stay cocky and we're going down."

Nicky giving him the look again.

"Hey, skip the eye cheese, Nick. Look, I'm watching my ass . . . and *trying* to look out for you too, since you're not."

"I want my dough, that's all. You ain't gotta watch out for me. Now look, I'm tired of the tongue-waggin', I want that five K. And I been thinking, I really oughtta get five on top of that, make it a split, make it right. Since you wouldn'ta got any of it without me."

Listen to him! "You kidding? You deserve a bonus for coming along and shooting Harris?"

"I just told you why. And I'm telling you this, buddy: it's bad business to fool with me."

Christ. That movie again.

"You're nothin' but a chip shot, Jacko. You don't wanna fool with me."

The only way to possibly convince him things aren't hunky-dory is to tell him someone saw them, someone *knows*. But Jack can't bring himself to sign Dana's death warrant—not at this point, when he's pretty sure she's too scared to talk anyway.

"All right," he says, "I'll get your money tomorrow. The five grand."

Pay him off and hope for the best.

saturday, may 19

Candy just hopes to make it back to Portland. Alive.

Coming out to the coast with Nicky was the stupidest thing she's ever done. They were having fun last night, zipping on crank last night and she wasn't thinking too good. It was sometime around midnight when he said Let's do another line, drive out there, tear it up and come back in time for you to get to Girls Girls Girls tomorrow night.

Why not? He wasn't talking about love anymore, he just wanted some fun.

But this afternoon he's acting like he owns her. Not saying anything about getting her back in time for her Saturday shift, her moneymaker. He's overcooked on meth and he's mad.

Her mind's eye sees a newspaper headline: "Portland Prostitute Murdered In Oceanside." A small headline, a brief story. Page three of Metro, maybe, in the column on the left along with other short items nobody reads.

Not that Nicky's a killer, not as far as she knows. Relax. He's just a little crazy from being up too long, doing too much crank. Knows he can take it out on her, for now, because he's got the wheels. She's here until she makes a decision to walk out, hike to the highway, put her thumb out and try to make it back to Portland, eighty miles.

Right. As if he'll let her walk out.

He's been in a snit since 4:00 A.M., when she happened to ask him to pay for everything up to that point: two jumps and a hummer. "What, you don't trust me? I got plenty, don't worry, I ain't gonna cheat you."

Now he's mad because she didn't act thrilled during his big caveman hump. "You didn't say anything," he grouses. Imbecile, wanting to hear how fantastic he is. Ooooooh, Nicky! It's so big, gonna split me wide open, I've never had anything like it!

He's a little boy, no matter how big and bad he thinks he is. They're all little boys. They're the studs, you're the porn queen.

Why'd she get into this life?

She thought she was cool, telling her dad to go to hell and dropping out of Franklin during junior year when a guy named Brad told her she could move in with him. Crappy little apartment, but so what? *But now what?* she remembers asking herself not long after, watching TV one night while he was out getting drunk. She ended up staying with her friend Jary briefly, getting stuck with the rent when Jary moved out, getting evicted and moving in with another friend, Harmony, and Harmony's big black stud-man Tre. That was it. Turned out they were running an out-call service and she could pay her share of the rent and expenses by going out a few nights a month. Easy. *You're "Candy" now, not Kay*, Tre said, and she said *Fine, whatever.*

One thing led to another.

The worst sign of all, now, is that Nicky's back to "Why can't we be together? Why not give up all that and let me be your sugar daddy? I can afford you, and we get along, and I *know* you like the tool."

She tries to reason. "We've talked about it. It's nothing against you and surely nothing against the tool, nothing wrong with that—"

"Nothing *wrong* with it?"

"I mean it's the best. The biggest and the best. But I've tried to explain, I've got my life and I wanna do what I wanna do. I wanna get some money together and go to community college and then chiropractic school. Instead of massage therapy."

"Gimme a break. You don't need all that. You don't need any job as long as you're with me."

"But it's what I want. And you're not always so flush, are you? What's going on, a lot of wrecks lately?"

"People are always smashing their cars. I work as much as I want. I can set you up, believe that."

"I don't want to be set up. I want to be unfettered."

Unfettered! It pops out, a word she picked up two or three months ago. It's been hanging in the closet, as her vocabulary book says, waiting for the right occasion.

But this isn't the right occasion. Nicky hates it when she uses words. He'll probably accuse her, again, of thinking she's as smart as Pam Gramm.

But right now his thoughts are back to crank. He's telling her about times he's worked on cars for thirty or forty hours straight, getting a week's work out of a few lines, then crashed for fifteen hours. And then done it again.

Which reminds him, it's about time to snort a line.

Candy says no, she'd better not, and he doesn't need any more, does he?

"I *want* some more."

Afterward, as usual, he gets testy again. Bugging her about June again—"your *girlfriend*," he says, all sarcasm.

"Let's not talk about it. You just wanna be mad."

"Wrong."

"And you don't need me anyway. You don't need any woman, any *one*. You need to spread that big ol' tool around, fella."

"Wouldn't need to if I had you. Wouldn't want to. You're the—the—"

"I'm nothing special. There are—"

"—the penultimate babe," he blurts. "The penultimate."

She can't help smiling, and she's afraid she's going to burst out laughing.

"What's funny?"

"Nothing."

"What's funny?"

"Nothing. I'm laughing at myself." Nice recovery. "You use a good word like 'penultimate' and it reminds me why I wanted to expand my vocabulary. I was with this old Portland State professor, this old potato trying to get into my head, and I told him I felt like a 'social piranha' sometimes. He busted a gut laughing. He finally explained that a piranha's a carnivorous fish and I probably meant 'pariah'. The next day I went and bought *Thirty Days to a Better Vocabulary*."

"You lie. You're laughing at me."

Reading her mind. Shaking her up. Her skin's hot, her mouth working: "All right, I thought 'penultimate' was funny. But look, everyone misuses that one. You mean you think I'm hot, right? I'm even better than the ultimate? But that's not what penultimate means. It means next to last, like 'November is the penultimate month of the year.'"

He gets up out of the chair, embarrassed. "Let's go out. Get some coffee or something."

Stupid of her, to embarrass him. Not that she meant to. She was trying to smooth it over.

On the way down the hill to the café, trying to change the mood, she remarks on the bright sunny sky over the ocean, but he ignores her and goes back to it. "Why do you do that with words? Study 'em?"

"The professor, that old fart. Laughing at me and calling me his little ol' man-eater, his piranha. Every time he said it he was reminding me he was a professor and I was a dumb whore. That's why. I work on my vocabulary so I'll be minimally articulate, that's all."

Mistake. "Minim-m-mini-*hell*," he snaps. "Why do you talk like that? Why not talk so people understand?"

"I'm sorry. But I want to understand other people, too, not have people talking over my head. Not make a fool of myself."

Wrong. "Is that what I do, make a fool of myself?"

"I didn't mean that! Come on, forget this! Is this why we drove all the way out here?" They're down the hill now, the café a few steps away, but suddenly she doesn't want to be trapped facing him across a table. "Can we walk on the beach instead of getting coffee? You mind? I need some exercise."

"You want exercise, we can go back in and I'll exercise you."

"I need fresh air."

"Fresh air, hell. But if you want, what the hell."

"It'll be good for us."

He brightens slightly when they hit the sand. Looking down the beach he says, "Might as well go all the way down to those rocks, huh, if you want exercise?"

"Fine with me."

It's blustery, bracing, and she feels great by the time they reach the rocks.

After staring out to sea for a while she asks if he wants to jog back.

He ignores it, still gazing out.

"Nicky?"

What he says when he finally looks at her—he hasn't heard a word she said—is, "Wanna make some money, man-eater?"

"Not here."

"Come on. No one can see us." Tipping his head toward the houses back off the beach. "You think anyone's standing at the windows with binoculars?"

"Sorry. I've already got charges against me in Portland, I don't need the Oceanside cops out here."

"How 'bout for double? Two hundred bucks for what, a minute or so? That's if you make it happen, don't pull off as soon as you get me going."

"Sorry."

Not what he wants to hear, and for a moment she's scared again, imagining police out here, a murder scene, an ambulance scooting across the sand, news teams, a juicy story about a prostitute beaten and strangled on the beach. But suddenly he's smiling. Smirking. "Three hundred?"

"Do I hear a thousand? I said no thanks!"

"I've got a thousand." Reaching into his jeans.

"No! Don't you hear me? Let's go back to the room, we'll do whatever you want, but not here."

"A *thousand dollars?*" Holding out a fistful of cash.

Candy shaking her head. "Let's go back. You'll save a lot of money and we won't get arrested."

# # #

After she's earned a mere hundred and wiped off, he lies there smiling.

"So, mister?" she says. "How is it you had a thousand dollars to spend on a minute or two?"

"No big thing. Just working. I told you I can take care of you if you'll let me."

"Come on, tell me. You got any idea how much you've spent on me in the last week alone?"

"It's only money."

Candy's too tired to push it. Too tired and too wired all at once, the awful feeling when you've been up too long doing too much crank. No wonder Nicky gets psycho, doing this three or four days at a time. She wonders if she can possibly drift off and catch a nap. A long day and night ahead.

Why's she here?

Early on, working for Tre and Jary and getting into dancing and modeling on the side, she knew she couldn't do it forever. She focused and got her GED two years ago, finishing up just a year after her Franklin class. Thought about college: maybe a nursing program, but probably community college first, PCC. The idea of chiropractic came when someone sent her to Fat Matt for weed a few months ago, this guy dealing to put himself through Western School of Chiropractic. Well, why not? She liked words but couldn't see herself as an English teacher, anything like that. . . . But it hardly mattered. She was making money, she was turned on to meth, she'd lost her way. . . . She thinks she's got her head on straight now, she can start at PCC in the fall . . .

"Hey!"

Her eyes snap open.

"What're you doing?"

"I need some rest. I gotta get some rest."

"Like hell. We came out here to party. Let's do another line and *do* something."

"I can't, not now. Please—"

"*Hey!*"

Her eyes snap open again and he's glaring down at her. Eyes wide and bloodshot, his skin pasty, teeth dirty, hair stringy. "We came here to party, remember? Come on, you want a line to pick you up? Booze? What do you want?"

"A shower," she says. "A shower and a nap."

"Let's take a shower, then. Have some fun in there."

"Please. I just want to soak and wash myself good."

"Why not make some money, though?" Leering at her. Grabbing his fat wallet off the nightstand, waving it in her face.

"Please, Nicky. I've made enough. We can do something later. Okay?"

sunday, may 20

Max drove Dana home Friday night after drinks, dinner, and hot-tub sex at his house; and drove back wondering if everything was as good for her as for him.

Emptied the last inch of wine from one of the glasses on the kitchen counter, went upstairs, brushed his teeth, undressed, turned out the light and lay down.

Heard a crinkling sound when his head hit the pillow. Reached underneath and grabbed the paper, whatever it was, and turned on the bedside lamp.

It was a homemade card, a sheet of thick paper folded in thirds, the writing surrounded by bright colored-pencil stars, flowers, hearts, smiley faces. The writing itself was childlike, an adolescent mix of printing and cursive, full of loops and swirls, circles over the *i*'s. But so what?

Dear Dear Max,

I'm thinking about your eyes and the kindness in them. How your touch is warm and gentle and perfect to me. Last night laying next to you, just kind-of breathing you into me and watching you and touching you—wonderful! You excite and calm me all at the same time. I don't want to try and figure everything out right now, I just want to go with it.

She had to have written it that day. She had to be talking about last night after they walked in Grant Park, talked about the future, went back to her place, drank wine by candlelight, looked in on the sleeping girls, lay down. . . .

What's happened? I'm confused about "Love" and "Being in-love" and "True Love" and "Lust" and "Wanting Love" and "Dealing with it all," well, just a number of things.

All right, so she's not a practiced writer. What does it matter?

You wanting to be with me and your gentleness and how you are with me is a gift of such love. Thank you! Thank you!

I asked my sister one time about sharing your life with someone and she told me "When you can not imagine your life without that person— when they fill your life," that's how you know. That's what is happening here, Max. You fill my life.

I will stay.

Dana

The greatest weekend of his life, even though it's mostly just hanging out. It's hanging out with *them*.

Dana brings the girls over Saturday morning. A quick trip to Starbucks, then home to get organized for a drive out to the coast. At Seaside it's *moments:* Dana explaining seagulls to Emily, romping in the shallow surf with Liz, marveling at seashells . . .

A long, long day, time stretching out the way it does when every minute is special.

Back at his house in the evening they hang out, the girls splashing and whooping in the hot tub, Max videotaping for posterity, imagining a day twenty years in the future when they'll all—a family—revisit the beginning. Max and Dana drinking frozen daiquiris and tending burgers on the barbecue, sneaking kisses and gropes when they go inside to refresh their drinks. Talking about the article in the Big O that morning about the best U.S. cities for singles, Portland a so-so number 31—Max saying it won't ever be an issue for either of them again, hopefully; Dana giving him those eyes and saying she hopes not, too.

He hates letting them leave later, even though they're coming back in the morning.

He goes to bed bursting with feelings. And as if it hadn't already been one of the greatest days of his life, he hears a crinkling sound again as his head hits the pillow—something underneath—and his fingers find an envelope and he knows she's still with him, even though she's gone.

When did she write it? When did she slip up here and leave it?

Dear Dear Max,

You fill me! I love being with you just sitting or just watching you thrills me I am totally serious. I get so scared sometimes. I want this so badly.

I want to be happy and for you to be happy. I want to be sure you know me. I don't want you to find out that you are disappointed in me because we didn't give it enough time and you might find out that I'm not all you thought I was. I want us to be so good together—to LAST to love & laugh and grouch and smile and hold and live forever content with each other, To like each other.

Dana

She's not John Updike. So what?

And it's *So what?* more than ever when, a few minutes later, not quite dead to the world, he hears the doorbell, gets himself up, looks out the window fronting the street and sees her car down there. Scoots down the stairs in the nude, cracks the door and finds her smiling at him, *glowing*. She leans in and kisses him. It's drizzly out and she's wearing a yellow rain slicker like school kids wear, maybe Elizabeth's.

"What're you doing?" he says. "Come in!"

"Come out! It's warm!"

Come out? But of course there's not much danger. None across the street, where it drops off into the slough, and Matt and Bridget and their baby on the left are lights-out and the Tandlers on the right, the same. He steps out and sits down, naked, in the wicker rocker on the left, Dana taking the other.

"I hated leaving earlier," she says.

"I didn't want you to."

"And I've got to get back soon, but I had to see you." Up out of her chair, coming to him, straddling him, dropping down on his lap and suddenly unsnapping the slicker, revealing nothing underneath. "Wanted to make you feel good"—reaching for his swelling pecker, the naughty girl.

Wow. Beautiful, and sweet, and naughty naughty naughty. And she will *stay!*

# # #

Hearing her old Civic pull up Sunday morning he pops out on the porch, thrilled to see little Emily springing out of the car and racing up the sidewalk—flying into his arms, saying she missed him last night, missed him! Teen-queen Lizzie appearing next, playing it cool but clearly glad to see him. Finally Dana, radiant. Max knowing it can't get any better than this.

Strawberry pancakes at Strudel House. A walk down to Sellwood Park, where they swing on the swings, chat with a young couple pushing twins in a double stroller, take a few pictures in front of some dogwoods. On down to the river, fool around a while, then back up to Sellwood for lunch at the Mexican joint.

All afternoon, it gets better and better. The squirt-gun fight. Old maid, with the deck of cards his nieces left last summer. Max and Dana doing curry stir-fry for dinner, the girls baking butternut cookies. Moments: Dana sharing Emily's excitement over a bird's nest they spotted in the apple tree; Dana doing Dylan's classic "Isis" when it comes on KGON, every word, with dead-on enunciations and even Bob's squint and scowl; the girls laughing no end when Max walks into one more squirt-gun ambush. Moments he knows he'll never forget, videotaped or not.

After dinner, after dark, Dana finally says they've got to go, she needs to get the girls ready for school tomorrow and their three nights with their dad. Max is deflated—but only for a few seconds, until she says "Do you want to follow us home? They want you to, and then you and I can have some time together after they go to bed."

It can't get any better.

# # #

Sure, she's been with other men, but he can't believe she's ever looked at any of them the way she looks at him. Telling him, "You're wonderful, Max," as they lie on the spread-out sleeping bag on the floor of her little living room, in the flickering light from the vanilla candle on the end table.

"No," he says, "but I'll try to be. I love you and I—"

"I love *you*, Max."

"—and I want us to be together, all four of us. Get up in the morning, have breakfast, get the girls to school, we go to work. Dinner together at night, homework, TV, bedtime." Like the first year or so of his second marriage. "And then just us, like this."

"It sounds perfect. I only wish . . ."

"What?"

". . . wish I was coming to you . . . *better*, you know? Younger, prettier, not . . . not *damaged*. Not scared."

"Forget it. Haven't we talked about this?"

Funny, he feels so lucky to be with her, to maybe have a future with her, then suddenly he gets a note from her or she starts talking this way and it's like *he's* got the power. Insecure? Her? He realizes how little he knows her.

"I guess we've talked about it," she says.

"We have, and I keep telling you you don't have a thing to worry about. You know what they say, that everyone's the product of everything they've seen and done and been through, and in your case the product is fantastic. You've been through a lot and survived it all and you're stronger for it. You know what you want, what you don't want. There's a serenity about you, like you know who you are and know you can get through anything, with or without a man. It's not like you *need* to be with someone, or you'd still be with one of 'em. That's why I'm so flattered you want to be with me."

"Awww."

"It's true. Give yourself some credit."

"I do—some—but I don't know if I'm what you deserve. You're important, you've done so much, you know all these big people, and I'm just me. I'm a *hairdresser,* I'm almost forty, I—"

"I'm *past* forty. And you're thirty-six, right? Which isn't almost forty. You look maybe thirty, with that angel face and this great body. Get a grip, huh? Hear me: the way I feel about you is the feeling people go to the wall for, change their lives for."

He can hear Paige laughing. *Ha! Change your life? You're the king DA first, a human being second—a distant second!*

"My job's gotten in the way in the past," he says. "Some people say I need it more than I need love or anything else. But it's not true. If the job starts coming between you and me I'm outta there. Gone."

"But I don't want that, Max. I want you to do what you love, what you're good at, what you make a good living at."

"But none of that matters if I don't have a bigger reason for doing it. Someone to be doing it for. Someone to share it with."

I have no idea what you're doing! Georgia, wife number two. *You're home, you're not home, your moods go up and down, and I have no clue! You tell me nothing!*

"You're the one, I'm positive," he says.

"I'd like to be, Max. I'm just not very sure of myself, what I have to offer. I remember seeing you with that lawyer lady—Paige, was it? So good-looking and so—"

"Forget her. *She's* someone whose career comes before everything, which is what she accused me of. You're a *woman*-woman, she's a fast-track professional with the woman buried a few layers down. With you it's all right there: feelings, tenderness, sex, vulnerability, motherhood, everything. *You're* right there. With a lady lawyer it's a struggle to get past the lawyer."

"Oh, Max . . ."

# # #

Badly, she wants this to work out (if the trouble goes away). She's thirty-six years old and still careening from one disaster to the next. Not as pretty as she used to be, with lines in her face and body parts sagging— she won't be attracting men forever, surely not the kind who can take her away from cramped apartments, claptrap cars and low-paying jobs.

If only the trouble goes away.

And if she can get used to Max's lovey stuff. Or if he'd get over it. It's embarrassing, especially when you know he's not seeing the real you. He goes on and on about what a great person she is. (CLANG!) He stares at her and goes on about how there's never been such a perfect arrangement of the 128 facial muscles. About her dreamy eyes, full of love and wit and intelligence. (Intelligence!) About her body.

"I can't believe we're doing this," he's whispering now, in bed. "Can't believe I'm the lucky one. Geez, your body . . ."

Her saggy thirty-six-year-old body.

"I adore you, Dana Waverleigh." Whispering in her ear again— he's big on whispering. "I can't stop saying it."

"Oh, Max . . ."

She does want something to last with a man, but it's so hard. They want you too much, or not enough. They smother you or don't pay attention at all.

Or they turn out to be druggies or crazies. She thought she was going to freak out last year when she saw Wayne in his car out on Eighty-second and that nightmare time came back: the screaming, the intimidation, the physical stuff. Seven years ago, and it only lasted three months, but she was an instant basket case when she saw him.

CLANG! *You still haven't told Emily about Wayne? She doesn't know she and Elizabeth are only half-sisters? You and Brian let her go on believing he's her father too? What happens when she finds out?*

She's got no idea what happens. She just doesn't want to upset Emily now.

CLANG! *Do you ever think beyond today? Ever?*

What will Max think when he gets to know her?

CLANG! *You've got an irresistible surface, but there's a huge void inside.*

"Unbelievable," he says, "that marriage never worked out for you. Guys never knew what they had."

"I'm not perfect, Max. I keep telling you."

He doesn't hear. "Unbelievable that anyone would let you down. That they'd *let themselves* let you down, once they had you."

Giving her the Soulful Gaze again.

She hates the labels but it's all too familiar sometimes, everything everyone's saying and doing. Herself included.

"Why hasn't it worked out?" he asks. "Hard to believe . . ."

"I don't know. Sometimes I think it's because I'm too much of a dreamer. Because I'm always looking for that crazy, perfect, shoot-for-the-stars kind of love." Something someone said sometime, she can't remember who or when or why. "You know?"

"I know."

"And now, maybe . . ."

CLANG! *Everything you've said about this bigger-than-life love of ours, and now you're walking out?*

monday, may 21

It's the nutcase, the last person Jack wants to see. Screaming into the lot, hopping out of his mean machine and bopping toward the office, a slimeball in biker boots, worn-out jeans, and his prized jean jacket over a Planet Hollywood T-shirt.

"Yo, Jackpot!" Bopping in, flopping down in one of the customer chairs. "Whuddup?" Tripping, for sure. Eyes way too wide, way too bright.

"Whuddup," Jack says, "is I'm working."

"Don't look like it. Nobody around."

"Vinnie's around somewhere, handling customers. I'm doing paperwork."

"Oh. Nothing important, huh? 'Cause we gotta talk."

"Man," Jack says, "you shouldn't be coming here."

"Whatsa problem? Things're cool, far's I can tell."

"We don't know that. I keep telling you we're better off if we're not seen together. Then if something points 'em to one of us, the other one's not automatically linked."

The stupid, doped-up grin. Mossy teeth he probably hasn't brushed in a month. "Nothing gonna touch us, my man, trust me."

"*Trust* you?"

The grin vanishes instantly, a scowl moving in like storm clouds. He'll start doing Edward G. Robinson any minute.

"They probably don't have anything yet," Jack says. "It'll all probably go away if we just be cool. If you stop coming around here. If you stop doing that meth and spending money. If you just work, lay low, act right."

"I'm working fine. 'Course, I could use more work to *do*. Keep me busy, man."

"I talked to Vlasitch this morning. He'll bring you something this week."

"That's good. '*When I was thirty-five, it was a very good year*' "— the fool up out of the chair doing his ridiculous Sinatra, his fist up to his mouth like a microphone. "—*It was a very good year . . . to beeee an ar-teest of in-de-pendent means. . . .*'"

If he was any dumber you'd have to water him once a week. Jack can picture him doing these poses and performances in front of a mirror: Little Caesar, Sinatra, probably Robert De Niro in *Taxi Driver*: "You talkin' to me?" Probably Stallone, too—shirt off, oiled up, flexing. Although Jack's pretty sure Nicky doesn't work out much anymore, too gone on dope.

"But for now," the fool says, abruptly dropping Sinatra, "I want the rest of my loot."

"Excuse me?"

"The rest of my fair share. Half. We talked about it."

"*You* talked about it. Look, we agreed you'd get a third, and you got it."

"But I been thinking. Only a third for me? Fifty-fifty sounds more real. Because you wouldn't have a dime of it without me. You'da never gone over there."

"Wait a minute—"

"You wait a minute, Jack. Fair's fair. The way I see it I still got five grand coming, which I could use right now. I had a big weekend." In front of the desk now, staring down at Jack.

"Easy, big fella. Be smart. We're in this together, remember."

"*You* be smart. Don't be a hardhead. My old man used to say a hard head makes for a sore ass."

"Righto. But remember this: If anything happens to me, it could easily track back to you. Especially with you coming around here all the time, us being seen together."

Nicky laughs, not that anything's funny. "Why we arguing, Jacko? Why don't you just gimme the five Gs and we're good?"

"I don't have it. Besides the fact—"

"Don't have it? You kept twenty that night."

"Ten I owed Vlasitch, the rest to bills. Besides the fact I don't owe you. You had ten grand coming and you got it."

"I figure you used me, Jacko, same as you been using me to do cars for cheap. Well, that stuff don't go no more, not with me it don't."

Jack remembers it from *Little Caesar*.

"Remember," the nitwit says, "a hard head makes for a sore ass."

tuesday, may 22

A week now, and all the clichés still apply. Max is floating. He's walking on air. He's on cloud nine.

All the love songs apply, even the sappy ones. Especially the sappy ones.

The whole thing disorients him. One minute he's sure they'll last forever; the next he's positive he's on borrowed time, because she could have anyone.

Sometimes he adores her, his angelic girl. Other times he suspects it's mostly about the sex. Such a naughty girl! What a rush he got Saturday night, when she went home with the girls but came back later wearing the yellow rain slicker—*only* the slicker, it turned out.

Then Sunday she seemed embarrassed about it, afraid he'd think she's trashy. Max, astounded by her insecurity, kept holding her, assuring her she's the best thing that's happened to him in years. Dana giving him the loving eyes, saying "I can't believe it. I've made so many wrong choices in my life, it's hard to believe this could happen."

Last night she was strong again and *he* felt unworthy, wondering aloud "What'll I do when you leave me?" She didn't want to hear it. "Stop, Max. That's not going to happen. Do I have to *show* you how I feel, again?"

No, he told her; he believed. The way she looks at him, the things she says, how can he not?

They're white hot. She goes braless when they're together and Max can't lay off her. Even when the girls are around they're constantly slipping around a corner, Max running his hands up under her shirt, Dana reaching for his knob and promising him a good time later. At her apartment, after the girls go to bed, she runs around in nothing but a long T-shirt, her hair tied up in a twist that drives him crazy, her bare neck looking so succulent he wants to take a bite out of it.

So what if she's a wee bit neurotic? It turns out she doesn't like him kissing or even touching her neck, doesn't even like the gentle stroking and kneading that lots of women crave. On a late-night walk she shakes out from under his hand, saying she just . . . she just . . . but can't explain. Did someone throttle her, one of the jerks in her past? Max wants to know, but doesn't want to ask.

So what if she's afraid of flying?

So what if she doesn't like being in a car unless she's driving? "It says something about my trust in you," she says, "that I ride with you and I'm not *too* nervous."

So what? We've all got our quirks.

So understanding, Max! Or is it just that she's the hottest thing you've ever gotten your hands on?

So what if he was raised upper-middle-class in Irvington and she was raised lower-middle, or prole, in deep southeast Portland, the area known as Felony Flats for the high concentration of probationers, parolees, dopers, and assorted losers living in the cheap rentals out there? So what if she and the girls play would-you? It's not quite like Howard Stern asking some bimbo if she'd suck her father for a million bucks, but the same idea: Would you eat someone's barf for a hundred dollars? Would you drink pee-pee?

So what? She's his radiant girl, doing pretty well considering she grew up poor, with nutty parents—a mother who was putting her down when she wasn't giving her the silent treatment, a father who obsessed about the end of the world and eventually sold their little house and bought a shack out in McMinnville on the theory they'd be safer there when America's enemies started dropping bombs on the cities. So what if she never went to college and there's not much in her little bookcase except self-help, a few romance novels, and some children's books she says she still reads because they're happy and positive and fun?

She's pretty wonderful, considering. And who's he to judge, given his track record?

Because the sex is the best ever, right? Because of the way she wraps those stretchy legs around you and coos in your ear, right?

No. Not only. Not by a long shot. It's because she makes him laugh, whether by showing him the Dental Probe or doing Dylan or imitating her southern-belle cousin in Alabama.

It's the way he feels when the Civic pulls up in front of the house and Emily bolts up the walk and bounds into his arms saying she's missed him.

The way he feels when Elizabeth tells him she's never seen her mom so happy, no man's ever treated her right, she's made such bad choices—until now.

Flattered, is how he feels.

More than ever, tonight, after he reads Emily a bedtime story and turns out the light and says good night and, as he's leaving the room, the little voice says "Max? I wish we could live with you. . . ."

It's so much fun at your house and down at the park. . . . I hope you and Mommy get married and we can be a family."

In bed with Dana a few minutes later, still glowing, he tells her about it. Tells her he sometimes regrets not having kids of his own, but becoming part of her girls' lives would be the next-best thing.

"It's not too late, Max."

Huh?

"For a child of your own. If you really think you want to be with me . . ."

"You know it."

"I've always wanted one more. I've got two that're pretty great despite all the turmoil, but I've always wanted to do it right. With the right man. Does that make sense?"

Whoa.

"You'd be great," she says. "The girls love you. Em talks about you all the time. You're already the closest thing to a father to her."

"Except for her father," Max says, straining to keep perspective. "She seems to like spending time with him every week."

No reply.

"Sweetie?"

"He's not . . . not . . ."

"Sweetie?"

"He's not her father, Max."

Huh?

"Em thinks he is, but he's only Lizzy's father. Em's is someone I never want to see again, someone I was only with for a few months. I get scared even thinking of him. I saw him in his car once, after *years* had passed, and I started hyperventilating so bad I had to pull over. . . . I know it sounds weird," she says, and kisses him—tentative, like she's wondering what he' s thinking.

He's not sure what to think.

"A man I got involved with after my first marriage," she says. "I got pregnant right away, before I realized what he was. I got out of there but I wanted the baby, which turned out to be Emily. I spent months in court getting custody and making sure this man wouldn't be in our lives at all, not that he wanted to be. He never paid child support but that was okay, even though I had no money and no skills to make a living at the time. Just so he was gone."

Kissing him again, in the dark, as if to make sure he hadn't run away.

"There was a time when we were so desperate we moved in with Brian, my ex, Elizabeth's dad—an architect making good money, a nice guy just trying to help. Pretty soon we realized Em thought he was her father too, not just Lizzy's. We didn't know how to handle it. I wasn't sure how Em would react when I explained. I know it's crazy, I know she's got to find out, but . . ."

She goes quiet, as if she's afraid Max will dump her for sure now.

Max thinking, *It gets stranger and stranger. But such a babe, and such sweetness in her, and after so much turmoil she's got to be desperate for some stability, for someone who's not an absolute asshole. Don't be so nervous.*

He'll ignore the possibility that she's one of these people who *enjoy* turmoil.

All he knows for sure is that he's got a woody that's about to burst. "I love you," he says, and her eyes glisten, and she reaches for him. . . .

"Let's do something with this, Max."

# # #

She feels crazy, dreading what will happen if they catch Jack and whoever was with him that night.

And what's happening with Max is making her a nervous wreck. She's afraid he'll find out what she's really like, and run.

She feels like two different people. Sometimes she's so happy, so sure of everything, with Max talking about buying a house bigger and nicer than his rental and marrying her; the next day she feels like a criminal or something, an imposter, a nutty little nobody that no one like Max would ever want if he knew her. The stardust phase will pass, the lust will fade and he'll realize her "inner light" (his term) exists only in his imagination, her "priceless" face is nothing special, the body he raves about is just an ordinary, aging body, her mind is nothing.

The clang and clatter of the past. When he gazes at her and says she looks so young, she wonders if it's because she's never grown up. Never had a career, never worked at a marriage, never read the newspaper. No wonder she hasn't aged: she's still a kid, as Amy says.

Every nice thing he says makes her feel bad. Reminds her of something someone else has said, someone who knows her better. When he says her daughters are wonderful, a tribute to her parenting, she hears Amy: *"Any expert would tell you the girls are being affected by this life, even if it doesn't show up for years. What're you doing, dragging them from one of your soap operas to the next? If you're not wrapped up in some new man and ignoring them, you're crying about a breakup and they're trying to comfort you. I know, I know, people say they're so mature—no wonder! They're the parents here, Dana, you're the child!"*

When he talks about how bright they are . . . CLANG! *"What'll happen to them without a college education? They'll be in trouble, all because you preferred to scrape by on child support all these years instead of working and putting money aside."*

When he talks about getting married and growing old together, she remembers overhearing Elizabeth on the phone last fall, during the fling with the lumber broker: *I like this guy, but he probably won't last. My mom tends to go from one man to another.*

It makes her crazy. She knows she should just give up men for a while, all men, and try to sort things out. But she's not going to throw this away. Max is a nice guy, interesting, fun, good in bed, good with the girls. He's important, one of the big shots in the DA's office, and Roop says he'll probably be *the* Multnomah County DA one of these days.

She might not have any idea what love is, but when you're thirty-six, with two kids and no money, this is close enough.

Now, if only the trouble would go away.

part two

thursday, may 24

Nicky pulls into a space at Kozy Kabin, the daily/weekly/monthly doper motel where Cannonball and his latest meth chick are staying. Three or four familiar heaps are parked near number 12, everybody probably slamming crank inside. A bad idea, coming here, but he needs to be around people—keep himself in reality, keep from getting wiggy over it.

It.

It hardly seems real.

But it happened. He did it. He still feels the jolt up and down his arm. (Which he didn't feel at all after he blasted Highwire Harris. But that was only one shot.)

He hears voices in 12, knocks, calls out "It's Nicky!" A few seconds later he hears the click of the lock and the door opens. Sylvie. She's tripping, looks bad.

Does he look that bad? He's still tripping hard.

He's sorry he came. Cannonball and his new chick, Tony, Sylvie, Bobcat, Rude—at least a dozen people sprawled on the beds, on the floor, in the chairs over on the kitchenette side. Cranksters. Losers. Of course he's a crankster too, but that's not all he is. He works, he keeps himself up, he's got some pride. This is nothing but ponytails, shaved heads, earrings, nose rings, dirty clothes, black leather jackets with straps and chains and studs. Everyone dirty, smelly, stupid, doing way too much meth.

Which he, for one, is going to cut way back on.

He's tripping now, though. No idea how many lines he's done today, or how many shots of Rebel Yell. One rush after another, almost a continuous wave.

He should rip outta here. Not a good scene for him, especially after what's happened. These losers attract cops. The last thing Nicky wants is—

What's this?

Her!—Pamela Gramm!—talking about him on the TV mounted on the wall! Not knowing she's talking about *him*, of course, but reporting what happened!

Red dress, sleeveless. Great arms.

Talking about "unknown assailant or assailants." "Murders in Dunthorpe," it says at the bottom of the screen.

"Nicko!" someone behind him yells. "Wanna slam, my man?"

It's Rude, over at the table with some scrawny girl, ready to shoot up. Pimping him, knowing Nicky doesn't like needles.

Nicky's dizzy. Too many lines today, too much Rebel Yell since . . . *it*.

His arm still tingling.

Did he really do it?

Yes. Pamela Gramm's talking about him on TV. Except he can't make out what she's saying.

Tripping *hard*.

Wondering how her arms would feel, wrapped around you.

". . . blew 'em all away," someone on the floor is saying.

Hey, he didn't plan on shooting anybody. (Doesn't remember what he did plan, but he sure as hell didn't expect those kids to be there.)

Why'd he take his gun, then?

He had to be out of his mind over there today, in the big house. To go there at all. To take his piece. Sure he meant to do something.

But just to *tell* her. *Keep away from Candy, you carpetmuncher.*

He did tell her, pointing the .40 right between her eyes.

So why'd he shoot?

# # #

The last couple weeks, since Oceanside, Nicky had tailed Candy quite a few nights before it occurred to him she might be seeing her girlfriend in the *day*time. If she really had a girlfriend, which he had a feeling she did.

Day before yesterday he waited up the street from her duplex early in the morning, saw her come out at nine (looking better in sweatshirt and jeans than in her hotsy nighttime outfits) and followed her to a café down Twenty-third Avenue, then to Gold's Gym, then to Safeway and back home. No sign of a carpetmuncher.

Yesterday she went to the café for breakfast, to Music Millennium on Twenty-third, back home. Came out again a half hour later, looking fine in a pink blouse and short white shorts, showing off the legs. Taking off in her car, Nicky following.

". . . *June Ohlander was twenty-nine years old.* . . ." On the TV now, Pamela looked the foxiest he's ever seen her, standing in front of the big rich house with the white columns. You can't see the lawn on TV but Nicky remembers it, big as a football field inside those walls and green as a pool table.

"*. . . The children, both pronounced dead at the scene, were Andrew, age five, and Debra, three.*"

For the longest time yesterday he stared across that lawn from the road, waiting for Candy to come out, wondering. Two hours he waited before Candy and a woman with short dark hair came out the side door. Definitely friendly, the way they were talking and laughing, and when they hugged and kept hugging Nicky knew what they'd been doing inside.

". . . Man, I'm zoned," someone's groaning behind him. . . .

". . . Some kinda baaaaaad man they're talkin' about . . ."

"*. . . Ted Ohlander, June's husband of seven years, is a senior account executive at Pacific Crest Securities in Lake Oswego. . . .*"

Pamela's babe-alicious, no doubt about it. Foxy, classy, the makeup just right, the cute pointy chin, the arms, everything. And Candy dares to criticize her? Candy the cocksucker? Candy the carpetmuncher?

Well, there's one dyke's carpet she won't be munching anymore.

# # #

"*. . . Again: Portland police detectives and personnel from Multnomah County's Major Crimes Team have been here at the scene since shortly after the bodies were discovered. . . .*"

Is Pamela wearing the famous diamond ring, big as an ice cube? He can't tell, she's holding the microphone in her right hand.

"You all right, man?"

It's Little Tina, Cannonball's newest crank whore. Sores all over her neck and arms from scratching, probably all over her skanky body.

"Just checkin' out this stuff on TV," Nicky tells her.

"They cut in on *Oprah*," someone's saying.

"*. . . were discovered by a friend of June Ohlander who became concerned when Mrs. Ohlander failed to show up for their scheduled racquetball game. The friend was unable to reach Mrs. Ohlander by phone and drove to the house. . . .*"

What dictionary words will the carpetmuncher have for *this?*

"Nicko! Got you a line here, if you don't wanna slam!"

He needs to get out of here. Cranksters, losers . . .

"*. . . the brutal murders of a young woman—a wife, mother of two—and her two small children . . .*" Pamela giving it the sad voice, the sad face, like they always do.

And there's the ring! The gigantic stay-away wedding ring, as she waves a guy in a suit into the picture.

"*. . . Max Travis, senior deputy district attorney and coordinator of the Major Crimes Team . . .*"

"Cops all over that place," someone's saying.

But they don't have a thing on him! Nobody else in the house at the time, nobody outside, and those houses were so far apart there's no way any neighbor could make him. Five minutes later he was back down by the Willamette with the fishing pole he left there before. When he got back to his rig he cut the doctor gloves into little pieces and fluttered them into the wind as he drove off.

"Two little kids," Sylvie's saying. "Wow."

Well, those kids were *there*, that's why. He didn't expect them to be, he didn't expect a dyke to have any kids. But there they were and what was he supposed to do, say hi? Ask 'em not to yell when he shot their mommy, don't tell the cops?

He needs to get out. Maybe no danger here, but gotta be careful. Be cool.

And cool is what he is. Even now. Especially now, because crank makes most people crazy but it makes Nicky focus.

Know what you have to do and then do it, that's all.

He's gotta go to bed, is what. Smoke some weed first, slug some more Rebel Yell, whatever it takes to go to sleep.

On TV Pamela's still in front of the big white house, foxy as can be in the red dress, babe-alicious even when she's so serious.

Did it really happen?

Yes, because she's right there talking about it and his arm still feels weird, but otherwise it all seems unreal.

"*. . . bodies are still inside. They were found in the kitchen, according to a police spokesman, where June Ohlander was baking cookies while her children ate lunch. . . .*"

# # #

Dana had planned on meeting Max at the Veritable Quandary around six today, whenever she could get there after work. Elizabeth was going to look after Em for a while, pop a pizza in the oven.

Max called at four saying he couldn't make it, he was on his way to a murder scene, he'd call when he could.

At the salon they turned on the TV. Two local stations were already live at the scene, a ritzy house in Dunthorpe where a woman and her two kids had been shot dead in their kitchen.

She left at five-thirty, picked up the girls, stopped at McDonald's to feed them. At home she had a drink and the girls watched reruns. She wondered what it was like for Max, being in the middle of it, seeing the bodies. He's seen lots of them. She can't imagine.

She can't imagine lots of things. Things are so strange. Highwire Harris gets shot, now this. All kinds of things in between, here and everywhere.

It's past nine when Max finally calls. He says he'll be at the scene a while longer, he's not sure how long, better not wait up.

"Will you come over whenever you can?"

"I don't have any idea when it'll be."

"It doesn't matter." After last night she needs some reassurance. "Come whenever you can, you've got the key. Wake me if I'm asleep."

"I could. But like I say—"

"Don't you want to? Have a drink and relax after all that? And I want to hear."

"All right. But I can't say when."

"It doesn't matter."

No answer. Noise in the background on his end.

"Max?"

"Sorry. Detectives talking to me."

"I love you, Max."

"Me too, but I gotta go. I'll see you when I can." And he clicks off.

Leaving her uneasy. All right, he's in the middle of all that, but it unnerves her that he doesn't care about seeing her tonight. Last night shook her up. After he left she lay there wondering if she was on the verge of blowing the whole thing. Suddenly seeing 145th Street clear as day, the shabby little house she grew up in, all the shabby houses. The creepy one with the curtains always drawn, the one the kids were supposed to stay away from because of "petty files." She used to hurry past on her way to the bus stop, on her way home later, wondering about "petty files," all kinds of dark meanings attached to the phrase. It was even scarier when she found out it was a group home, three *pedophiles* living there, and that the windows were covered so these bad men couldn't look out and see the kids. She started taking the long way around, avoiding that house. She avoided it forever after, and when she moved in with Jack after high school she promised herself she'd never go back to a neighborhood like that.

But tonight she's seeing 145th again, all too clearly.

# # #

"It's always bad," Max says, "but especially when there's kids."

"Let me make you a drink."

It's two in the morning. She gave up on him at midnight and finally slept, escaping the vision of drawn curtains at the pedophile house, but suddenly she's awake, Max sitting on the edge of the bed in his suit pants, Oxford shirt, and loosened tie.

Terrible, he says, following her out to the kitchen. The woman and her kids dead, blood everywhere . . .

But all she can think about, mixing two heavy screwdrivers, is that it took him so long to get here.

"I waited up till midnight," she says. "I was sure you'd be here by then."

"We were out at the scene till then. Longer than I thought, but the crime scene is crucial. What you do there can make or break your whole case later. Everything has to add up: cartridge casings, bullet holes in walls, angles of bullet holes, hairs, blood, prints. Or else you end up in trial a year later wondering how you missed something, why you didn't spend longer at the scene. One guy beat an aggravated murder charge because what we assumed was a leak in the roof turned out to be a hole from a stray bullet."

"I thought you'd call."

"I told you I'd come when I could. I said to go on to sleep. I think I said I probably shouldn't come at all."

"But I wanted you to."

"That's what you said. And I wanted to. I stopped for a beer with the detectives when we got back downtown and then I came right over."

A beer? How bad did he want to see her if he stopped for a beer?

But don't get crazy. Don't. He's been looking at dead bodies all day. And he's here now.

"I'll go," he says, "if you're mad at me."

"No, don't. I'm sorry. I'm not mad."

"I've got to be back downtown at seven in the morning."

"Stay here, then. You've got a suit in my closet."

"I don't know. Let's just sit down, okay? I'm whipped."

On the love seat he drops his head back, lets out a long breath and stares at the ceiling.

Just tired, or exasperated with her?

"Max? I'd like to hear about it."

"You said you saw it on TV. You don't want to know any more than TV gives you."

"I'll tell you if it's too much. You promised not to shut me out of what you do, remember?"

He finally looks at her. "Trust me, you don't want to know. Every murder scene leaves me with snapshots that'll be in my mind for the rest of my life, and if I describe this one you'll have 'em too, images you can never shake."

"But does it help you, maybe, to talk about it? I want you to know I'm here for you, I'm supportive—"

"I'll be fine. No point in giving you nightmares."

"Well, but . . . Will you be able to sleep?"

He drains half his drink and drops his head back again. "Not yet."

"Anything I can do? Talk? Listen? Rub your back?"

"I'm fine. Maybe I'll fall asleep if we lie down."

In bed he's so distant he might as well not be there at all, and she can't help feeling ticked again. She's tempted to roll away from him and just be quiet, get his attention, make him come to her—but tells herself, *No, grow up, don't play games. Remember what he's been through. You can't imagine.*

"You're great, Max," she says, and squeezes his hand.

Nothing.

"I feel so lucky to be with you. I respect you so much, the job you do. And I want to be supportive, however I can."

"Thanks, sweetie."

That's all.

But just as she starts thinking maybe there's a good reason *his* relationships haven't worked out, he turns toward her. "I love you. You know it, don't you? You're the best, and not only because you do 'Isis' better than Bob and you like your chicken burned like I do and you make me hot hot hot. You're the sweetest, is why."

Is he just trying to make up?

But why should he have to make up? He didn't do anything.

"Sweetie?"

"I want to be, Max. Sweet. I try to be."

"You're wonderful, believe me."

She'll try, but she's not sure how wonderful either of them is. Two people no one's latched on to yet, and things are already weird between them.

friday, may 25

Seven A.M., Central Precinct. Chief Tabb, DA Johns, ADA Stormin' Norman, Max, Veronica from the state crime lab, lead detectives Haynes and Morales.

Veronica, with a diagram of the Ohlanders' kitchen and a dozen gory photographs, explains what happened.

"I'm sure the killer shot the children first. They were eating their sandwiches at the table, Andrew in this chair and Debra here. One shot killed Andrew—he was probably first. I'm pretty sure the wound in Debra's neck was next—she was moving, probably getting off her chair, and the killer missed her head. You can see the spatter on this wall where the blood shot out of the artery in her neck. But this wound didn't kill her. She's crawling this way, toward her mother, as the killer takes care of her—of Mrs. Ohlander. He puts her down with the shot to the chest, then puts the two in her head. Then he notices Debra's not dead—she's crawling toward her mother, which accounts for the mess on the wall here. Where he goes back and finishes Debra."

You never get used to it.

Glancing around, Max sees everyone else shaking their heads, too.

Back at the office afterward he starts reading the transcripts of the detectives' first interviews, but it's not easy with his VCU guys dropping in to hear what's going on, Stormin' Norman coming in talking about putting a second lawyer on the case (Max says no), detectives calling, reporters calling. Pam Gramm from Channel 2, who lucked into the story yesterday, shows up in person, acting like she and Max are tight because she's been sending him Christmas cards since they got acquainted during the KOIN Tower trial three years ago. As if it wouldn't occur to him she was simply trying to cultivate a source.

But even when he gets through the interviews and detectives' reports, he doesn't have any idea what these murders were about. You look at the spouse first, but even if Ted Ohlander were crazy enough to kill not only his wife but his own children too, he'd been at his Lake Oswego office yesterday and didn't even go out for lunch as far as anyone knew; he'd have had to do a Spider-Man trip out the window and down the side of the building, drive home, wipe out his family, drive back and spider back up the building and in. Not likely that he hired someone to do it, either. Everyone so far has told the detectives the marriage was good, and Max saw for himself that Ohlander was a wreck yesterday—he'd have to be an Oscar-worthy actor or a world-class sociopath to have faked it, and nothing indicates he's either.

Maybe it was another home invasion gone wrong, like what happened at Roop's. But Ohlander swore there was nothing missing. Besides, home-invasion types aren't usually murderers, just dopers or dimwits needing cash or something they can turn into cash. They'll usually run before they'll kill anyone, much less two little kids.

Who knows?

# # #

He skips the autopsies to meet Dana at her place for lunch. She got insecure again last night, and before he went home she asked if they could please get together at noon today, stay connected.

Her car is already out front when he gets there.

She comes to the door naked.

Lunch turns out to be a peanut butter sandwich he eats on the way back downtown.

# # #

"Psychodrama," his dear friend Merlene says. It's midafternoon, they're in Starbucks behind the courthouse.

Merlene always brings it straight. No hidden agenda, either romantic (she's gay) or professional (she's a senior deputy just like Max, head of the Career Criminal Unit).

"Say good-bye," she says. "Lose this woman."

"But I'm in love. Madly."

"Emphasis on 'mad' as in madness. You *love* her? You're out of your mind, you realize, or else you wouldn't be talking this way after . . . how long, a couple of weeks?"

"Or else she's the one, finally."

"Sure. The perfect match. We know your history of disasters, and hers is even worse, yet within two weeks you're talking about getting married. And maybe having a kid? Real smart, yes siree."

"Okay," Max says, "granted, if a friend came to me with this story I'd probably tell him to run like hell. But would it be fair, if I hadn't met the woman? And even if I had, I wouldn't know what the two of them have, how they feel when they're together, all that. So what do I do when it's *me,* and it's so fantastic, so intense?"

"You run. She's had three marriages that didn't work? If the men left her, that tells you something. If she left them—"

"She did, I'm sure."

"Which should tell you she'll leave you too."

"I don't think so." *I will stay,* her card had said. "I mean, not necessarily. I'm pretty convinced she wants it as much as I do. Wants to do it right for a change."

"Maybe. For now, anyway. But even if so . . . we're prosecutors, and what do we know about behavior? About future behavior?"

"All right, all right. The best indicator of future behavior is past behavior. Fine, but this is different. I've never felt anything like this, and I'm pretty sure she hasn't either."

"Because of the intensity?"

"For one thing."

"You know what someone said about that? That it's the *in*appropriateness of two people for each other that makes a relationship intense. For a while."

"Great. You sound like my second wife, the therapist."

Which ends the conversation, Merlene shrugging and changing the subject to the WNBA, women's basketball, some point guard she's got a crush on. Max nods and half listens, as always for each other.

He *wants* Dana, that's all. He's picturing her in her living room after the girls go to bed, walking toward him in the candlelight wearing nothing but a T-shirt. The tight body, slim shapely legs, translucent skin, soft blond hair up in a sexy twist. He's supposed to give her up because the intensity might mean they're *not* a good match?

Bottom line, Dana could have any man she wanted. He drops her and she walks into the Quandary the next day and with one look, one twitch of that ass she's got some U.S. attorney sniffing around, some newscaster, some moneyman. The line forms here, guys.

He'd never forgive himself.

# # #

Candy had to be nuts to wind up at Nicky's "getaway" with him, this sleazy doper motel way out toward Gresham.

Nicky saying, "I got somethin' for you, 'member? You ain't seen this bad boy for a while."

"I told you, I'm out of the business. I'm not that kind of girl anymore."

"What kind you gonna be, then?"

"I'm still thinking about it. But not that kind."

"Thinking about it since when?"

"The last few weeks. Since the bust and the prostitution charges, anyway."

"What're you talking about? We got together a buncha times after that."

What's she doing here? How dumb is she, letting him sucker her out here to smoke some crystal? Believing him when he said she didn't have to put out?

She didn't want to see him again after the trip to Oceanside. And didn't. He didn't call—maybe he knew he'd scared her. Maybe he was dead, all the crank he'd been doing. She didn't really care, as long as he was out of her life.

How bizarre that he appeared this afternoon, just when she was thinking about him again. Thinking about crystal meth, anyway. She's been going crazy since hearing about June yesterday, and as she stepped out of the duplex for a walk in the rain, she found herself wondering *Where's Nicky when you need him?* She was halfway down the block when she heard "Hey!" and turned and he was trotting toward her, the big goon. Not looking too good. But looking cranked-up, which was exactly what she wanted to be.

"I don't have any with me," he said. "But if you wanna take a ride I can fix you up."

"Let's go. I'm not up for anything else, though. I'm not in the business anymore."

" 'Cause you're in love with a woman?" Grinning at her with the dirty, uneven teeth.

"Because of the bust. I'll only get probation 'cause I don't have a sheet, but if they get me again they'll come down on me."

Now, sprawled on the bed after two hits of crystal, he's asking if she's really quitting the business, that work she likes so much. He's smirking.

"What's the difference?"

"You're so good, that's all. It'd be a shame."

All she can think is: *June's dead!*

The day before yesterday—day before yesterday!—they were lolling and laughing in the deep pillows on the big bed, June calling Teddyboy at work to make sure he wouldn't be surprising them. . . . Now she's dead!

"Not even gonna work strip joints or model underwear anymore?" Nicky says. Up off the bed, coming this way, not quite steady.

"Nothing. None of it."

"Gonna do what, then?" Beside her now, behind her, near enough that his stink hits her. His fingers in her hair. "What's my girl gonna do?"

"I don't know. I'm thinking about it. But the sex stuff is over."

"Except if it's love, huh?"

"What?"

"Except if you're in love. Like with your girlfriend."

"Please, let's not go there."

"No?"

Behind her, he moves to her left. One hand lifts his shirt and the other pulls her face to his hairy belly. Something tells her not to pull away.

"Well, it's a good idea," he says. "I told you you should quit. You don't need it. You know what I'm saying?"

"Nicky, let go."

"Know what I'm saying?" He tips her head back so she's looking up at him. " 'Member I said I'd take care'a you?"

"And I said—"

"*You* said"—jerking on a fistful of her hair, his face suddenly mean. "You said a lotta stuff. One thing, you told me you like the tool but you had a girlfriend. A *girlfriend!* That still a problem?"

"Nicky, stop!"

He does stop, lets go, like he suddenly realized what he was doing. "All right . . . You want another hit? . . . It's great seeing you again, you know it?"

"No, no more . . ."

"Wanna have some fun, then? I got cash. I know you like that cash money."

"I told you I'm finished with that. . . ."

"Forget cash, then. That doesn't mean no ballin', does it?"

"Please. You asked if I wanted to trip and I said yes, but that's *all,* and you said okay."

"Did I? Maybe I was talking a little trash, like you talk it to me."

"I—"

"What, you thought we were gonna trip and not party a little? Come on. You know how I get. Trippin' does it to me, you do it to me—put 'em together, I'm hornier'n a four-peckered billygoat."

Why'd she come here?

Why's June dead? *You still believe things happen for a reason?*

"Easy money," Nicky's saying. "I drop my pants here and you

just close your eyes and open that mouth, you don't hardly have to move. Huh? Better yet, you don't charge me for it."

She's afraid. June's dead. People get killed, insane things happen.

"How much have I spent on you?" he's asking. "*Plenty*. You don't think you owe me one? With all the ones you do for free? That spade basketball player—"

"Don't—"

"But that's love, right? The ones you do for free?"

Tears in her eyes.

"You crying now? Whatsa matter?"

What's she *doing* here? But there's no way out. Dead bolt on the door, chain lock too, he'd grab her before she could run. . . .

She can't stop crying. Remembering the day before yesterday with June, lolling and laughing, such fun, talking about how amazing it was they'd gotten together—

"Hey!" He yanks on her hair again, snaps her head back, forces her to look at him. "What's this crying? You said you wanted to party, we came out here and now you act like you've lost somebody near and dear! What the hell's that about?"

She's too scared to talk.

"I think you're being clever, trying to get outta here after you smoke my crystal. And that just don't seem right to me, you know?"

"I want to go home. Please"—trying to stand up—

"*Down!*"—snarling that he'll *rrrrrrip* the shittin' stuff out of her shittin' head—

saturday, may 26

In the office Saturday morning Max is wiped out, after another night without much sleep. Thinking, It's too familiar, a woman getting weird when he's on a big case. He skipped the autopsies yesterday to see her during her lunch hour, then went over there last night after working late—had drinks, lay down with her, felt good. But there was the sense that he *needed* to be there or her insecurity would take over again. So strange, this insecurity in a woman who could have any man she wanted.

Which reared its ugly head again when he said he'd better not stay all night, he needed to get some sleep. She said she was feeling left out of his life.

"What, you think I'm *avoiding* you?" he said, and tried to explain that this is how it is at the start of a major murder investigation.

She reminded him that he keeps promising the job won't interfere with them.

I said I'd try not to let it interfere. But this is, uh, slightly major.

She pouted a little and said she was used to seeing him every night, getting some attention.

Max hid his irritation—tried to—and repeated that this is how it is sometimes. He *didn't* say that at times like this, most people's needs suddenly seem incredibly petty. Micro. A woman and two children get slaughtered, survivors' lives are changed forever . . . and you're feeling insecure? Get a grip!

Didn't say it. Promised they'd go to Batty's barbecue Sunday if she still wanted to.

She said yes. Acted contrite. Said she knows he can't say much about his cases but she'd feel better, more connected, if he told her something.

In the end she took him to bed, rocked him, things were good again—but when he said he'd better go home, get some sleep, she turned chilly again.

He drove home thinking maybe Merlene's right.

Barely slept. Thinking that even if Merlene *is* right, the idea of breaking up, of someone else grabbing her, is unbearable.

But hey, you're Max Faxx, up to your eyes in a triple homicide. Pull it together.

# # #

Pam Gramm, Channel 2, is a lightweight who manages to see the big picture on occasion. Like now, after lucking into a big story.

She called around nine asking if she could come over. Now here she is, as made-up and put together as always, but there's something different about her. Probably the fact that she's got something to sink her teeth into for a change.

"It was just timing," she says. "The day-shift reporters were wrapping up when the report came in, the anchors were getting ready to go on the air—no one available, so they called me at home. I got dressed and got over there."

Poor thing, A lightweight who, despite being a lightweight, seemed to be going places after Channel 2 brought her to town a few years ago. She had the blond hair and blue eyes and a not-too-bright look that seemed to sell. They plugged her in as a reporter, then made her a weekend-news anchor, and it looked like a matter of time before she got the coveted weekday anchor spot. But it hasn't happened yet. Her bimbo-ness outstrips her babe-ness. She can read the news but it's pretty clear that's all, she's just reading it, she doesn't *get* it, she's lost if the teleprompter goes down. She's more suited for *Entertainment Tonight,* something like that. Max will never forget the poor thing pushing her microphone in his face after the KOIN Tower sentencing: "Mr. Travis, do you think three hundred and twenty years is enough, considering what this man did?" *Do you think three hundred and twenty years is enough?* Max thinking, No, I'd be more comfortable with four hundred.

She's sent him Christmas cards ever since. At first he thought she was interested, but they've kept coming even since Pam Pinney became Pam Gramm. She wants a source, that's all.

"What's happening?" she asks now. Wanting a scoop for the news tonight.

"Not much. We don't have anything yet. The detectives are talking to everyone they can."

"Nothing? Really?" With a tilt of her head, her confide-in-me look.

"Nothing so far. We're going to have a bunch of Explorer Scouts fine-tooth the yard, see if there's anything there. I don't know what else to tell you."

She doesn't push. She seems to realize that's all she's going to get.

Max, ready to be done, just sits. Anything else?

In her off-the-record mode she says, "It was ugly over there, wasn't it?"

"Ugly."

"I had a hard time. Was I okay? Did you see the news later?"

"From what I saw you did fine."

"I'm not used to seeing bodies carried out. And *children* . . . I don't have any of my own, not yet anyway, but I've got nieces and nephews. . . ."

"You're right, it was pretty bad."

"*Bad* bad. Who would *do* it?"

"I wish I knew."

"The husband?"

"The detectives are talking to everyone."

Careful. If he's anything but vague, she'll spread misinformation all over the place. *Senior prosecutor Max Travis says authorities suspect Ted Ohlander in the brutal murders of his wife and children.* . . .

"It seems like they had a perfect life," she says. "I don't see how it could be Mr. Ohlander—I talked to him. One of the detectives said it was probably a robbery that went wrong."

"Probably. Possibly."

" 'Probably'? 'Possibly'? Well, I can see you're not going to trust me with anything." Her flirty smile. "I thought we were buddies."

"I don't know anything more than I'm telling, Pam. Call me later on if you want."

"I will."

# # #

It wasn't Ted Ohlander, but they can't rule out anyone else. Can't even rule out the possibility that Ohlander hired someone to kill his wife—not the kids, but they happened to be there.

Not that Max believes Ohlander's behind it, but he always gets twitchy when he keeps hearing how perfect a marriage was. All these interviews on his desk—with Ohlander, in-laws, friends, neighbors—everyone talking about how happy the couple was. How pretty and kind and sweet and generous June Ohlander was.

Of course, everyone's shocked after something like this, grief stricken—who's going to say an unkind word? A natural reaction. It was the reaction after Gil Fitzhugh out in east county was clubbed to death in his basement two years ago. Christian man, good Christian wife, four perfect kids, perfect world. Then it turned out Fitzhugh's wife not only had a scumbag boyfriend but talked him into doing the job, promising him they'd live happily ever after on the $416,000 life-insurance payoff.

Sex, drugs, or money—every murder case has one of those elements, if not two or all three. Max is pretty sure this one wasn't about drugs. *Maybe* it was about money—a bungled home invasion, like everyone wants to believe. But the cynic in him, or the realist, keeps coming back to sex, somehow. Love. Sex masquerading as love. The marriage not as perfect as outsiders want to believe.

Of course, he's been wrong before. All too often.

sunday, may 27

Nicky always wondered about Pamela's legs. She's so great looking you'd expect her to be perfect all the way down to some cute little toes, but you never know. Until a few weeks ago he'd seen her sitting behind that anchor desk. Then they showed her interviewing a butterfly collector, the two of them walking around the guy's garden, and she did have awesome legs. Top to bottom, she's awesome.

A runner, he found out when he started investigating. Good. He likes a woman who keeps her body up.

He finally fell asleep yesterday after the news, after hearing her talk about this "brutal psychopathic killer" on the loose. That made him mad but he'd been up so long he fell asleep a few minutes later.

Thirteen hours in the rack then, and he woke up this morning feeling brand-new. A few snorts and he felt even better.

He didn't know if her routine was the same on weekends, but he didn't have anything else to do. Took a long shower, powdered himself all over, put on clean Bermudas and T-shirt, got his hair right and didn't look shabby at all, if he said so himself.

Drove across town, up Fremont, and parked in the cul-de-sac across from her house.

On weekdays her husband, Milquetoast, leaves at eight-fifteen for his job at the power company, and within ten minutes the door opens again and she appears, cute as hell, all in white (sneakers, socks, shorts, T-shirt) except for a hot pink ball cap with her hair tied up inside. Bounces up and down in the driveway, then jogs off down the sidewalk, light-stepping, her fine ass jiggling just a little in the white shorts. Trots down to 122nd (Nicky staying well behind her in the rig), turns right and trots on down to the Starbucks. Gets her coffee and cup of ice water, sits at one of the plastic tables out front, drinks up and then trots home.

That's weekdays. But this is Sunday, she's probably lying around with Milquetoast, maybe won't come out at all.

He'll give it a few minutes.

# # #

Here she comes after all. Cute as hell doing her little bouncy-bounce in the driveway, loosening up. Taking off, now.

He doesn't need to follow, he knows where she's going. He'll wait fifteen minutes and drive down.

He checks his hair in the rearview. Combs it back, even though it's looking good. Looking *good,* Mr. Nick! She'll like your look, and if she gets to know you she'll see you're an all right person, too, not this evil psycho killer she's been talking about.

Cruising down Fremont a few minutes later he's excited, wondering if he's really, truly going to be face-to-face with Pamela Gramm.

Wondering if she wears the big sparkly diamond ring when she runs. So far he hasn't gotten close enough to tell.

He hits 122nd, turns into the parking lot in front of Starbucks, and there she is, sitting by herself out front. Sexy legs crossed . . . Mama, he could jump her right now. He drives on past, down to the end of the line of shops, so she won't be able to ID the rig.

Can he do it?

Now or never. She's right there, he'll feel like a puss if he chickens out.

Takes a deep breath. *Pamela* . . . Checks his hair in the rearview. *Pam . . . What do you like to be called?*

Go.

He locks up the rig and takes the sidewalk past a deli, pet store, pharmacy, fabrics.

Now Starbucks.

He's ten feet away from her, Pamela Gramm in person, in her white jogging getup and hot pink ball cap.

She glances up—maybe sensing someone there, maybe seeing his shadow on the sidewalk.

She nods at him!

"You"—pointing at her—"you're the lady from TV."

She stares back.

"Right?"

A little smile, a little nod.

"I thought so. I see you . . . I . . . I—I've seen you. . . ."

Stammering. And suddenly she's got a strange look, she's not smiling.

"Having your coffee?" It just comes out! *No, fool, she's doing laundry!*

She nods, but barely. She thinks he's a nut or something!

Wearing the diamond, yeah, big as an acorn.

"You're on the weekend news, right? Pamela Gramm? Pam?"

"I'm the weekend anchor, yes."

"And also . . .?"

"I do some reporting during the week."

"You do a good job."

"Thank you."

Those legs . . . crossed, right knee over left, the foot sticking out toward him. New white Reeboks and those shorty socks with the little pompoms at the back.

Man, she looks so *clean*. She'd smell great, even with a light sweat.

"Do you go by 'Pam,'" he asks, "or 'Pamela'? You say Pamela Gramm when you come on, but the other people call you Pam. I wondered . . ."

What the hell are you saying?

"Never mind. Anyway, I saw you sitting here and thought I recognized you. Wanted to tell you you're the best on TV, you should be on every night."

That gets a little smile, but she's standing up to go. Taller than he thought. Saying she appreciates the kind words—

"Definitely the best looking," he says.

"Thanks again." Moving around the table to drop her cup in the trash can. "Nice talking to you, but I'd better—"

"Run home?"

She gives him a funny look. "Nice talking to you," she says, and trots off—in the opposite direction she came from.

Afraid he'll follow her and find out where she lives?

Why'd you say that, fool?

# # #

Dana wondering, *When does it settle down? When does it get normal?*

But then, when has anything ever been normal for her?

She wants a drink, but there's nothing but beer at this barbecue.

She's going to lose Max if she doesn't pull it together. The way she's been acting lately, he'd be gone already if he weren't so infatuated. If he weren't so hooked on the sex. But he'll get over that, they always do, and he won't stick around then if all he sees is a crazy lady.

She gave him a hard time Thursday night for relaxing with the detectives before coming over—after he spent eight hours at a triple-murder scene! She made up to him with the lunchtime sex on Friday, but that night she wanted him to stay over and when he said he had to go home and get some sleep she got pouty again. When he called from his office yesterday she was sure he was going to end it. It turned out he only wanted to say hello and make sure *she* wasn't mad. She knew that was crazy. She had two drinks before he came over last night and shouldn't have had another one when he got there: this time she was the one saying she needed to sleep, saying she must have picked up a bug or something.

This morning, headachy, she waited for him to call, hoping she hadn't blown it last night. But he was sweet when he called, and seeing the sunlight out the window she imagined being over at his house, sitting on the front porch with the view of the river and downtown, or out on the back deck or in the hot tub. Not stuck in her little apartment. How nice it would be to walk over to that place in his neighborhood, Strudel House, for a Sunday brunch, not worrying how much it cost. Having a life! And he *is* a nice guy, it's not just the lifestyle. . . .

She told him yes, she still wanted to go to the barbecue at Bill Batty's house.

But it really hit her when they got here: how nutty she's been, what she's going to lose. These other lawyers—smart, accomplished people—treating Max like he's a mile smarter than they are, a mile more important. Treating her like *she's* something, because she's with him. Talking about him . . .

A preppy, egghead guy who talks like he's got a mouthful of

peanut butter: "Everyone remembers the time he stood up during jury selection, which usually turns into quite a process—Max stands up, looks around at the jury pool and says, 'Anyone here *not* have any common sense? Anyone with no common sense, please raise your hand.' No one did, of course. And Max says, 'Good, 'cause that's all you're going to need to try this case,' and sat down. That was it, that was jury selection. You know what that communicated to those people? It communicated absolute confidence in his case. It was as effective as jury selection can be. I'll tell you, I've learned so much from him. A lot of us, whenever he's in trial, sit in as much as we can. . . ."

An older woman, tall, gray hair: "He's so *real*. I remember Judge Keys talking about a guilty verdict he never expected Max to get. Calling Max a dirtbag—as a compliment! 'The dirtbag's dirtbag.' How he makes people so comfortable, makes a jury feel like he's their best friend, like they're all in it together. He puts on no airs at all, he doesn't *act* smart, and you know, that's a great thing. People can be around Max for a long time before they realize he's the smartest person in the room."

A woman named Susan, very friendly, probably gay, says she's worked several major cases with him. "Funny guy. Amazing guy. The first case we did together, the KOIN Tower case, I came in with my closing argument typed out, forty pages, which I'd been practicing in front of a mirror at home all week. . . . I made sure I got nine hours of sleep the night before. . . . Max comes in looking like he'd been out all night, with a few notes scribbled on a crumpled-up three-by-five card, and he stood up for second closing, the last word from the state, and absolutely enthralled that whole courtroom. The defendant, the defense, you could see they knew it was over. . . ."

Dana doesn't like it here. Hearing how smart Max is makes her wonder what he really thinks of her and how much he really knows about what's going on. Hearing someone ask him about his big investigation makes her feel ridiculous—the triple murder he's trying to solve while she complains about not getting enough attention! Seeing how important he is reminds her of Jack saying she always tries to soar with the eagles. Reminds her Max isn't another loser to play games with.

Amazing he hasn't seen through her already.

It's the sex. Always.

# # #

"You're something else," Max says. "You know it?" Sitting on the toilet lid in the Battys' upstairs bathroom with his jeans down over his loafers, Dana still straddling him.

"Am I?"

"You're the one, you know *that?*"

"Am I? This was fun, then?"

"You have to ask?"

"Just checking."

"Checking. Ha." Shaking his head, smiling like he still can't believe it. "Wow. I didn't know what the hell was going on when you asked me to come upstairs. Then, come in the bathroom? I thought you'd found a dead body or something."

"I didn't know where else to take you. But I was going to take you somewhere. I wanted to connect, after the way we've been lately, the way *I've* been. I was watching you little while ago, thinking how handsome you are, thinking what a brat I am sometimes—"

"Stop it. You're not."

"You wouldn't say so if I was."

"But you're not. You're the best. We're both trying to find our way in this thing, that's all."

She leans against him, chin on his shoulder . . . feeling dishonest, somehow, hearing the love and trust and hope in his voice. She's told him everything, she hasn't lied about anything, yet there's this feeling of fakery.

"Are we better now?" she says. "Can we start being better than we've been the last few days?"

"I think so."

"I'll be more understanding."

"You're fine."

"I've been a bad girl, but I'll be better."

"You're perfect. The love of my life, I think"—pulling back to look at her with the moony-spoony eyes. "People might think it's strange, us calling it love so soon, but when you know it, you know it, right?"

monday, may 28 (memorial day)

They're both flawed, both bringing some baggage to this, but it sure feels good.

It's been great again since yesterday in Batty's bathroom. It's as if the petty stuff the last few days reminded them how much they want each other, and that quick, red-hot session drove the point home.

He couldn't wait to get to the apartment after work today. Dana was home, the girls were here. They called out for a pizza, watched the *Seinfeld* rerun while they ate it, then Liz left with some friends and Max and Dana walked up to Grant Park with Emily.

Precious Emily, who doesn't even know who her father is. It still seems odd, but Max doesn't question Dana's parenting. What can you say when the girls are so bright, funny, thoughtful, all these good things? Their mother's done a lot of things right.

Max and Emily keep getting tighter. They talk, they laugh. At the park tonight he couldn't take his eyes off her. The simple joy and exuberance of this beautiful seven-year-old! The three of them were walking along when she suddenly took off running into the open space ahead—not running *to* anything, just bolting out ahead and *running,* burning off energy. Most charming thing he's ever seen.

He's tired, and facing a long day tomorrow, but Dana asked if he'd stay a while after the girls went to bed. He wasn't about to say no. Now they've poured wine, lit the candle and cozied up in the love seat.

She asks about the investigation. Still trying to make up for her impatience the first couple of nights.

"Not much happening yet," he says.

"Will you solve it?"

"I hope so. We're trying. But you don't really want to talk about this, do you?"

"I want to know what you're doing, what's on your mind. Will you find the person, or was this the perfect crime?"

"There's no such thing as a perfect crime. A killer always leaves something at the scene or takes something away from it, something that'll give him away. We just have to find it."

"And in this case. . . ?"

She seems sincerely interested, and Max sincerely wants to share whatever he can share. "Today's development . . . not that this'll help us find whoever killed these three, but it's interesting. The crime lab told us the killer might be the same person who shot Highwire Harris. The bullets were fired from the same gun, anyway, a forty-caliber. It doesn't help much, since we don't know who shot Highwire, but it means that if we crack either case we'll have a suspect in the other one, too."

tuesday, may 29

Jack's at his desk drinking coffee, debating whether to pull out his flask and spike it, when Dana calls, all shook up. "I need to talk to you, Jack. We need to talk."

It's the first he's heard from her since the morning he spelled things out, out by her car, after he tracked her down at the Thirsty Parrot and they spent the night together.

"We need to talk?" he says. "Well, talk."

"Should I? On the phone?"

Something bad, then. "Maybe not. Can it wait? Meet me at the house at noon."

# # #

When he pulls up she's waiting in her car. Still shook up, anyone could see.

Inside he takes her into the living room, sits her on the couch and gets to it. "So?"

"So what's *happening,* Jack?"

"What do you mean, what's happening? I thought you had something to say."

"Jack . . . These people who got killed last week, this woman and her kids that everyone's talking about . . ."

"Yeah?"

"My friend . . . boyfriend . . ."

"Yeah? The lawyer?

"He's a DA, that kind of lawyer. One of the big DAs."

"And?"

"He says these murders . . . He says there's a connection between this and . . . you know, Highwire Harris. Something about bullets, cartridges—cartridge casings, whatever—"

"Whoa. Hold on. Slow down, babe. How 'bout a drink? Let me get us one."

A quick trip to the kitchen for glasses and OJ and gin, like old times.

She chugs half of hers as soon as he pours it, then tries to explain. Her boyfriend is working these murders with the police, she says, and last night he told her these people were murdered with the same gun that shot Highwire Harris.

Jesus Christ. Nicky. Jack knew he was crazy, but—

"What's *happening,* Jack? What's going *on?*"

"Easy, babe. Drink up. Relax." But he's sweating.

"Jack!"

"Let me get this straight. They're saying whoever shot Harris is the person who killed the lady and her kids? And you think I know? . . . You think I—?"

"*You* didn't, did you? You told me you didn't, that morning . . . you said it was the other person . . ."

"It was *not* me. I never shot *anyone.*"

"I believed you, I still believe you, but whoever it was—I mean—"

"*Babe,*" Jack says, taking her hands. "Slow down. Settle down. Take a deep breath."

"You said if I ever say anything . . . Oh, Jack, I never would, but I'm scared of getting pulled into something anyway!"

"Babe, no"—holding her now as she sobs against his chest. "We'll work it out, babe. I'll find out what's going on. Just believe me: I've never shot *anyone.* And even if the person who shot Harris did kill these people, they don't know who it is, right?"

"But Max says—he says Highwire c-could wake up and say something."

"He won't say anything. He won't *know* anything. Roop didn't."

"Max says maybe Highwire knew your friend, whoever was with you. Maybe that's why he got shot, something between them."

"Listen to me, babe. First of all, this guy's no friend of mine. And I'm sure it's not the same person anyway." He told Nicky to get the hell rid of that gun and he figured the fool traded it for some meth or something, which would mean some other doper killed these people. "All right? Trust Jack, babe. But you've gotta do your part now, too."

She pulls away, eyes wide. "I've gotta do what?"

"Just keep doing what you're doing, fucking your Mr. Big. Stay with him, whatever you do."

She's bawling again. Basket case. Jack wondering how the hell he ever got into this. Why he brought a brain-dead stoner like Nicky in.

When the bawling eases he tries it again. "Now, listen. You keep this guy happy. You stay with him. And pay attention. Find out what you can find out."

"Jack . . . I don't want—"

"Just pay attention, and you and me'll be in touch. Now, the guy's happy with you? He wants it to last?"

"I—I—he says he's in love with me."

"Well, keep it that way. Meanwhile, you tell me every single thing."

# # #

Max remembers her from the murder scene: Bonnie High, June Ohlander's racquetball partner, the one who found the bodies. Nice-looking woman, nice person. Calling to find out if they're making any progress.

Not much, he says.

"That's what I keep hearing on the news, but I wondered. I keep hoping you've got something and just aren't saying. It's been five days. What I'm afraid of is . . . you always hear that most murders are solved in the first two or three days, and if they're not solved by then they're usually not solved at all."

Max senses something. "Something about the investigation bothering you, Miss High?"

"I . . . think I should talk to you. I don't want to but I should. If you're not getting anywhere."

"Is there something you didn't tell the detectives?"

"Can I come and talk to you?"

"I can send the detectives to you. I oversee the investigation but they usually handle the interviews."

"I'd rather talk to you. You seem like a sensitive person. Not that they aren't, but the way you went about your job that day, the way you came over and talked to me after the detectives were finished. . ."

Max remembers. Remembers her more clearly now. She called 911 about the bodies and was waiting when he and the MCT and the media showed up. He listened to part of her account to the detectives. Early thirties, dressed in sweats and Nikes for the racquetball game that never happened. Unmarried—divorced, Max assumed. Not a stunner but certainly attractive, and one of those people whose manner makes her more appealing yet.

Smart, too. Knows a sensitive guy when she sees one.

He tells her to come on downtown, they can talk.

# # #

Naturally she turns out to be "of the one true church," as Merlene likes to say. It hits him before she's been in his office two minutes. It's why there's no ring.

And he's pretty sure she's come to tell him about the underbelly of another "perfect" marriage.

"I'm not sure I should be doing this . . ."

"Of course you should. If you know something that could help us."

"You see it coming, don't you?"

Max shrugs. "An imperfect marriage, I'm guessing. You were a good friend and you knew."

She's nodding. "Just promise me you'll handle it with some sensitivity. For her husband's sake, her parents'. . ."

"I'll try."

"I came to you because I'm pretty sure that if I tell a detective, the whole world will hear on the five o'clock news."

"Possibly."

"And I'm not even sure it's true—that there was someone in her life. I hope you can find out, and maybe what I tell you never has to become public. If it gets out but then ends up having nothing to do with what happened, I'd want to die."

"I'll be as discreet as I can be, Miss High."

"Bonnie."

"Bonnie. Thanks for coming in, Bonnie."

"I had to, didn't I?"

"I think so. I'll try not to make you sorry." He tells her about the great O'Leary, ace investigator in the office, as trusty and discreet as they come. "If you don't mind my sharing with him—him only—he'll check out whatever you say and let me know. Me only."

She thinks about it a little more, then finally gets to it.

She met June Ohlander at SportsNation last year. They hit it off. Started playing racquetball, taking saunas and Jacuzzis, eating together afterward. Bonnie didn't try to hide anything ("not that I came on to her"), and she was pretty sure June suspected she was a lesbian. It turned out that was what had intrigued June in the first place. When she finally asked the question, Bonnie was honest. From that point, it was what they mostly talked about. June confided that she'd wondered about herself ever since a night in college when she and some girlfriends got drunk and she wound up in bed with one of them. Nothing "happened," but she'd always wondered after that, always been curious. She told Bonnie she thought certain women were beautiful, sexier than any man.

"Of course lots of women have the thought but never take the step," Bonnie says. "Maybe June never would have, either, except for her husband. But last fall she found out he was having an affair with one of his secretaries, and that did it. First she just cut him off—physically, emotionally, every way. Then she started thinking about what *she* wanted, for a change. What she might want to explore, at least."

Another storybook marriage. It explains the outdated birth-control pills the detectives found.

Bonnie says June debated endlessly whether to act on her "feel-ings, curiosity, whatever," and that in February or March she hinted that she'd placed a personal ad somewhere. In the last couple months Bonnie got the impression something had happened.

"You only 'got the impression'?" Max says. "She didn't tell you?"

"Not exactly, but I was pretty sure. She talked about a whole new way of seeing things . . . the things a lot of people say when they come over. Something was definitely different. She was happier, she had a shine. . . ."

wednesday, may 30

Nicky needs to sleep, sleep, sleep and then lay off everything—not just crank but the weed and booze too, everything. Maybe not completely off weed and booze, but definitely crank. He gets bloody noses from snorting it, sore throats from smoking it. His head feels like it's on fire. He sees things. Wants to fight, wants to hurt people.

He needs to sleep sleep sleep and then get straight and figure out what's happening.

Although he's pretty sure everything's cool. Shooting the spade happened so fast it never seemed real in the first place, and now it's been so long it's almost like it never happened at all. You hardly see anything about it in the paper or on the news anymore. Maybe the cops have dropped it.

From what you hear on the news, they don't have a clue about the thing last week, the carpetmuncher and her kids.

And there's no way a whore like Candy is gonna convince the cops she got raped the day after, not by someone she's fucked so many times before.

Yeah, it's all good.

Because *he's* good. Plenty good, pal.

Now, keep it up. Get some sleep. Lay off the stuff. Eat. Work out.

Be careful. Always.

Use the brainpower.

He remembers Jack calling last night, wanting to get together later to talk. Yeah? What does that mean? And what does it mean that he wants to meet at a tavern instead of at his house, when he's the one who keeps saying they shouldn't be seen together? Must be scared to be alone with him.

Or, maybe all of a sudden he figures they're scot-free on the robbing and shooting, he's not worried anymore.

But if that's it, then what's to talk about?

Maybe he finally talked to Vlasitch and arranged for some cars. That'd be good. Nicky could use the work.

# # #

Jack's waiting in one of the high-back booths in the Rumpus Room when Nicky walks in. Already into a drink. Looking all serious.

Nicky slides in across from him. "Whuddup, Jacky?"

"Not much. What's up with you?"

"Same ol' stuff. Pretty smooth."

"Great."

He's not in the mood for chitchat. Sits there looking weird while Nicky locates their waiter, waves him over, orders a martini.

"Martinis, now?"

"Why not? Gonna drink, might as well get to the point."

"Your man didn't."

"Huh?"

"Little Caesar. Edward G. Robinson. Remember? 'I don't touch the stuff.' Your man worried about messing up."

Vlasitch, he says. Wanting more money for every stolen car from now on, and claiming Jack owes him more for what he's done in the past. Making some threats. "I don't know what he's thinking," Jack says, "but I'm not sure I want to find out the hard way."

"Get blown up."

"Exactly."

"So what're you thinking?" Nicky likes it, that Jack might take things in his own hands. It's the only way.

"You still got that weapon?"

Wow. Nicky leans across the table and drops his voice even lower. "You serious?"

"You got it or not?"

"I got it. You really gonna do him?"

But Jack doesn't answer. Suddenly he's leaning back, giving Nicky a whole different look. Like something clicked, something happened. *"You've still got that forty-caliber?"*

Now Nicky gets it. Sonofabitch suckered him. "What I mean is—"

"You've still *got* it? I told you to get rid of that thing!"

"All right, I got it, so what? You want it or not?"

"No, I don't want it! And *you* better get rid of it!"

"Why's that? Why you havin' a hissy fit, Jacko?"

Jack's looking around. Finally comes back to Nicky, but instead of answering he takes in a long, deep breath and lets it out sloooow. Pissed off. "You wanna know why?"

"Duh. Yeah, I wanna know."

"Well, think about this. The cops think that whoever shot Highwire Harris is the one who killed that lady and her kids in Dunthorpe last—"

Nicky's already shaking his head no no no, not me. "Not me.

Uh-uh. You think—? Nuh-uh, I don't know *nothin'* about that, if that's what you're thinkin', no way. No chance, Lance."

"None, huh?"

"*What're* the cops saying exactly? And who told you what they're saying?"

"Friend of a friend. Friend of someone who knows a cop. Doesn't matter. Just tell me—where's the gun?"

Mama. Nicky didn't expect any of this, coming here. Gotta think, gotta think. "I gotta pee, I'll be right back," he says, and slides out of the booth.

# # #

Think fast.

Jack setting him up?

It's not impossible.

Nicky steps out of the bathroom, peeks around the corner, sees the back of Jack's head over the top of the seat. He slips out.

Outside he hurries around back, to his rig in the lot. Unlocks, opens the door, reaches under the seat for the iron Jack's so worried about. Sticks it under his belt, lets his T-shirt hang out to hide the lump, and walks back inside.

Jack starts up again as soon as he sits down. "What the hell're you thinking, man? I said to get rid of that gun! Where the hell is it now?"

"Whatsa matter, Jackpot, you scared? Your pussy hurtin'?"

Jack ignores it. "So? So"—looking around, keeping his voice down—"*did* you do that lady and her kids?"

"I don't know what you're talkin' about. Man, Crackerjack, you look like you're 'bout to mess your pants. I swear, you *pose* at bein' cool, but you ain't nothin', you know it?"

Jack just looks at him, shaking his head. Maybe realizing he's better off keeping quiet.

"Whuddup, Crackerjack? What if I did it? *You* didn't, so why you shakin'?"

Jack still not talking, just looking at him.

Nicky, with a plan, looks around like he's worried someone might hear them. "Maybe we better go outside. Come on."

"Nah, we're good here. Now, listen—"

"I said let's go out."

"Nah, just keep your voice down. Now, tell me what the—"

"*Hey.* Jackpot." Getting his attention. "I said let's go outside. 'Less you want your beautiful life to end right here—which it could, 'cause I got my hand on that forty. Right down here. I can see it, 'Used-Car Dealer Shot Dead in the Rumpus Room.' Pamela Gramm talking about it on TV. That what you want? No, I didn't think so. Now, leave some money and let's go. 'Less you wanna take a chance."

Jack's not that dumb. A minute later they're out in the lot, getting in the rig. Jack saying Be cool, everything's cool, just ditch the piece and things should work out.

"Question is," Nicky says, "are *you* cool? Or do I gotta worry about you?"

"Worry about me why? Look, I'm on your side. Didn't I call you so we could get together and I could tell you what I heard? I don't know if you did the lady and her kids or not, but—"

"But you think you know. Am I right? And for sure you know what happened with Harris, so I'm thinking maybe I'd be better off without you around."

"Come off it. Like I'd give you up."

"Like you wouldn't. Who you think you're talking to, some retard?"

"Just lay low, is all I'm saying. Ditch the gun and lay low, it should all pass."

Nicky smiles at him. Jack, the brain, praying for his life now.

"They think it was the same person," Jack says, "but they don't know who. So they're nowhere. If you just be cool they probably never will know."

"If *you* be cool. But how do I know you will be?"

"Come on. What'm I gonna do, go tell'em 'I know this guy shot Highwire Harris 'cause I was there too'?"

"I don't know. I'm just saying don't forget which side you're on, Jack Smack."

"I'm cool, don't worry."

"Better be, Jacky." Nicky lifts his shirt, showing him the .40, and gives him a little Rico: "Jacky? This game ain't for guys that's soft, ya know."

"Damn, man! Get *ridda* that thing! *You* better remember this isn't any movie. You know?"

"I know. And I think we're good, it's all good. Take a chill pill, brother. You said yourself it'll all work out."

"If you wise up, I said. But is that gonna happen? I'm not sure you've heard a word I've said. Well, listen to this. One other thing. Why you better get serious."

"Yeah?"

"Listen good: someone saw us that night."

Which gets Nicky's attention, damn right. "Who did?"

"It doesn't matter. They recognized me, not you. They don't know—"

" 'They'?"

"It doesn't matter. What matters is—"

" *'They'*? They recognized you but not me?"

"Look—"

"Your girl, right?" The bitch. Nobody else Jack would try to protect. Probably didn't *see* 'em, but she knew what was happening—

"Listen, Nick—"

"*You* listen, Jacko . . ." Pulling up his shirt and jerking the .40 out of his waistband.

"All right, all right . . ."

"Good. Now tell me every little bit."

And Jack tells plenty, if not everything. Says the bitch came walking down the sidewalk toward the house as they ran out that night. Recognized Jack, even with the mask, but she's got no idea about Nicky. You're safe, Jack says.

"But we'd both be safer without her, am I right?"

"No, no, no. She'd never turn me in and she didn't recognize you. And I talked to her, put the fear of God in her, told her she'll get dragged in if it ever comes out. It'd also be *dumb* to cap her, considering she's balling the DA on the case and he'd be all over it. Considering she's getting information from the guy, like how they've connected the Harris thing to the murders. What do we gain by capping her?"

thursday, may 31

Dana's felt crazy before, but never like this. Max snapping at her one day, stars in his eyes the next. Her wanting to run one day, wanting to latch on the next.

But all that seemed like nothing when he told her about the bullets, Monday night. She got through the rest of that night (glad, that time, that he wanted to go home and get some sleep), but she came unglued Tuesday when she told Jack and he said it was serious now, *serious,* and she had to stay with Max no matter what and report every word he said about the investigation.

That night was freaky: Max all gooey again while she struggled to hold it together. When he asked what was wrong she told him she'd had a bad day at work. She didn't go anywhere near the investigation, and he didn't offer anything.

Yesterday, with Liz and Emily still at Brian's, she called him and said she couldn't see him, she needed to do the Thirsty Parrot with the girls, one was moving to L.A. and this was their last night together; then she just stayed home, drinking screwdrivers and going crazy.

Tonight was Mom's birthday party out at "the farm," her folks' dump in McMinnville. Max had wanted to finally meet the family, but she left him a message around four, a lie about Mom not feeling well, not feeling up to meeting anyone.

She and the girls did drive out there, unfortunately.

She's a wreck when they finally get back to the apartment at ten, her head still clanging from the abuse.

And the phone's ringing as she unlocks the front door. She'd planned on coming in and unplugging it so Max couldn't get through, but Elizabeth, typical teenager, bolts in past her to snag it.

"Mom! It's Max!"

No choice but to take it.

He says he's missing her, can he come over for a while?

She says she's tired, she needs to go to bed, she wouldn't be any fun.

He says he won't stay long, it would be worth the drive just to tuck her in and kiss her good night.

She says she's sorry, she's just too upset: "My family got into a bunch of crap." Which is true.

He says he'd like to comfort her, what's a lover for?

She says, really, she'd better just go to sleep.

He sounds hurt, says it seems like forever since he's seen her, he's starting to wonder if she's losing interest.

Stay with the hotshot, whatever you do. You hear me?

"No, Max, I'm not. Come over, then."

# # #

He lies beside her in the dark in his jeans and button-down, stroking her cheek, kissing her. "Beautiful," he's saying, "and the sweetest girl in the world . . ."

CLANG! *So you're beautiful, so what? Beautiful and wacko! In five years you'll just be wacko!* Someone a few years ago—the football coach?

Sweet? Beautiful? A great mother? All these things Max says she is? Good thing he wasn't a fly on the wall at her folks' place tonight.

It started right away. One of the girls must have mentioned Max when Dana went to the kitchen for water, because as soon as she reappeared Amy pulled her into the den asking, What? A new boy-friend? Not the guy who owns the bar but *another* one?

Perfect Amy, who moved out of the house on 145th the week she finished high school, just like Dana had, and who only dated two or three guys before she met perfect Adam. Adam was perfectly boring, too, but his father owned Paint Your Wagon and he was in line to take over. He did, soon after they got married, and they bought the big house and went to Bible study and raised perfect kids and did all the right things, Amy doing volunteer work and fund-raising and yes, listening to Dana's sad stories and inviting her and the girls to move in every time things fell apart. Only rarely passing judgment. (CLANG! *Maybe you like abuse, Dana. Maybe you think that's what you deserve. Maybe you gravitate to jerks because they reinforce the low opinion you have of yourself.*)

But she passes judgment more and more these days, probably because her perfect little life keeps being perfect. Which is probably why Mom and Dad agree with everything she says.

Tonight Mom appeared in the doorway while Amy lectured Dana about a parent's duty to be a role model. To not be a slut, she meant. Mom heard the last part and (of course) agreed with her.

Dana wasn't ready for the double team, wasn't ready for any of it. What would they say if she told them she's not only gotten involved with another man but there's no way it's going to work out with him, either?

She told them what a great guy Max is, what an important guy, and that they've talked about getting married.

Amy acted shocked. "Marriage? You've known him a few weeks and you're talking about marriage?"

"Marriage?" Mom said. "Dana, listen . . ."

She covered her ears.

"Well, that's mature," Amy said.

Mom came and put her arm around her, like she cared. Pitying her, probably, more than caring. Dana shook free.

Amy: "You're actually thinking about getting married again? Because he's important and makes good money?"

"Because he loves me."

"Loves you? So soon? Mom, have we heard this before?"

She covered her ears again.

# # #

"My sugar. My love." Max gazing down at her. "I knew it the first night."

He likes the sex, that's all. Amazing, how it makes even smart men stupid.

On the phone he said he just wanted to kiss her good night, he wouldn't stay, and now she wishes he'd get going. She can't stand him looking up and down her body like she's some kind of goddess, whispering sweet nothings.

Finally, knowing what he wants, she whispers "Can we do it before you go, Max?"

It's a relief to turn over and bury her face in the pillow.

". . . can't believe I'm doing this with you," he's saying. . . .

friday, june 1

"How'd you find me?" she wants to know.

Kay Henson, street name Candy. Twenty-one and an eyeful, not your typical hooker except for the overdone makeup. Makeup she hardly needs, with a face and youthful skin like that.

"My lead investigator's a genius," Max tells her. "Guy named O'Leary, used to be a cop. He can find anyone. We had information that Mrs. Ohlander might've placed a personal ad and he worked it from there."

It took O'Leary less than twenty-four hours from the time Bonnie High came in and talked to Max. *Rose City Review* let him into their personal-ads archives. He listened to the voice-mail responses to an ad under the heading "June Swoon" ("Attractive bi-curious WF seeks discreet, curious other") and traced one to someone calling herself Candy. His connections at the phone company told him the number belonged to a Katherine Henson, and records showed numerous calls between that line and the Ohlanders' in the weeks since the ad appeared.

Henson also, lo and behold, showed up on the computer with a recent prostitution bust and the business handle Candy.

"I asked him to go see if he could find you," Max says, "and he came back yesterday saying he did and that you were very nice, cooperative, and you'd be coming in today. Which we appreciate. We'd all like to solve these murders. I'm sure Mr. O'Leary told you which ones I'm talking about. You know what I'm talking about."

She does.

"We've been told that June Ohlander might have, ah, expanded her circle of friends in the last few months of her life. You know what I mean?"

She does.

"I don't know if this angle has anything to do with the murders, but we don't have much else at this point."

"It's fine. I want to help if I can."

"She and her children were brutally murdered, after all."

She looks away, out the window.

"Let's make sure we're clear," Max says, and brings the photo of June Ohlander out of his drawer, slides it across his desk to her. "This is who I'm talking about. You knew her?"

She glances at it and quickly looks away again, out the window, nodding.

"All right. Can you tell me about it, Miss Henson? I can see it might be hard. . . ."

A tear at the corner of her eye, now. Rolling down her cheek as she stares out.

And suddenly she loses it. Her lips tremble, her face contorts, and she's up out of the chair and gone.

When Max catches up to her down by the elevators she's sobbing, her eye makeup's running. She manages to say she'll talk, she will, but she's too upset now—can she please, please come back on Monday?

# # #

Dana's coming apart. Last night was too much, Max all moony about her after her family reminded her what she really is—nutty, self-centered, slutty. All day today she wondered how to avoid seeing him tonight.

But she can't avoid him. Jack called as soon as she got home from work, asking what's going on, and when she said she didn't know he said she'd better find out, *tonight,* and be at his house at noon tomorrow with the latest.

She paged Max and he called a minute later. Struggling to sound normal, she asked if he wanted to come over tonight, spend some time together after the girls went to bed.

Now, ten-thirty, they're having drinks on the couch. Max telling her how glad he was to see her last night, glad to be able to comfort her after she got upset out at the farm.

It's enough of an opening. "I was glad too," she says. "I didn't want you to think you had to come, but when you got here—"

"I wanted to come."

"—when you got here I was happy. I just didn't want . . . I mean, you've been working so hard lately. . . ."

"But I've told you, I don't want to lose my life to work. I don't want to lose you."

"You're not. You won't. I'm afraid of losing *you,* the way I've been."

"Forget that. We'll just keep trying, huh? I'm just in this phase, this investigation . . ."

"I know you are. But it won't be forever. Right?"

"I hope not. No, it won't be."

Ask. It's like Jack's watching, talking into her ear. "How's the investigation going, anyway? Any progress?"

"Nothing great. Nothing much. I had a woman in today who might be able to give us something, but she broke down and walked out. I chased her down and she said she'll come back, but who knows? It might take a subpoena, and even then you can't make people tell what they don't want to tell. Although I don't think it'll come to that with this woman. I think she'll come back and talk to me."

"And she could help?"

"Not for sure, but she was a friend of Mrs. Ohlander and she might be able to point us some way or other, I don't know."

Dead end.

But Jack expects information. And it's for her own good, too.

"The other night you were excited about bullets matching the bullet that hit Highwire Harris . . . cartridge something-or-other. . . ."

"Cartridge casings, shell casings, yeah. They match. But they don't tell us who the shooter was."

"So, still no idea?"

"Nope. And it's not looking good. Most murders—the ones that are ever solved—are solved in a day or two. The longer it goes, the colder the trail. This trail could be getting cold." He finishes his drink and gets up to go for a refill. "There really *isn't* any trail," he says over his shoulder, "unless this woman can help."

saturday, june 2

At noon Saturday Jack leaves Vinnie in charge of the lot and heads home to meet Dana, find out what's up.

She's waiting in her car in the driveway. Looking scared as she gets out, even though she's obviously had a drink or two. Looking pretty good in jeans and the old brown shirt with the colorful little birds stitched into the front. Not that Jack's interested. He doesn't care if he ever sees her again once he's out of this mess.

"You look upset, babe." Taking her hand, walking her inside.

"It's just all this . . . all this . . ."

"Come here and sit down, babe. Talk to me."

On the couch, looking at her, he wonders if she's a genuine mental case, not just another neurotic woman. He remembers when she called him, crying, at the end of her second marriage, saying her parents and her sister Amy were talking about having her committed if she wouldn't go into counseling. (Funny coming from her parents, out there in the country stockpiling canned food for the apocalypse.)

He reaches out and holds her hand. And remembers, yeah, she used to be hot. Looked like an angel the first time he ever saw her, little fourteen-year-old freshman. The night of the first football game, of course, he found out she was no angel—Jack watching from the stands, suspended from the team after the first car-theft bust; the two of them leaving at halftime and making out in Steve Stell's basement while a bunch of others drank grain alcohol upstairs. He could have nailed her but he's always been glad he didn't, glad her first time was in the backseat of her dad's car, in their driveway, her dippy folks in the kitchen with no idea.

"Talk to me, babe."

She just stares off, looking like she's about to cry.

"Dana Marie?"

"I can't do this, Jack!"

He pulls her to him, pat-pat-patting her back and telling her it's okay, okay, gonna be okay if she does what he tells her.

"I can't! I can't even be around him anymore!"

"Your boyfriend?"

"Yes!" She pulls back, looking at him through watery eyes, bottom lip quivering—not a pretty picture.

Jack's not in the mood. "Straighten up, babe. Come on."

She doesn't get it. He's not even sure she heard him.

"Hey! Straighten up, I said!"

Focusing now. Haunted eyes. "Jack, I didn't *do* anything! It's not fair!"

"Yeah, you did. You did plenty. At least that's my story if I'm approached, and I'll be approached for sure if they get this maniac that did the shooting. He'll give me up in a heartbeat. And I'll give you up. So I suggest you get your mind right and do everything you can to make sure they don't catch him. That means tell me every little thing so I can try to make sure. You hear me?"

She bawls.

"*Hey!* Listen to me! This can all work out, but you gotta shape up! You shape up and this all goes away, you live happily ever after with your DA guy, you—"

"No, that's over! I—"

"He's what you're looking for, isn't he? Your ticket out of Palookaville?"

# # #

All because of Nicky Nutcase. Take him out and your worries are over.

But Jack's no killer. He's still got the .45 he picked up when he first thought of robbing the bar owner, but except for the one time at the range he's never fired it. The thing scares him; all guns do. If he's even in the same room with one—even if it's up in a closet, or lying on a table with no one near it—he half expects it to go off somehow and shoot him right between the eyes.

He hates keeping it around, but it hasn't been out of reach since Nicky pulled the .40 on him outside the Rumpus Room on Wednesday. Nicky's too scary now. Until that conversation he was so cool, so sure the trouble would all pass, but things changed when Jack told him, number one, that Dana saw them that night, and two, the DA had connected the Highwire Harris shooting and the Dunthorpe murders. Jack convinced him he'd only make things worse by killing Dana, but ever since then he's wondered if it occurred to Nicky that he, Jack—the only one who can tie Nicky to the night at Roop's—is the one who should be erased.

He'll keep the .45 handy.

Or . . . be proactive, take *him* out, and your worries are over.

Talk to Vlasitch, he'd probably do it for laughs.

But then Vlasitch becomes dangerous.

Beautiful. This is what Jack gets for being slick, trying to pull off a stickup.

Slick, all right. He should have gotten the clue back at Franklin when they voted him "Most Likely to Wind Up in Vegas." It was cool at the time, winning a little dough on World Series and Super Bowls, but later he suspected the people who voted had a different idea— that he was shifty, something like that. And why not? He'd had the second auto-theft bust by then.

"First to Do Time," they should have said. Real slick, to grab that Mustang a couple years later and wind up in real court, the old judge saying first convictions rarely result in jail time *but since you have two juvenile convictions for auto theft and seem to be a slow learner, Mr. Nitzl, I'm going to give you a year to think about it.*

Definitely slick.

sunday, june 3

Gotta lay off today, Nicky thinks. Today of all days.

Nothing this morning, anyway, not when he's on his way to see Pamela and feeling good. Finally got some good sleep last night, even on Tweety's crappy bed with the gas-station light blinking outside.

Wearing just his blue satin drawers, he stops in the bathroom for a good long leak, then heads out front. Tweety's in the kitchen—wearing nothing but cutoffs himself, so proud of the stupid spider-web tattoo on his stomach. He's at the stove turning some scrambled eggs. Got some toast, too, just popped up.

"Tweetybird!"

He turns. Not smiling. Still mad about last night—Nicky showing up saying he wanted to stay a night or two, which was fine, but later saying he'd take the bedroom and Tweety could sleep on the couch.

But what's the little booger gonna do? He's got no friends except a few punks, he's glad to have someone around, and he's always thought Nicky's too cool. As he turns this way, carrying his plate to the table, Nicky can see he wants to forget last night and be buds again.

Tough titty, said the kitty. That chow looks too good.

"Here," Nicky says, swinging a leg over the back of a chair and pulling up to the table.

"Huh?"

"Bring it here. Yeah, that."

"Huh? It's my breakfast! It's all I got!"

"*My* breakfast. Put it down here. Gimme that fork."

# # #

Well, maybe a skimpy little line, to get sharp. After all, this might be the day he meets Pamela. A good day. Got some sleep, had some breakfast, took a shower—a little line and he'll be perfect.

She'll be surprised to find out he's not the horrible guy she keeps talking about on TV. Yesterday she went on and on about the whole city being terrified, this monster still on the loose. Please. The whole city? Because three people got killed? Please. One lady plus two little kids that never knew what hit them.

In the rig he takes the 122nd exit, pulls into the empty Pizza Hut lot, grabs a *Penthouse* off the floor and lays out a line. Not exactly a skimpy one, but he'll only do the one.

Aaaaaah. Suddenly the bright morning's even brighter. Blue sky, white clouds, yellow sun . . .

Pamela. Wow. On the news yesterday she looked her best ever, in a blue dress with a white border around the neck. So clean, like she just took a bath and put on fresh makeup and would smell so good.

So clean, so proper, such a good girl . . . yet, he always thinks of the old *Saturday Night Live* Weekend Update, the hot blonde at the anchor desk giving the look and hinting she didn't have any panties on under there.

He tosses the *Penthouse* on the floor and pulls out. Almost time, if she's on schedule, and she's always on schedule. Nicky looking forward to her little bouncy-bounce in the driveway before she takes off, which is his best view of her great legs. (Except for that closeup at Starbucks last Sunday, wow!)

She's early. He's on his way up Fremont, a few blocks from her house, when he spots the hot pink cap coming down the sidewalk.

Don't want her to notice him here! He swerves to the right, turns off on 142nd Place, pulls over and waits, watching her pass in the rearview. Swings around, gets back on Fremont, goes up to 144th and turns right. He can still get down to Starbucks ahead of her, easily, and be sitting there with coffee like he's a regular.

# # #

He's sitting in a back corner with a newspaper when she comes in. She's catching her breath, waiting in line behind some senior citizens. She's pink in the face, shiny all over with a light sweat, cute as can be with the cap pulled down low on her forehead. Tasty, tasty. That monster ring, like a stay-away sign, makes her even tastier.

She pulls money out of her shorts, gets her coffee and ice water, carries them outside and sits at the same table as last time.

Okay.

Be natural. Act surprised to see her again.

He gets up and walks out.

"Pamela!"

She's sitting there, three feet away. She looks up.

"Oh. Hello."

Sit down? Something tells him no.

He was going to ask her what she's drinking, which of Starbucks's thousand kinds, but now it seems weird. "How's the news?" is what comes out.

She doesn't say anything, just sort of looks around.

Did he really say that, How's the news?

He shouldn't have cranked up.

Her cute little leg's crossed over the other one, the one foot sticking out with the little pompom thing on the back of her sock.

"Drinking coffee?" he says. "When you're hot?"

"Just a short espresso. After the water cools me down."

Is her mouth puckery like Candy said? Not really. Candy's full of it, the whore.

"So, what's the news?"

She looks at him like he's strange. He already said that!

He's afraid she's going to get up and leave. He sits down. "I saw you talking about the gangbanger and the baby getting shot." Last night, after the psycho killer bit—a drive-by down in the 'hood, some Crip wounded and a baby accidentally killed. "That's bad."

"All this killing is bad," she says. "It's one after another."

"But a baby, that's terrible."

She doesn't say anything. Just looks at him . . .

Now what? Something, before she leaves!

"How 'bout this rich lady and her kids? This psycho killer?"

"That one, my God . . . Who did *that,* and for no reason anyone can figure?"

"You got kids?" he says.

"No, but I've got friends who do, I've got nieces and nephews—"

A cop car swings into the lot and pulls up to the curb, within spitting distance. An old cop and a young one get out.

His gun's in the rig.

But they're just going in for coffee. He's paranoid from the crystal, like Jack says. They got nothing on him.

But it's good to be careful, stay alert. Like he told Jack, the stuff makes him sharper—

She's getting up! "Nice talking to you. I've got to—"

"Hey, you didn't drink your—"

But she's trotting away.

monday, june 4

Kay Henson, "Candy," calls Max at nine sharp, apologizes for Friday afternoon and promises to come in by noon.

She shows before eleven, wearing black jeans and a shiny, silvery top. Apologizing again as she takes the same chair in front of Max's desk, saying she sincerely wants to help if she can. Thanking Max for not relaying what she said Friday to the detectives, "if you really haven't."

He assures her he hasn't and asks her to pick up where she left off the other day.

She looks him in the eye and talks. Yes, she had a relationship with June Ohlander. Yes, June had been angry at her husband, one reason she was exploring her feelings for women in the first place.

What Bonnie High said last week.

Yes, it got sexual between them, but not only that. It was special. Henson had been surprised, last year, when she enjoyed her first experience with a woman—not only because she got paid well for it—and later she enjoyed close encounters with two others. "At that point I wasn't sure what I wanted—what I *was*, if you know what I mean. Even though I like men."

She says she thought about it a lot, she looked at personal ads, and something made her respond to "June Swoon" in the *Review* back in March. They got together and connected right away, having lunch at Foothill Broiler. After their second lunch they took a walk up in Forest Park and wound up hugging, kissing—"then she called Ohlander, to make sure he was at work and wouldn't be coming home, and we went to the house. Lay down on their bed. It was wonderful. She said she couldn't stand being there with him anymore but this was 'sweet,' how it felt with me. That was the start."

"All right."

"We had feelings, you know, it wasn't just the sex. There was no money or anything."

"All right."

"Just so you know."

Max likes her. Not just her looks, her killer body, but *her*. She's no intellectual but no dummy either—using words like "ambivalent" and "insensible" without trying too hard—and like lots of working girls she's clearly got street sense. The shiny silver top, the overdone makeup, an indefinable something in her face tell him she grew up lower-class, and he knows she's a hooker, a stripper, but she's not pretending otherwise. He senses she'd be a lot of fun in the right circumstances.

But the information she provides doesn't seem to lead anywhere. June Ohlander had a secret the last nine weeks of her life, but there's no indication it had anything to do with the murders.

Well, at least he won't have to pass this stuff on. He promised Bonnie High he'd keep any revelations to himself unless they seemed to lead somewhere.

He's about to let Henson go when he thinks to show her a picture of Roop. If there's actually a connection between the home invasion at Roop's and the Ohlander murders, there's at least a possibility that Henson is the common denominator.

"You know this man?" Sliding a color shot of Roop across his desk.

No.

So much for that. There's hardly any point in showing her the shot of Highwire, who just happened to be in the wrong place at the wrong time.

"Well, I don't know what else," he says, ready to thank her and send her home. Then, what the heck, he pulls the Highwire photo out of his drawer and drops it on the desk.

Which gets a reaction.

She stares at it. Glances up at Max, then stares at it again.

"You know him?"

"Yeah. Highwire. We went out."

"Dated?"

"Yeah."

"Business?"

"No. Because I wanted to."

"When? How long? How often?"

"The last few weeks. Up until . . . you know, what happened to him."

"And it wasn't business?"

She shakes her head, looking down at the picture again. "I liked him, he liked me. Not the feelings June and I had, but we had fun. We laughed a lot."

"So you were seeing them both? Highwire Harris and June Ohlander?"

"Yes. But neither one very often."

Still. She saw both of them, and now Highwire's in a coma and Ohlander's dead. Coincidence? Not many law-enforcement people believe in coincidence.

Then again, whoever shot Highwire hadn't gone looking for him. Two guys went to Roop's house looking for cash, and one happened to be a psycho racist and Highwire, black, happened to be there. There's nothing saying that was anything *but* a coincidence.

"Been dating anyone else the last few months?"

"Not *dating*. Customers . . . I don't call that dating, even though I know that's how cops refer to what people like myself do. Cops and probably DAs too, huh?"

Max lets it go. "Has anything happened to anyone else you know?"

"Not that I know of."

# # #

But something reminds her of a john, a meth-head who got crazy with her a couple of times.

"Yeah?"

But she's afraid to say who.

"Afraid he might do something if he finds out you've talked about him?"

"*Oh* yeah. He'd do something."

"It's come up? He's got reason to think you might talk about him? There's something you might talk *about?*"

"Nothing special. But if there was, and if I did, he'd do something, all right. *Oh* yeah."

"All right. It's true, he might do anything if he's into crank. But help me out here. I can always get you protection if you need it."

She wants to believe him. They always do, but they're scared. She stares out the window.

"Talk to me, Kay. This guy's been rough? Hurt you?"

Once, she says, but she doesn't want to talk about it.

"Doesn't surprise me. Half our violent crimes these days, meth's involved. If he's into it like you say, he's capable of anything, including the murders we're talking about."

She finally looks at him—but only for a second. Her eyes flit around again, around, finally settling on the Stones poster.

"He won't know we've talked," Max says. "No one knows we talked Friday and no one knows you're here now. I'll have my investigator check him out very discreetly, Mr. O'Leary I told you about. This guy'll never know."

"And? What'll that do?"

"Depends on what we find. Maybe we won't find anything indicating he was involved in what happened to either Harris or the Ohlanders, in which case there's no problem and this won't go any further. If we do find something we'll deal with it, but trust me, please, I won't endanger you. If we get as far as talking to him, we'll do it based on information we get from this point forward, not on what you're telling me."

She considers. Wanting to do the right thing, but scared.

"We don't want someone like this running around, right? Think about June. Her children. Think about Highwire."

She's thinking. Looking out the window again, biting her lip.

A peep, finally.

"Excuse me?"

"'Nicky,' I said."

"'Nicky'?"

She makes herself say it. Clearly. "Nicky Bortolotti."

# # #

Dana's been a wreck since Saturday at Jack's house, when he threatened to tell the guy who shot Highwire that she saw them that night.

She went home after that, told the girls she didn't feel well enough to see anyone, sneaked the booze into her room, closed the door, unplugged her extension, lay down and drank until she dozed off. She woke up with a headache so bad she knew she wouldn't fall asleep again all day. Awful day! The girls kept knocking, asking what was wrong and if there was anything they could do, and she kept telling them no, no, not even letting them in. When she finally let them in later she immediately lost it, seeing the unsuspecting faces and wondering what she's been doing to them all these years. (CLANG! CLANG!) The girls asking what's wrong, hugging her, comforting her like so many other times. Lizzie, who's seen so many men come and go, asking if things were okay between her and Max. Yes, yes, she said, even though she knows it's over between them. If she even survives.

She lay there all night praying for sleep. Tortured, knowing a young woman and two little kids would be alive today if she'd done the right thing after seeing Jack and someone else tear out of Roop's house and down the street.

Yesterday was more of the same. Every time the phone rang she knew it was Max. It got even worse when she finally called him. He asked if he could come nurse her and she said she'd rather he didn't. He said she's been different lately, it felt like she didn't want to see him at all, what was he supposed to think? She told him nothing had changed but she felt sick and looked terrible and just wanted to lie there alone; hopefully she'd start feeling better and they could get together tomorrow night.

This morning she had to go to work, she's called in so much

lately, but she was a mess. She almost cried when a snippy old lady complained about a tiny uneven place in her cut.

When Max called and said the investigation was moving ahead—"We've got a name"—she knew she couldn't see him tonight. She knew he'd wonder why not, and she knew Jack expected her to find out what's going on, but there was no way she could handle it.

The girls are with Brian and she'd like to just unplug the phone tonight, have a drink, lock the world out, but Max might show up. She's got to get out. As soon as she gets home she calls Ivy, one of her Thirsty Parrot friends: Wanna do something?

Ivy's game, of course.

# # #

Messages on the recorder when she gets home at midnight:

"Hi, girls—Dana, Emily, Liz . . . Oh, I forgot, the girls're gone tonight. Sweetie, are you there? I know you haven't been feeling well—I'm wondering if you're okay. You're probably just taking a bath or something, but please give me a call when you can, let me know you're all right. Love you. 'Bye." Seven-oh-six P.M., a few minutes after she went out.

Next: "Sweetie? I guess you're asleep, or you turned off your ringer. I called earlier and didn't hear back so I'm wondering. I'm sure you're fine, I just miss you, haven't seen you forever. Anyway, call me if you get the message, otherwise I'll just hope to see you tomorrow." That was 10:19, the machine says, about the time she was dancing with the carpenter at the Candlelight Room.

Next: "Beautiful? I'm sure you're asleep—I hope you are, I hope nothing's wrong. It's getting late, I'll stop calling, but I'd sure like to know you're all right. Please call if you get any of these messages tonight, no matter what time. Anyway, you're the best, and I hope to see you tomorrow. G'night, sleep tight." Eleven-thirty-two, a half hour ago.

She lies in bed hoping to fade quickly, escape her thoughts. A drink? No, she's had plenty, besides getting high with the carpenter—which hit her like a ton of bricks, first time she's smoked in years. . . .

CLANG! *You'll screw anyone, won't you?*

# # #

She hadn't even known the guy an hour. Malcolm? Some odd name. Malcolm, she's pretty sure. Sat down with her and Ivy at the Candle-light Room, chatted them up, asked her to dance.

Another script. If she'd stopped to think while they were dancing, she could have predicted the rest.

Her hands sliding up under his wife-beater T-shirt during the slow dance, up his big strong carpenter's back—what was he supposed to think? His strong hands moving down her back, cupping her buns and pulling her against his big boner. Pretty clear what was happening.

I've got a little headache, she said at the next break. Not meaning anything except that she had a headache, but . . .

Want some fresh air? Wanna walk around the block?

They walked a few blocks, stopped under a streetlight looking at each other, hugged.

Mmmmm, he said.

Mmmm. What's that I smell on you? she said.

That smell good? You want some? Good for headaches.

It might help. Haven't smoked in a while, it might be fun. . . .

It's in my van. You wanna go?

Script! Go to his van, get high, then go someplace. . . .

But look: a rolled-up egg-crate mattress in the back of the van, along with a big toolbox, three or four saws, a carpenter belt hanging from a hook. They sit there cross-legged, smoke a couple of hits. . . . The kiss . . . Her fleeting thought of Max and the real world, and then just letting go. He unrolled the mattress—Malcolm?—their clothes came off—

Brrrrriiinnnnnggg! The doorbell, shocking her.

She's paralyzed. The luminous clock on the nightstand says 12:23.

Anyone but Max, she's fine. But it's probably him, worried about her, and he's got a key. And she smells like cigarettes, booze, dope, sex.

She's up off the bed, into the bathroom, into the shower. Not even waiting for the water to warm up.

A minute later she hears the bathroom door. "Sweetie?"

"Hi!"

"You okay? I've been worried. I kept calling and—"

"I'll be out in a minute! I couldn't sleep, I thought maybe a warm shower—"

"Where have you *been?*"

"I can barely hear you, Max! I'll be out in a few minutes, all right?"

tuesday, june 5

Maybe he'll wise up someday and give up women altogether.

Not quite sure why he's suddenly so uneasy about Dana, but he is. Probably the fact that there always turns out to be something wrong with anyone he falls for. And with anyone who falls for him.

So what is it with Dana? Sometimes she's so *there*, so completely with him, but sometimes he can only wonder if he's said something wrong, done something. . . . Or does it have nothing to do with him? That's even scarier, the idea that he's his same wonderful self but she's so different.

He wonders about her. It's easy to see why she attracts men, but why doesn't anything last? Is he missing something, something he should have seen by now? Maybe Merlene's right: maybe he's been so wrapped up in her looks, the hot sex, the fun they have together, that he hasn't paid enough attention to what she's said about having crazy parents, about so often feeling scared as a kid, about things that scare her even now. What does all that mean? Or does it mean anything?

Has she even been different lately, or is he imagining? Is he simply *expecting* things to go to hell, since they always do?

It's all going round and round in his head—Max staring vacantly at a stack of subpoenas on his desk—when O'Leary appears in the doorway, something on his mind.

"Yes? Something on your mind?"

"Nicholas Bortolotti."

The meth-head Kay Henson talked about yesterday. "What about him?"

"Operates a body shop like your source said, a fourth-rate joint out on Johnson Creek near Two-oh-five. Doesn't get much business from Allstate or State Farm, I'm sure. The kind of place teenagers go after they get drunk and roll their Camaros."

"Any sign of Bortolotti?"

"Not one."

"So?"

"So, not much. He's not in the computer"—no criminal record. "Rents a place out in doper country, Hundred fifty-fifth and Persimmon, one of those old houses way back off the road with No Trespassing signs all over. No sign of him there either. No message when you call the number, which isn't in his name, by the way. No utilities in his name. No credit cards. Driver's license, but no registered vehicles."

One of these ghostmen, almost doesn't exist. You always wonder about them. The more normal someone is, the more you can find out about him, because he's not trying to hide anything—it's when you start turning things over but come up empty that you start wondering.

Not that it necessarily means anything at all.

Either way, Max reminds himself when O'Leary leaves, he's got a lot more to think about than a shaky romance.

#

Dana wants to cover her ears! Run away from all of it! Quit her job and move into Amy's again, where Max can't find her! Where Jack can't, where no one can!

But no. Anywhere but Amy's.

Brian's.

Except then he's all over her, wanting her to give him another chance, and she feels so guilty, feels like she has to sleep with him. . . .

She can't go on like this!

She's all snarled up again, about to cry again, when Max calls, asking about getting together tonight.

"I can't."

"Busy?"

"Yeah." Think of something, fast! "With the girls. . . ."

"Yeah? All night?"

"I'm not sure."

"What's going on?" he says.

"Going on?"

"It feels weird. Between us, I mean. It's different."

"What do you mean?"

"You don't think so? I hardly see you lately—"

"We were together last night, Max. And it was good, wasn't it?" After her shower. The sex.

"I wouldn't have seen you if I hadn't gotten worried and gone over there. You're always busy lately, or not answering your phone, something. I don't get it."

"I've had things to do. My mom's birthday. Then I felt like crap all weekend, and—"

"I wanted to come over and nurse you."

"I know, but I . . . I . . . when I'm sick I'd rather just be sick. I look awful and I don't want you to see me that way—"

"Don't worry about that. You don't ever look awful, anyway. I don't know, I'm just wondering what's happening. Can you tell me?"

"I don't think anything's happening, Max. I don't think anything's wrong."

"No?"

"No."

She wants to *run!*

wednesday, june 6

O'Leary drops in saying he still hasn't located Nicky Bortolotti. Asks if he should try to locate this "Jack" that Bortolotti mentioned to Kay Henson a few times, guy who runs a car lot out on Eighty-second. Henson thought Bortolotti might have done some work for him.

Check him out, Max says, lacking any better idea.

A half hour later O'Leary's back, an odd look on his face. "Jack Nitzl, the guy's name is, N-I-T-Z-L. Owns Executive Motors, out there between Astro Gas and Furniture Liquidators. Remember the TV ads, 'One-Dollar Down Payment'?"

" 'We care more about your future than your past'?"

"That's the guy. Probably hoping no one looks too closely at *his* past, or his cars."

"Why's that?"

"He showed up on the computer. Two juvie convictions for stealing cars, then one when he was twenty-one that got him a year at Inverness."

"Anything else?"

"Well, what I said about the cars on his lot . . . There was an incident five weeks ago, which Winkle just explained to me"—the DDA in charge of the Auto Theft Task Force, downstairs—"where these Russians, known car thieves, shot up a car lot but the owner wouldn't ID 'em. This guy Vlasitch and a couple of his stooges? Vlasitch is the one—"

"—who blew up the man in Vancouver last year, right?"

"A guy who supposedly owed him money, right. Blew the car sky-high. Actually *told* people about it, but they were all too scared of him to talk. Likewise, it sounds like this Jack Nitzl was too scared to say it was Vlasitch and his friends who shot up Executive Motors. Someone saw it and called in, the blues picked 'em up within five minutes and took 'em to the lot, but Nitzl claimed he'd never seen 'em before, didn't have any idea what it was about."

"So?"

"So why did Vlasitch shoot up Nitzl's lot? A known car thief, a guy who's known to kill people who cross him. My guess is Nitzl owed him money."

"Hmmm."

"Yeah. Bortolotti's got a low-rent body shop, Nitzl owes a car thief—it starts to add up."

"Which takes us where, as far as Bortolotti and the Ohlander murders?"

"Probably nowhere. It only tells us Nitzl, this buddy of Bortolotti's, has been in some trouble with the biggest car thief in the metro area."

"And? Anything else?"

"Well . . ." O'Leary, who's never hesitant with Max, hesitating.

"Yeah?" Max says. "Well?"

"All right, there's a little more about Nitzl that might interest you."

"Bring it."

"It'll interest you, but you might not like it."

"Let's have it. What the hell."

"If you say so. All right, what's her name again, your lady friend?"

"Dana Waverleigh, L-E-I-G-H."

"What I thought. All right, you want it?"

"I'm getting a feeling I probably don't, but yeah, come on."

"Nine years ago she's in a car with Nitzl, eight in the morning . . ."

Pow. Blah blah blah, O'Leary goes on, but Max barely registers it.

". . . cited for careless driving," O'Leary says. "Report says he was rolling through stop signs, speeding through a residential district and a school zone. He was asked to test and blew a point-oh-six, just below the limit. Either he was still half-drunk from the night before or he's a guy who wakes up and pounds a couple to start his day. And Dana Waverleigh is named as a custody associate, is all." Meaning she was in the car. "Nothing to do with murder or stolen cars," O'Leary's saying, "but I thought I should tell you."

# # #

At first Jack thinks it's about Vlasitch and his goons shooting up the lot last month—this guy O'Leary showing up at the lot, bringing out picture ID showing he's an investigator with the DA's office, saying he wants to talk.

"You wanna talk about those jerkoffs shooting out my windows, shooting holes in my inventory?"

"Not that," the guy says. Slim, gray-haired, softspoken guy probably in his fifties. "I'm aware that happened, but no. Those charges were dropped, that's all over."

"So what's up?"

"I need to locate Nicky Bortolotti, and I heard you might be able to help."

Jack's instantly defensive, not about to take the explanation at face value.

"Word on the street," the guy says—odd way of talking, barely moving his lips—"is that Bortolotti's in danger."

"So why'd you come to me?"

"We can't locate him, and someone told a detective you're a friend. We don't know who else to ask."

"Who's this someone that said I'm a friend?"

"I don't know. I didn't get that, and either way, when it's street talk there's a good chance the name an individual gives the detective isn't his real name. All I can tell you is that we've heard Mr. Bortolotti might be in danger. We just want to find him, that's all. Possibly relocate him, provide protective services, something."

Jack gives him a shrug.

"He's not at the address the DMV has for him," the guy says, "which is an apartment he apparently moved out of last summer. He's not at his place of business, either. He still operating Nicky's Body on Johnson Creek, as far as you know?"

"Far as I know."

Jack's heart is thumping. Maybe someone *is* after Nicky—lots of people probably have reasons—but Jack smells bullshit. Maybe this O'Leary's checking *him* out, not looking for Nicky at all. Maybe the whole thing's coming apart.

"So you don't have any idea how I can find Bortolotti?"

"Not really."

"A message number, pager, anything? We're trying to save his life."

"Sorry."

"Know how he gets around? What he drives? Seems he doesn't own a vehicle."

"I've seen him in different ones. I think sometimes he drives cars he's supposed to be working on. At his body shop."

"You see him very often?"

"Almost never. Calling us friends is a stretch."

"You know anyone who knows him? Family? Anyone who might know how to find him?"

"Sorry."

# # #

You were cool, Jack thinks afterward. But suddenly he's sweating even more than he did during the conversation. Wondering if they know anything.

Maybe they know everything.

From Dana?

No way. She's scared to death.

Then who?

No telling.

But doesn't Jack *want* them to find the nutcase? If they nail him for killing the lady and her kids, Jack's not involved at all. Worst-case scenario, they somehow nail him for shooting Highwire Harris during the robbery and he gives them Jack, hoping to catch a break—but Jack denies everything, and what can they do?

Best-case scenario, they *suspect* Nicky for one or the other and approach him. Chances are he'll be tripping on meth and packing a gun. He's Edward G. Robinson, Little Caesar: *You want me, you'll have to come and get me! No two-bit copper'll ever put any cuffs on me!* Shootout. He's dead. Jack's worries are over.

Tough call. Do you clue him in and hope he believes you're trying to protect him?—but risk having him come after you anyway, since he figures you're the only one who can dime him up for shooting Harris? Or forget it, and risk having him find out from someone else that they're looking for him?—in which case he *will* come after you, figuring you dimed him up.

Maybe best to call him.

#

Jack's on the line saying somebody from the DA's office came around looking for him a few minutes ago. "Said someone told a cop we know each other, and wanted to know if I could tell 'em where to find you."

"Find me why?"

"He said the cops heard someone's talking about taking you out."

"*Who's* talking about it?"

"He didn't say. He wasn't giving up much. Said they want to find you and offer you protective custody, that's about all."

"Protective custody? What, a jail cell?"

"I guess that's what it means. Anyway, what's going on? Someone mad at you?"

Nicky's suspicious. "You, maybe?"

"Gimme a break. Seriously, who you been jerking around?"

"Nobody. I got no idea. So what'd you tell him?"

"Said we're not that great'a friends, I haven't seen you for a while, and if you weren't at your house or your shop—since I knew he already checked there—I didn't have any idea."

"You sure, Jacko? That's all?"

"Trust me."

"Yeah. I trust you, all right." Should've iced him after the conversation in the Rumpus Room lot the other day.

"I didn't know if he was being straight or not. Maybe they're looking for you for something else, you know what I mean, and—"

"Ain't no way. They got nothin' on what happened to that spade. Unless you told somebody."

"Right. Like I'm gonna say something. I was there too, remember?"

All right, Jack probably didn't say anything.

Probably. Still . . . should've iced him *that* night. You'd have had all the money and wouldn't have to worry about him now or ever. This is what you get for being a good guy. For being soft, like Rico said. It was Rico's downfall, not taking care of Joe Massera and his girlfriend before they squealed.

There sure wouldn't be any uproar if Jack Nitzl disappeared.

# # #

Hard to believe. That Dana could be so . . . so . . . so *low-life*. And maybe much more, much worse.

But there's nothing to believe, not yet!

Then why's Max walking around the house in dazed disbelief, doing shots of Johnnie Walker?

It was nothing O'Leary said when he reappeared in Max's office just before five, back from visiting Jack Nitzl's car lot. Nitzl's a little slick, he said, a little seedy, but that's a used-car dealer. Average looking, still has his hair, wears a cheap suit and assumes people won't notice his threadbare socks. Serious nail biter. Not a huge success, by the look of him, his dinky office, cheesy little lot with the banners strung around it.

He was surprised to see the DA identification, O'Leary said, but not all that surprised. Acting at first like O'Leary must have come to talk about the Russians shooting up his lot a few weeks ago. O'Leary wasn't sure if he was faking it or not. Wasn't sure, then, if he bought the story about Bortolotti being in danger; wasn't sure he'd care, if he did believe it. He took O'Leary's card and said he hasn't seen Bortolotti for a while but he'll sure call if he does.

Jack Nitzl. Cheeseball. But a cheeseball who had Dana in his car at eight o'clock one morning nine years ago, meaning a 90 percent chance they'd spent the night together. *Maybe* she was a stranger, a hitchhiker or neighbor or cousin Nitzl was giving a ride to work, but . . . Make it 98 percent they'd spent the night together.

It's over.

The fantastic body, the legs wrapped around him, the coo in his ear—it's all over.

He should have known. Suspected, anyway.

Suspected what?

Something. He doesn't know exactly what.

You're not even sure anything's wrong.

Little things that would have added up if he'd been willing to see, if he hadn't been blinded by the smile, the body, the rockin'-sockin' sex. How about her "Would You?" game with the girls, asking each other if they'd eat someone's barf for a hundred dollars? Low-life.

But he overlooked that, and the crazy parents, and the neuroses . . . telling himself those little details weren't nearly as meaningful as the big picture, the cosmic place where the two of them connected.

Yeah? What level was that, considering they've never talked about much besides what happened today, and the girls, and how thrilling it was to be together?

You putz.

He remembers Merlene asking, incredulous, *How can you possibly believe you know anything at all about this woman, so soon?*

Well?

Maybe he'd know more if he'd asked more questions. Or if he'd listened more carefully when she talked, instead of just groping her and thinking about the bed-rattling sex to come.

He should have been suspicious the night he started giving her a short version of his marriages and divorces and she said *We don't ever have to talk about the past, Max, it's probably better that way.* Lord only knows what-all she hasn't told him.

But you don't know! Worst fears, that's all!

No? Then why's she been so weird lately? Sure, she was sick all weekend, but other women would have wanted you there.

But remember how she made love Monday night, when you showed up late and she got out of the shower all warm and tender and wrapped you up? Come on! You're just paranoid because so many other relationships have exploded!

Maybe, maybe not. Maybe he wouldn't feel this way if she hadn't been in a car with a half-drunk used-car salesman at eight o'clock one morning nine years ago.

# # #

Where is she? No answer when he calls, just Emily's cute message (wrenching, suddenly) on the machine.

He's jittery, restless. He needs a new murder to work on, right now.

How sick is *that?*

Johnnie Walker. Johnnie Walker. When you need a friend.

No answer again, just Emily's message.

He thinks: Bortolotti-Nitzl. Nitzl-Dana.

No. You don't even have a solid Bortolotti-Nitzl connection. And maybe Dana hasn't even seen Nitzl in nine years. She's never mentioned a Jack. A Brian, a Henry, some others, but no Jack that he can recall.

He punches in her number again.

No answer, again.

# # #

Quiet on her street as he comes around the curve, a half hour later.

But a light on, behind her curtain. She's there, maybe.

Why doesn't she answer the phone, then?

No cars in the street except for hers, the downstairs lady's, the van from across the street and a vintage Volvo.

Why didn't she answer the phone?

Someone's with her.

He drives past, thinking it through.

Maybe she's *not* there. She took the bus somewhere, or got a ride. Leaving a light on is normal.

Around the corner he tries again on his cellular.

Emily's message again.

Is she cooing in someone's ear, too busy to answer the phone?

Is she in there *hurt? Dead?*

Looking for an excuse to go in.

Feeling like a stalker.

Go home.

Pulling up across the street, thinking the hell with it. Getting out. Crossing the street, the sidewalk, the small square of grass.

All quiet.

Under the porch light he silently turns his key in the lock. Inches the door back—

—sees the security chain across the opening, and knows she's here. With someone.

Quietly pulls the door shut, scurries back across the street, gets in his car and drives home. Mortified.

part three

thursday, june 7

If the end's coming, it's coming. But Nicky Bortolotti's not about to give himself up. *You want me, you'll have to come and get me!!!*

What he's going to do is meet Pamela Gramm, in case this really is the end. He made up his mind after Jack called yesterday. He got hold of Beaner, the Mex, and arranged to use his house today, maybe a few days. It's rundown and doesn't smell too good but it's out of town, nobody too close, and Beaner's got infrared sensors all around the lot and closed-circuit video monitors inside to let him know if anybody's snooping around. (Investments you have to make when you're using a stolen farming permit to buy fertilizer and chemicals for meth production, storing it in your dilapidated barn and retailing it to people who cook the shit up.)

He's up before seven, showering and getting ready, spending extra time on his hair. Snorts a line to get sharp and leaves Tweety's before eight, Tweety polite but definitely glad to see him go.

Hot outside. Steamy. Rare for Portland, the kind of weather that frizzes your hair up if you're outside very long.

At Starbucks he grabs the table out front where she usually sits. There's an old couple sitting a few feet away, so he'll need to tell Pamela he'll waste her right here if she doesn't keep her voice down and be perfectly cool.

He's not sure what he'll do if she doesn't. Say, if she figures he wouldn't dare shoot her with a bunch of people around, and says something like *Excuse me, I'm going to go inside and call the police.*

But he doesn't think she'll test him. Show most people a gun and look like you mean business, they'll pee themselves and do what you say. Like Al Capone said, you do a lot better with—

Pamela! Here she comes, right on time, all in white except for her pink ball cap. Bringing her knees up high, getting the most out of her run. Cutting across the parking lot now, coming this way.

Noticing him, he can tell, but pretending not to.

"Hey," he says as she steps up on the sidewalk. Like "Hi," not rude or anything.

"Oh. Hi."

"Coffee?"

"Just water. Too warm." She's at the door, wants to go in—

"I wanna ask you something," Nicky says. "If I could. But go ahead, get your water, I'll be here."

She goes on in. Maybe a little uneasy, but tough titty. He doesn't plan on hurting her unless she forces him. He's crazy about her, why would he hurt her?

Two minutes later she's back out. Pausing, but not sitting down. "You wanted to ask me something?"

"Yeah. Can you sit down a minute? Drink your water?"

"I need to get going."

"Aw, have a seat."

"I really can't. No time."

"Bull," he says, keeping his voice down. The old folks nearby are reading the paper, not paying any attention, and he lifts his shirttail to show her the grip of the .38 sticking out of his jeans. "You're a babe and a half," he says, low, "but this here'll mess you up."

Her eyes get big, and meet his with a new look, with respect. He nods toward the other chair and she sits down.

Like Al Capone said, you get better results with a smile and a gun than with a smile alone.

"Good. Now, see the four-by-four?" Nodding toward it, nose-up to the sidewalk, with the Ohio plates he took off a Winnebago in the Lloyd Cinema lot last night.

She's staring at him, can't even talk.

"Let's take a ride," he says. "Just a little ride, then I'll drop you back here."

She probably doesn't believe him, but tough titty.

"Now, I'm gonna follow you over there, to that sliding door on the side. Right behind you, me and my friend here. You're gonna open that door, which I know you can do with those good strong arms. Right?"

She can't talk. Probably peeing herself.

"Open it and get in and lie down in back. I got a blade, too— you make a sound and I'll cut your tongue out. Be hard to read the news then."

She's frozen like a statue, her beautiful blue eyes wide.

"*Now,* Pamela."

She moves.

He follows. The old folks don't even look up. The old man's reading the comics.

She opens the sliding door and gets in, exactly like he told her. He's right behind her. Slams the door behind him.

She's on her knees on the carpeting, facing him. "P-please . . ."

"Lay down."

"Please."

"Lay down, Pamela. I'm not gonna do anything. Unless you don't lay down. That's your way of saying you don't mind dying right here." Reaching under the seat for the bone-handle knife that scares most people into acting right.

# # #

He knows she can't see anything from back there, stretched on the floor, except some of the blue sky. He does a couple of turns around the parking lot before pulling out onto 122nd, so she won't have any idea which way they're going.

Pamela Gramm. Pam, as all the dips on the newscast call her. Right here, close enough you could reach back and touch her. Tasty as tasty gets, and ready to do anything you say.

But many fields to conquer first, as Jack likes to say. One thing at a time. Focus.

He turns right on Siskiyou, cruises a few blocks, turns left, left again, and comes back to 122nd. Down to the entrance to 84 East. Takes the 136th exit and cruises down to Kmart, with the big parking lot that's still almost empty an hour before opening. He parks out in the wide-open spaces.

Scoots back to where she's lying just like he told her to, looking good and scared.

"Easy, Pamela. I'm not gonna do anything. Just this"—reaching in his pocket for the eyeshade he bought last night, the kind he wore for daytime sleeping when he used to work nights at that dairy. "Put this on."

"No. Please—"

"*Yes,* please."

She gets the message.

"Good," he says when she's got it in place. "Now, you move it, you even touch it, I might have to cut one'a your pretty fingers off. Speaking of fingers"—taking her left hand and pulling the big diamond ring off—"I don't like this very much."

Pulling out of the lot a few seconds later, he rolls down his window and pitches the thing.

#

It's over. Incredible. She changed his life—he knew it, knew this was it—and now it's over.

Jack Nitzl. Whoever the hell he is.

Driving away last night Max instinctively noted the plate on the vintage burgundy Volvo, the one car on Dana's block he didn't recognize. It's a violation of office policy to get into DMV records for personal reasons, of course, but everyone does it once in a while and the first thing he did this morning was run that plate. Not that he expected anything.

John Harris Nitzl.

Jack Nitzl.

He sat here stunned. It was early, still quiet, but inside his head it was all noise, confusion, nightmare.

Well, at least it explained what's been going on, how weird she's been.

But no, it didn't explain anything. It only verified that *something's* been going on.

Finally, heartache and disbelief gave way to anger and focus . . . Max Travis receding, Max Faxx emerging. Instinct taking over, his mind working the connections and possible connections.

The connection the shell casings made between Highwire's shooting and the Ohlander murders. Kay Henson's connections with Highwire, June Ohlander, and Nicky Bortolotti.

Bortolotti-Nitzl. Nitzl-Dana. Dana-Roop.

Bortolotti-Nitzl-Dana-Roop? Was it possible?

A few minutes later it came to him, how to find out. He called Roop. Yes, Roop said, he was free this afternoon; yes, he'd like to play cops-and-robbers; sure, he'd come up around one.

Max, afterward, staring out the window again. Hearing the old song again: "*. . . I believe in you. . . .*"

Finally got up and—what he should have done a long time ago—took the elevator down to the first floor of the courthouse, to Multnomah County Records, and requested divorce decrees for Waverleigh, Dana Marie.

# # #

Jack wasn't fooling last night. Telling her she'd better call Max today, arrange to see him tonight, find out the latest.

She finishes a dye at quarter till twelve, drives home, slams a gin and tonic, gathers herself, and dials Max's cell phone. Gets him at the food court in Pioneer Place, noise behind him.

How's he doing? she asks.

Working. Busy. Grabbing a piece of pizza to take back to the office.

Is he busy tonight? Can they get together?

He doesn't know. He's kind of busy.

"I'd like to see you. Will you try? Will you call me if you can come over?"

"I'll try."

He sounds so cold!

"Or I'll come to your house," she says. "We can sleep together, at least."

"Don't you have the girls?"

"I can leave them. Lizzie's old enough."

"You shouldn't do that."

"I want to see you. I want to be with you."

"Oh?"

"Max? What's happening? You sound . . ."

"I sound what?"

"Not like you. Not very loving. I want to see you, but . . ."

"Yes?"

"I know you were upset because we haven't been together much lately, and now I'm trying to make it happen but . . . I don't know. I don't know what's happening."

"I called last night," he says. "No answer."

"I had to go out. A friend needed to talk, she's having a hard time."

"All right. Whatever."

Quiet.

"Max? Are you mad at me?"

"Not mad, just confused. And I don't need confusion right now, everything that's going on."

He sounds *hard!*

She's going to cry. He's a good guy, they could have had something, but suddenly she's in this position of lying to him, using him, taking advantage of how he feels about her.

"I'm sorry, Max . . . It's me, not you. . . ."

"I agree. Something happened to you, I don't get it."

"I know. I don't know, I get scared. . . . I just know I want to be with you tonight."

"Uh-huh."

"Can I please see you?"

He doesn't answer, there's only the Food Court noise behind him. She pictures him in the noon crowd, grabbing pizza to take back to the office so he can keep working. A solid guy with a clear conscience, like most people.

"Max? Will you please come over later? I get the girls back this afternoon but we can have time after they're in bed. I want you to lie down with me, hold me. . . ."

Nothing, even when she mentions lying down.

"Max?"

"I'm here. But what'm I supposed to think about all this? You say you love me, you talk about having a *baby,* and then all of a sudden you didn't want me around."

"It wasn't that I haven't wanted you around! I haven't been feeling well, I haven't been any fun to *be* around, I've been ugly, I—"

"All right, whatever."

"But it's not all right! It sounds like you're *finished* with me! Are you? You won't come over tonight?"

"I didn't say that. I said I'm confused and I don't need confusion right now. I don't know. I wanted to see you last night, talk things out. I kept calling and kept getting no answer."

She remembers the phone ringing over and over as she sat there with Jack. "I . . . was out with my friend, then stopped for groceries to get ready for the girls coming back, then I went to bed. I still don't feel great."

"Maybe I shouldn't come over, then."

"Please! I'm over the bug, I'm just a little tired. Please come see me. I'm feeling insecure about us, I guess. I still can't understand what you see in me, but when we make love I feel better. . . ."

CLANG! *You lie!*

# # #

Max sits at his desk waiting for Roop, staring vacantly at the over-priced slice of pepperoni pizza. He's got no appetite anymore.

Can I please see you tonight, Max? The little innocent voice.

But he's not only angry. He's sad, he's hurt. The idea that the sunny future they imagined—*he* imagined—is shot to hell, a mere three weeks and what, three days after that magical Monday night at the Quandary, in his hot tub, in his bed . . .

Roop walks in just in time, celebrating the sunny day with a loud Hawaiian shirt. "Ready to rock?"

Max dumps the pizza in the trash and gets up. "Let's go."

They take Roop's Lexus and twenty minutes later they're cruising past Nitzl's car lot out on Eighty-second. It's every bit as cheesy as O'Leary made it sound, with the little colored pennants and the "One-Dollar Down Payment" promise underneath the bold Executive Motors sign.

Two minutes later, in the Dunkin' Donuts lot across the street, Max instructs Roop to sit tight until he gives the signal. "Let me check him out. When I start stretching my neck like I've got a crick, come on over."

He wants to see if Nitzl has any reaction to the sight of Roop, and if Roop recognizes anything about Nitzl—movements, voice, anything. See if there's any chance Nitzl was one of the masked men at Roop's house that night.

Max crosses the street and walks into the little glass-enclosed structure that passes for Executive Motors headquarters, a bell announcing him as he opens the door. The guy they saw outside when they drove by, presumably Nitzl, appears from behind a cheesy bamboo partition. Fake hearty, sticking his hand out: "Yessir! How are ya? What can I do for ya?"

Max shakes and says, "You got cars?"

"Have I got *cars?*" Waving the hand, taking in everything outside. "Something you wanna see?"

"Cars."

"Well, let's go look at cars, then. I guess my salesman went for some lunch. . . ."

Mid-thirties. Hair not receding but seriously thinning. Nervous guy, despite the cheery patter—nails gnawed down to nothing, nicotine-stained fingertips on his right hand.

Outside they stroll toward the Volvos. Max asks him, "How's business?"

"Not bad, not bad. Now, any special model you like?"

"Don't know much about 'em. Just happen to know a guy, who swears by 'em. Says they last forever."

"Well, I happen to have a few."

Did he have those nasty hands all over her last night? Did she fuck this piece of garbage?

Forget it. You're Max Faxx now.

"All these here," Nitzl says. "Different models, different years."

"I see." Max tilts his head back, rolls it around, stretches his neck.

"Any of these do anything for you?"

"Maybe. What's a good deal?"

Glancing across the street and seeing Roop coming out of Dunkin' Donuts, heading for his car.

# # #

At his desk Jack lights a smoke, his hands shaky, and uses his cell phone to call the salon.

"Hair on Burnside," the girl chirps.

"Gimme Dana."

"I'm not sure I can. Can she call you back? She's doing a dye."

"I need to talk to her. Tell her it's Jack."

"I'll see," the bimbo says, and puts him on hold.

What the hell's going on? That's Roop out there!

Dana comes on the line. "Jack? I'm in the middle of—"

"Don't tell me what you're in the middle of. Listen, what the hell's going on? I've got *Roop* here and—"

"Where?"

"Where do you think? And I want to know why. He been looking for a car?"

"Jack . . . No . . . I mean, I don't know, I haven't talked to him. . . . I can't talk right now. Where are you? Let me finish and I'll—"

"You *stay* on this phone, you hear me? Now, I want to know what the hell's up. I told you to get together with your boyfriend and find out what the hell."

"I did! I talked to him just a little while ago about getting together tonight! What's happened?"

Jack glances outside, where the guy he was talking to when Roop showed up is still looking at Volvos, and Roop—he's positive it's Roop—is talking with Vinnie. "What happened is Roop's here, like I said. You hear me?"

"I heard you, but I don't understand."

"All I know is I'm out here trying to sell a Volvo when this guy pulls in in a late-model Lexus, cream colored. Is that Roop's car? And does he wear ugly luau shirts?"

"He—he's got a Lexus."

"I knew it was him." Ever since that night, he knew he'd never forget the face.

And knew—he'd thought it through a hundred times—knew the only way Roop could ever hope to identify *him* was by his voice.

"Luckily I saw him before he came up and started talking to me. And luckily Vinnie showed up, so I don't have to deal with him." Vinnie, praise the Lord, getting back from McDonald's just as Jack spotted Roop and turned away from the Volvo guy in midsentence, panicky, *Excuse me, I gotta take care'a something.* Had to get *away.* Here came Vinnie, stuffing fries in his face, and Jack grabbed the Mickey D's sack and said go help the guy in the shirt. Came in here and got on his phone, to look like he actually had a reason for walking away.

"I don't know what's happening, Jack. I was going to find out tonight. I called Max like you said, he's coming over later."

"Jesus Christ. All *I* know is I got Roop out here talking to my salesman."

#

He sees Vinnie leave Roop and head for the guy in the suit who's looking at Volvos, probably pissed about Jack ditching him.

Roop wanders over to the BMWs.

It's got to be the craziest coincidence ever, Roop showing up here. Can't possibly mean anything. Jack finally takes a chance— goes to the squawk box and says, "Vinnie . . . Phone call." Three quick words is all, the guy can't make much out of that.

He's back at his desk a minute later when the bell sounds, Vinnie coming in. A few seconds later Vinnie comes around the partition, baffled. "Who called? They musta hung up, none'a the lines are blinking."

"Nobody called, forget it. Who's the guy in the pineapple shirt? What's he want?"

"Just looking. Says he needs a second car but he doesn't know what. I finally told him to let me know if he wants help."

"What'd he say?"

"He said he would. Let me know."

"I mean *before*. All that time you were with him."

"Oh. Not much. Cars, the weather . . . You going back to that guy?"—nodding toward the one Jack walked away from when Roop showed up.

"He want help, or's he just passing time?"

"I'm not sure."

"Go find out. Help him if he's ready, otherwise tell him to let you know when he is. I'm getting out of here for a few—*Christ*." Stopping short as he sees Roop coming this way. Bolting up out of his chair, gotta get the hell *out*, telling Vinnie "Help this guy, I'll be in the bathroom." Hearing the bell as he darts back to the can. Short of breath as he locks the door, turns on the light and sees his pale face in the mirror over the sink.

It's happening. What he thought would never happen.

That investigator sniffing around yesterday . . .

He drops the toilet lid and sits down. Sweating through his shirt.

Remembering the year at Inverness so long ago . . . So long ago, but seems like last week . . . County jail, so-called easy time. Easy, sure. Guards wearing shank-resistant vests; "guests" (as the guards sarcastically called them) wishing they had them too. Jack swore he'd never go back.

Then *why?* Why rob someone at gunpoint, especially with a cranked-up Edward G. Robinson wannabe as a partner?

The walls in the little bathroom are closing in.

But when do you dare go back out there? What if Roop's sitting there?

# # #

Finally.

Pamela in there waiting for him, in Beaner's bed with the clean sheets Nicky put on while she was in the shower. Pamela Gramm. In there naked, all his.

He smoked three hits of the crystal a minute ago, he's feeling good, and it's finally time. He gets out of the chair and walks to the bedroom.

Dark in here: tin foil over the windows, only a little light from the lamp he moved to the corner farthest from the bed. But his eyes will adjust in a minute.

Even though it's plenty warm, summertime, she's got herself under the covers, all except her head and the one arm with the wrist cuffed to the bedpost. Doesn't want him looking at her.

Scared, he can see as he approaches. The whites of her eyes.

"Don't worry, Pamela. I won't hurt you. Unless you make me. Be nice to me, I'll be nice to you. I haven't hurt you, have I?"

Terrified eyes.

"Have I?"

She shakes her head.

"All right then."

He sits on the edge of the bed. Puts his hand on her knee, through the covers, and feels her tense up, hears a little sound like her breath catching.

"Don't be scared."

"Wh-why? . . ."

He can't help smiling, he doesn't know why. "Why did I bring you here? You don't know?" Shaking his head like it's the dumbest question in the world. "Because you're the most beautiful woman I ever saw. And classy, and smart, and a nice person."

"But . . . but . . ."

"Easy." He pats her leg through the covers. "Relax. It ain't been so bad, right? I haven't hurt you."

No answer, just the big scared eyes.

What a face. Right here, in real. Close up. He made her get ready for him with a shower and the makeup he bought when he went out this afternoon, and she looks great. Scared, but great.

"Just relax, let me be nice to you."

But she's shaking under his hand. "Wh-why are you doing this?"

"I told you why. 'Cause you're so fine. 'Cause ever since I saw you on TV during that snowstorm I always thought . . . You really wanna know? 'Cause I'm gonna *die*. And ever since I saw you that time I knew I'd die happy if I could be with you just once. You understand that?"

Tiny voice, barely a squeak: "No."

"Because you can't see yourself like I do, like a man does."

"I don't understand why you'd—if you like me, why you'd—"

"Well, if you had any idea how fantastic you are—"

"Please!" And all of a sudden she's crying. "Please let me go! I swear I won't say anything! I don't even know your name, I don't know where we are—what *could* I say? Please!"

Nicky just looks at her. The beautiful face, the one arm stretched back toward the bedpost. Remembering the sleeveless red dress the day she reported the story, how great her arms looked—

"I don't know why you did this but it's not too late! *Please!* Just let me go and it's over!"

"That's what you say."

She'll say anything. Any of 'em will. He gets up and walks out, slamming the door behind him. Not gonna do it today anyway, he decided a while ago. Plenty of time. Nothing but time. Beaner's cool with him being here.

Then again, have a nice dinner, talk some, tell her you just want to do it once or twice and you'd probably let her go . . . maybe she'll feel different.

# # #

Max drives out to Beaverton and meets Barris, husband number three, for a drink at Beef & Brew. Better than coffee downtown, which they talked about when Max called him this morning.

Max orders a Beefeater martini, dry as the Sahara, and tells the waiter he'll want another one pretty quick. Barris orders Glenburnie. When the drinks arrive Max cuts the small talk and picks up where he ended the phone conversation this morning. *What happened to you and Dana?*

It pains Barris to talk about it. Naturally. He experienced the blue blue eyes, the coo, the flesh, the whole feel of her and the way she makes *you* feel: like you're the only one who ever mattered to her, the only one who ever will.

"I was so in love," he says. "But I had to wonder, from early on. She had a history of relationships she didn't stay in, marriages and relationships that didn't work out for whatever reason. And as soon as I mentioned marriage she wanted to talk about a prenuptial."

"Never a good sign."

"But I agreed to it, I don't know why. I made it conditional on her staying at least five years, which she didn't like, but what could she say? . . . She stayed nine months. She was fantastic for six and then suddenly she wasn't there at all. She just disconnected. When I pressed her she'd say I wanted too much from her and she couldn't handle it, stuff like this. I don't know—she'd say this, that, the other thing. Then it turned out she'd been seeing this old flame of hers. She even admitted she was crazy to have anything to do with this loser, this used-car salesman, but she said she couldn't help it, he was the love of her life. I couldn't believe it. She was even sort of embarrassed, saying 'What I probably need is ten years of therapy.' I said 'Well, why don't you get started?' but then she just laughs and says,

'I should, but I probably never will.' And then moves out. End of the marriage. Moves in with this loser, guy named Nitzl. Jack. I can still see the look on her face when she said it: 'Jack.' Must be the coolest guy in the world."

"Not hardly," Max says. "If it's any consolation."

"You know him?"

"Met him this afternoon, briefly. And I know a little *about* him."

"And you're not impressed. I'm not surprised. Which doesn't make for any kind of consolation. Quite the opposite, that she'd leave me for him."

"I'm sorry."

Barris shrugs. "Is this helpful at all?"

"Probably. Makes me feel like a fool for getting reeled in the same way, but it gives me an idea of who I'm dealing with. It's possible she's involved in some bad business."

"You mentioned an investigation?"

"Which I can't talk about. Yeah. It's only dawned on me the last day or so that she might be involved."

"Interesting."

Barris polishes off his drink and looks for their waiter. Max drains his martini, savors the olives, wonders where it's all heading. Who he got involved with. What else is behind the mask, behind the so-blue, so-innocent eyes.

Barris, with a faraway look, probably asking himself similar questions.

Yes. "I still don't know who she is," he says at last. "I was so shocked when she moved out I had to talk to someone, had to try to understand. I went to see her sister Amy. Which was strange, that conversation—I got the impression she'd tried to explain Dana before. I barely got started before she said 'I don't know if I can help you, but I can tell you she's *not* mentally ill, she's *not* drug addict.' As if people have been trying to understand her for a while. She said there's never been any stability or continuity in Dana's life, that she's been with different men and lived in something like thirty different houses and apartments in the last ten years. . . . This sister loves her, she wasn't trying to make her look bad, but she didn't have much encouragement for me as far as Dana coming around. Which I suppose a part of me was still hoping for. Crazy, huh?"

"Human, I think."

"All right, I like that better. Now, it got really interesting not long after that talk with the sister. When I'd started feeling relieved, almost, lucky it hadn't turned out even worse somehow. What happened, about a month after she moved out to be with her great love, was that her great love apparently lost interest, treated her badly, and she was calling me asking if we could 'work through things.' Basically, could we pretend she never lied to me, cheated on me, shit on me. As if she'd just stepped out for cigarettes and now she was back. Boy, I laughed. And then she actually went and got a lawyer and started making claims on my property, even though we hadn't been married anything like five years. Challenging the prenuptial *she* insisted on."

"I saw the file," Max says.

In the divorce papers Barris claimed unfaithfulness on Dana's part, *repeated and admitted involvement with an old boyfriend.* Dana cited irreconcilable differences and found a lawyer dumb enough or desperate enough for work to contest the prenup on those grounds, which were no grounds at all. And she looked worse than merely silly when all was said and done. *The court finds that the respondent was untruthful in her financial reporting and in her spousal-support affidavits. The court is therefore rejecting the respondent's petition to set aside the prenuptial agreement.* In other words, Dana got caught up in her lies and Judge Kuykendall threw her case out.

"If you saw the file, then you know," Barris says. "She'll do anything for money. She's been poor forever but she doesn't like to work. This hair cutting is the first real job she's had, as far as I know, and she must've only started that out of necessity after she left me and then her great love dropped her. She got the training sometime back but never followed through and got a job—I guess she kept finding people to support her, and in between boyfriends she'd survive with some baby-sitting, housecleaning, this and that. When we got together she *talked* about working but never did. She worked at coming up with reasons not to work. She'd say she needed to look after Emily, even though Emily had started school. She talked about us having a baby, which *might* have been sincere but struck me as simply a reason to stay home."

It's not too late for you to have a child, Max. . . .

"She can fritter away days and weeks doing I don't know what," Barris goes on, "and she doesn't care what anyone says about it. Her sister told me their parents would give her a hard time about it, and *she* used to, the sister, but Dana's in her own world. You probably noticed she keeps herself in nice clothes, and buys for the kids at thrift stores? She's certainly got her priorities. But you know, it's easy to lose sight of these things. Easy to get stars in your eyes around that girl. She comes off so sweet; she can actually *be* so sweet. . . ."

"It's true," Max says.

"But there's a mean streak there. Mean streak? I don't know. Call it an absolute lack of feeling, at times. I'll never forget the end. One Wednesday night she was, pardon me, blowing me on the back porch, but by Sunday she didn't want any part of me. Much later, when I found out she'd been seeing Nitzl, it turned out she'd run into him that Thursday or Friday. It was over for me right then, I just didn't know it till I caught her a couple months later. When I did find out and asked her to explain, she gave me this love-of-her-life crap for a few days, then she wouldn't talk at all. As if I was waaay out of line to think I deserved an explanation."

She came into his world, Barris says, made him feel like he was the only one who ever mattered, then cut him off at the knees and went on her merry way.

# # #

Pamela was nice for a while after Nicky let her off the bed, let her put her clothes back on, the undies and sports bra and white short-shorts and Save the Penguins T-shirt he bought earlier. They had a glass of wine and talked while she cooked the spaghetti and made the salad, Nicky sitting at the table in Beaner's breakfast nook. Not that she wouldn't have left if she could, but she seemed to realize he's not such a bad person. He was saying all those nice things, not only about her looks but what a nice person she is. *I was impressed how upset you were about the lady and her two little kids getting killed. They hardly even talk about it on the other channels anymore, but you still do.*

Maybe stupid to talk about that—it was the crystal talking—but it was exciting, and no, she couldn't possibly know.

She said it was such a horrible thing, she couldn't let go when everyone else moved on to the next sensational story. (He liked the part about everyone moving on. Maybe the cops are, too.) He asked her who she thought killed them and she said probably a stranger, a robber. Nicky said maybe it wasn't a stranger or a robber, maybe someone had a reason, like the lady's husband found out she was fooling around. Pamela said nobody knows and it's a horrible thing, that's all. He told her again he's always thought she's a caring person.

She said thanks, he seems like a caring person too, which makes it so hard to believe he'd do something like this. . . .

That was when he decided to take her on a date, probably tomorrow night, and asked what size dress she wears, what size shoes. He'll go out tomorrow and buy himself something to wear (in case someone's watching his house) and buy her a nice dress, shoes, whatever she needs. Then disguise her a little, dye her hair or cut it or get her a wig, and go out to dinner. Someplace out of the way, of course, but nice, like that hotel out at Multnomah Falls. Yeah. Take a little walk, look at the falls, have a nice wine and dinner, soften her up, *then* come back here and finally do it. Do it nice.

Tonight, leave her alone. Maybe don't even go in the bedroom again. Stay out here, watch TV. Take a walk, get some air, clear your head. She's not going anywhere, unless she can take that bed with her.

# # #

But how about after the date? After they get back here and do it?

Because he blew it today, he's pretty sure. Not by what he said about the woman and her kids, but the other.

You know about Highwire Harris?

Dummy! He'd taped her to the chair and gagged her before he went shopping, and she had a hard time breathing—pretended to, at least—and wrote a note on the tablet asking him to please take the gag off. He thought it over and told her okay, there was no one within screaming distance, and he'd turn Beaner's tape recorder on when he left for the store so he'd know if she tried anything.

He made the mistake just before he left. He was tripping hard and he reminded her not to try to scream for help; he was being nice, leaving the gag off, but if there was even a sound on the tape when he got back, well, *did she ever hear of Highwire Harris?*

Now there's no choice, really. No way he can let her go, no matter how sweet she is or what she promises about not saying anything.

So, what happens?

# # #

Soft summer night, Neil Young's "I Believe in You" on the oldies station, Max getting teary again as he drives over to her apartment for probably the last time. Remembering the nights (last week!) she gave him those eyes and said she felt unworthy of him and he told her to forget that, he loved her and absolutely believed in her, who wouldn't?

Idiot. Believed in her based on what? Those so-blue, so-innocent eyes? The smile? The coo? The hot body and what she did with it?

Based on sympathy? Because she'd had a hard life, little cutie from the wrong side of the tracks?

Embarrassing, that he wanted her so much he got played. And he's still not sure why she's been playing him.

All he knows for sure is that she's dreaming if she thinks she's going to pull off whatever she's trying to pull. *Max, can I please see you tonight? I'm feeling insecure about us but it's always better when we make love.* Meaning *You're so hooked on the sex that I can do anything I want with you.*

She wants to play? Well, she's never played in the big leagues.

He turns right off Halsey, right again in front of the Red Apple market, takes the curve around to Seventieth and spots her old Honda in the usual spot along the curb.

No vintage burgundy Volvo, of course, not tonight.

She comes to the door in one of her long T-shirts, bare underneath as always, the blond hair up in the French twist she knows he loves. Giving him the angel eyes. Planning to give him one of those rocket rides to the stars.

And he'll let her. He's dying to give it to her. Forget "making love," he wants to rock her. Then, when she thinks he's putty, he'll sit back and see how she goes about whatever she's up to.

The fat pink candle burning in the living room, as usual. Quiet, the girls in bed. The wonderful girls. He didn't come over earlier because he couldn't bear to see them, knowing he's not going to be in their lives after all.

Sure, he says, he'll have a drink. He can tell she's already had a couple.

She goes to the kitchen, showing him the legs. A minute later she's back, handing him a screwdriver and asking him to come sit on the love seat.

Curls up against him, legs tucked beneath her—a tasty morsel, as Roop said, no matter what else she is. Giving him angel eyes again. "I'm glad you came, Max, even so late. I'm glad you're here."

"Yeah?"

"The girls wanted to see you but I said you were working, I didn't know when you'd get here. Maybe we can all do something this weekend."

"Maybe."

"I'm just glad you're here. I've missed you."

"Yeah?"

Anxiety clouding her face, suddenly, as she realizes he's not melting. "What does that mean, 'Yeah'? You don't believe me?"

"I wanted to see you and them *last* weekend, and ever since, but I can't get invited."

"I was sick last weekend, you know that. I'm still not all better. We've talked about this, Max."

"I would've looked after you. Made you some chicken soup."

"The girls were looking after me. That's not what I want you for, to take care of me."

"What do you want me for?"

Stopping her for a second—but only a second. "You still don't know?"

"I thought I did. Now I'm not sure."

Confusion, now. "Max, are we fighting?"

"Are we?"

"If we are, can we stop? Can we be like always? Like before these last few days?" Scooting closer. "Please?" The coo.

"If you say so."

"That's all?" Finally realizing she's not directing the play. "What's going on, Max? Will you please talk to me?"

She *is* a babe, Lord, all curled up against him with nothing but the T-shirt on, ready to pull that off, too. And he's ready, ready to burst. But he just looks at her. Waits. Max Faxx superceding randy Max Travis.

"Talk to me, Max."

"About what?"

"About what's happening here. I thought we promised to always be honest with each other, but all of a sudden . . . I mean . . . Okay, we don't have to talk—maybe it's better if we don't right now. Can we go lie down? You're so distant all of a sudden, so different, it scares me. It's like we're not together anymore."

"You're saying we *are*, still? Together?"

"Can we just go lie down? Just *be?* It's always good when we just do that."

"Sure, let's go."

# # #

He can tell she's startled by the way he slams away, by the lack of sweet nothings, but he doesn't care now.

Afterward, for their different reasons (and he still doesn't know what hers are), they lie there pretending things are all right. But everything's different.

And he's sad. Wondering if there's any chance, *any*, that he's all wrong; if there's any way they can go back. And he knows there isn't, even though he's still far from knowing everything.

# # #

"So," she asks at last, "how's work?"

Ah. He knew she'd get to it. It's why she wanted to see him tonight.

"Just work," he says. "You know."

"The case? The murders?"

"Not much happening there. I'm working on other stuff."

"But weren't you making progress a couple days ago? You had some information?"

"Nothing much."

She doesn't know where to go next and they lie quiet. Max imagines Nitzl lying here last night. . . . Amazing. A fucking cheeseball is her kind of guy, her great love. A car thief, an eight-in-the-morning drunk, a chain-smoking, nail-chewing used-car salesman who's probably got more reason than ever, now, to chew his nails. Who was almost certainly part of what happened at Roop's house that night: no other explanation for him coming apart when Roop showed up at his lot today. So chummy with Max till then, with his third-rate salesman patter, but he spun away the instant Roop appeared, in the direction of nothing in particular, grabbed the McDonald's from the swarthy guy and bolted back to the office. Sat at his desk and made a phone call, shuffled some papers, finally just sat there. Finally got on the speaker and called the swarthy guy away from Roop—"Vinnie, phone call"—but Vinnie went in and never picked up a phone. They talked by Nitzl's desk, Nitzl agitated, and Max knew he'd recognized Roop. He was asking Vinnie what the *hell* was going on?

Any doubt was removed when Roop went in a minute later and Nitzl shot into the bathroom. Took the longest dump of all time.

"Are you mad at me, Max? Are we okay? You're so quiet."

"No, not mad," he says. And knows it's time. "Not mad, just wondering."

"Wondering?" she says. Hesitantly, as if she's not quite sure she wants to know.

"Wondering, yeah. How deep you're in this."

friday, june 8

Dana barely slept after Max left. Tossing, turning, obsessing, feeling things crashing down but not knowing how or why or what happens next.

Finally she got up and made a drink and sat in the dark, in the dead-of-night silence, remembering. . . . Max so strange, so remote; rough in bed like he's never been, not easing up even when she groaned, just doing it and then lying there quiet afterward. No propping up on his elbow and gazing up and down her body like it's the eighth wonder of the world, no sweet talk.

And then springing it on her: *I'm just wondering how deep you're in this.*

She wanted to call Jack after he left, maybe he could tell her what's going on. She knew she *should* call him. But she was afraid they might have her phone tapped, or that Max would call and find her line busy and somehow figure out she was talking to Jack, after she told him she doesn't *know* Jack.

And how stupid was that, saying she doesn't know him?

She sat in the dark for an hour, then lay in bed all night without sleeping a minute. Knowing she's going down.

But she didn't do anything!

# # #

No way she can work today. She's so jittery she'd jab someone's neck, lop off an ear. Go drop the girls at school, call Jack from a pay phone (listen to him rage when she tells him she didn't find out anything), then come back and . . . what?

Wait.

For what?

She's got no idea.

# # #

Max wakes up Friday morning knowing it's going to be a bad day, and that there are plenty more ahead. It's all too familiar: the knotted stomach, the anxiety, the emptiness. It lasted for months after each divorce and set in again when Paige dumped him—until, yes, a certain evening at the Veritable Quandary when a certain babe of a blue-eyed blonde sat down with him and changed everything. A night when he would have sworn he'd never feel this way again.

But he's an open sore again. On the drive to work the oldies station brings Roy Orbison: *Only the lonely . . . know the way I feel tonight. . .*

He surfs, only to come across Al Green doing "For the Good Times." Lord, it gets better and better. The good times. Her body by candlelight; Liz and charming little Emily chasing him with squirt guns; Emily saying she wished they could be a family; Dana's hilarious Dylan imitation.

He surfs again, only to land on Orbison again, "Crying" this time: *I love you more . . . than I did before*—taking him back to last night, all the conflicting feelings.

Stop. Turn the damn radio off. Go to work. Max Faxx. Sort this thing out.

Work. Job. Put your faith in something you can't lose, as a wise man said.

# # #

They're in McGowan's office, next door to Max's, when he walks in—McGowan, Witty, Batty, Cornell, all abuzz about something.

About Pam Gramm disappearing. "Norman came looking for you a minute ago," McGowan says. "Central Precinct called him saying she didn't show up at KATU yesterday, didn't make it home last night, never called her husband all day the way she usually does. Hasn't been seen since she stopped for coffee at Starbucks yesterday morning, the one off Fremont out in Parkrose. Husband called in last night."

"And Stormin' wanted me for what?"

" 'Cause you're Max, I suppose."

"I'm Max, all right," turning toward his office. "Pam, huh?"

Nice lady, even if there's something a little sad about her. He stops in front of his bulletin board and locates a card she sent him last year, a cartoon of a guy standing in front of a judge saying "Never mind what I *did,* Your Honor. I want to be judged for who I *am,* as an individual."

The cops'll find her—alive, hopefully. A TV personality, they'll be all over it. He's got has plenty to think about.

# # #

Over coffee at Seattle's Best a few minutes later, he tells O'Leary about yesterday at Executive Motors: Nitzl freaking at the sight of Roop, bolting to the office, finally hiding in the bathroom. "Roop sat down in the office and waited for him. I hung out on the lot in case anything went down. A half hour later Nitzl was still in the john and I knew he was one of the guys at Roop's that night. I wondered if one of the calls he made before he went into the john, after he recognized Roop, was to Bortolotti, to let him know they're hot. Be nice to get his phone records. Not only for yesterday, but ever since the night at Roop's."

"Assuming he was there."

"Which I'm now assuming."

"All right. Well, since we can't get a subpoena on an assumption, I'll see what I can do."

Meaning he'll talk to his people at the phone company. It's an old joke in the office, O'Leary's "people." He's got people everywhere.

# # #

Back at his desk, Max wonders if Nitzl's phone records will show much contact with Dana. Any. If not, then all he's got to explain away (the ridiculous shred of him that wants to believe they can have that sunny future after all) is the episode nine years ago, and Nitzl's car outside her place Wednesday night.

Yeah, that's all.

# # #

Jack's got that tone, he's *demanding.* "He said *what?* He wondered how deep you are *in what?*"

"I don't know, Jack. . ."

"Where the hell are you? What's all the noise?"

"In a phone booth. Outside Red Apple"

"Speak up. Now, he wondered how deep you are in what?"

"I don't *know.* He said it, that's all. And I didn't say anything, and he didn't say anything else, he finally just got up and got dressed and said 'bye and left."

"When you gonna talk to him again?"

"I don't know. He's at work now."

"Working *this.*"

"I don't know, Jack . . ."

"But you know which side you're on, babe, right?"

# # #

It's almost two, Max at his desk eating pizza from Food Court, when Kay Henson walks in. She's Candy, too, but today she looks every bit Kay Henson, a regular girl. Jeans and a denim shirt, the heavy makeup gone, long painted nails gone.

"You look different."

"I am. I'm at Fresh Start. Although"—quickly—"I don't expect you to tell."

"My lips are sealed." Fresh Start being a rehab house for hookers over in Northeast, where they go to transition from the life to something better. To get counseling, detox, hide from abusive or homicidal pimps, johns, whoever.

She looks good, but she's upset. "Sit down," Max says. "What's going on?"

"I was in my car and I heard something on the news a few minutes ago. . . . I came straight here."

"Heard what?"

"That this lady's missing, Pamela Gramm, Channel 2. I came straight here."

"Why?"

"I don't know, maybe it's nothing, but . . . Nicky. The guy I told you about. Nicky Bortolotti."

"What about him?"

"He has a thing for her. He'd talk about her. . . ."

She says that aside from his insane jealousy of anyone she, Henson, was interested in, Bortolotti had a crush on Pam Gramm. Rated her right up there with Cameron Diaz and Winona Ryder as a fantasy girl. Talked on and on about her—her name, her wedding ring, what she'd be like in bed.

"And he's so crazy sometimes, doing so much crank and all, I just thought I better come talk to you."

"I'm glad you did."

"I hate him. I lie awake every night thinking about June . . . those kids . . . what it was like for them. They were having lunch, just a nice sunny day, a regular day, and he comes in with a *gun*. I lie awake thinking what it was like . . . whether she saw him murder her kids or whether he murdered her first and then . . . Those poor kids . . . I *hate him!*"

# # #

Back from walking her down to the elevators, he calls Verdow at Central Precinct. "Phil? Anything on Pam Gramm?"

"Nothing. We're talking to people at the Starbucks, Channel Two, working it the best we can."

"Well, you might try to track down Nicholas Thomas Bortolotti, the same guy we wanna talk to about the Highwire Harris shooting and the Ohlander murders. I just got some information. Can you reach Haynes and Morales? We might have something here."

"I'll find 'em"—the lead detectives on Ohlander—"and I'll tell the guys working Gramm. What do you have on Bortolotti?"

"Addresses for a house he rents and this scummy body shop he operates, but we haven't seen him at either one lately. O'Leary's looked for him."

"Vehicles? Associates? Anything?"

"Not much. He doesn't have a record and he owns almost nothing in his own name. O'Leary talked to a Jack Nitzl, John Harris Nitzl, N-I-T-Z-L, an associate of some kind, but Nitzl played dumb. Probably for good reason, which is that he's probably involved in some of this with Bortolotti."

"Some of what?"

"I'm just speculating. Let's talk. I can come over there—"

"You been running an investigation on your own? Listen—"

"Just speculating, I said. I did go out to Nitzl's car lot yesterday. . . . Look, I'll tell you about it. Meantime, I can tell you Nitzl's not gonna say anything, no point wasting your time. Might not hurt to put a tail on him, but I'd focus on Bortolotti, see if he's at his house or this dump of a shop, Nicky's Body, out on Johnson Creek. I'll talk to Johns and see if I can get started on warrants."

# # #

Pamela's thankful he hasn't touched her, Nicky's sure of that. He's pulled the covers back and looked at her plenty, but that's it. She knows he's not just after sex. Well, he *is*—what, she's gonna ditch Casper Milquetoast and marry him?—but the point is he could have done whatever he wanted as soon as they got here yesterday and any time since, but he didn't, he hasn't.

What're you waiting for?

After their date. Make it right.

You outta your mind? Make it right?

All right, all right. Maybe it's crazy.

This minute, this second, he knows it's crazy, but then he starts thinking the other again. Too much crystal, his mind doing the thing where it jumps from one zone to the other. Tripping along in the red zone, things making perfect sense; then it's like a train jumping the track and landing over here, everything sort of green, greenish yellow, the voice in his ear.

Hard to get out of it, out of his head. Red: Take her out, have drinks, be nice, talk, eat, have dessert, drive back (her hand on your knee in the car) and she's all yours. Green: *You're nuts! You grabbed her, showed her a gun, showed her a knife, duct-taped her to the chair at Beaner's, cuffed her to a bed, said that about the spade. . . . It's over! No choice but to . . . you know. She can't go free.*

He's dizzy, on the way downtown to buy her a red dress and shoes and Lady Clairol dye and some nonprescription glasses. He pulls into a Pizza Baron lot, kills the engine, lets his head fall against the window, closes his eyes. The stuff sets your head on fire . . . Voices yammering at you . . . Red zone, green zone, train jumping the tracks . . .

Take her out, have dinner, then go back and do it all—whether she wants to or not, 'cause it's over, it doesn't matter. Then waste her and fly—

Gonna waste her?

Gonna tell her you are, or just sneak up and . . . ?

Then run, or put the iron in your mouth and be done?

Dinner. He was in the place once, the restaurant in the hotel out at Multnomah Falls. Dark wood paneling, white tablecloths . . .

He sees Pamela across the table, beautiful, candles, people around them having conversations, waiters in black and white coming and going. Reminds him of Rico getting into a tux before his big dinner with the Big Boy, grumbling that all he needs is a white towel over his arm.

Red again: Dinner, her hand on his leg on the drive back, the sex—

Green: Crazy. Rape, you're talking about. And then she has to die. You knew it before you ever grabbed her.

Or else you put the iron in your mouth and it's all over.

# # #

"What's happening?" Jack's demanding tone. "Have you talked to Travis?"

"I don't know what's happening, Jack. . . ."

She's got a headache, is all she knows. Stayed home from work and had too many drinks, scared to death. No idea whether to keep quiet and hope it goes away or tell Max everything—*I didn't do anything!*—and beg for mercy, for help.

As if he'd help her now.

"Jack, what's going on?"

"You were supposed to tell *me.*"

"I don't know! He wouldn't talk last night. He knows I'm in it, in *something,* that's all I know."

"Great. You been with the guy this long, and you're supposed to be finding something out, but you don't know anything. What's up with that?"

# # #

"What's up with that?"—and hangs up on her.

But forget her, handle this yourself. Jack sitting at his desk at the lot, listening to KXL for the latest on this kidnapping. Pamela Gramm—the weekend lady on Channel 2, Nicky's dream girl—hasn't been seen since yesterday morning. Police suspect foul play. Jack suspects a nutcase doper by the name of Nicky.

It could work out perfectly. Call the cops and say this nutcase had a thing for Pamela Gramm, always talking about what he'd like to do with her, all this . . . *and* you're pretty sure he shot Highwire Harris . . . *and* killed that lady and her kids in Dunthorpe.

The cops say, How do you know all this?

Jack says, Trust me. I'll bet the bullets match.

They'll realize he knows what he's talking about.

They'll know Nicky's dangerous. If they locate him they'll send a SWAT team—try to save Gramm if they can, but they won't give a rat's ass about Nicky. They'll take him out if they get half a chance.

Which would put Jack in the clear. Dana would be the only one left who could link him to what happened at Roop's, and she'll never talk.

Even if they don't kill Nicky, maybe they nail him for Highwire Harris or the Dunthorpe murders or both. Maybe the fool still has the .40 on him.

If he squeals on Jack, trying to make a deal, Jack deals right back: *I know someone who knows someone who knows Roop, and I told Bortolotti the guy kept a lot of cash in a safe at his house. I didn't do anything. I figured he's the type who'd do it, he'd get one of his crankster friends to help and then he'd probably throw a few bucks my way afterward. But I sure as hell didn't do anything.*

But do you really want to get into this at all? They'll suspect you right off. You want to go downtown and talk to a bunch of cops?

#

All the way downtown in her car, Dana's not sure she can go through with it.

It's not that she can't bear to do it to Jack, not after he's told her he'll give her up in a second if he has to. Not after all the ways he's proved he doesn't care about her. It's *What if they believe him, not me?*

But she doesn't have much choice now. It's all coming apart. It didn't all go away like Jack kept saying it would.

She finds a spot on Fourth, plugs the meter and walks down to the courthouse.

Through the metal detectors, and she's standing at the elevators. Does she go up?

If she doesn't, and it all comes crashing down, they *really* won't believe a word she says.

#

"You can dye it or I'll cut it," Nicky informs Pamela. "I bought dye 'cause I thought you'd rather do that. But whatever you want. Tell me."

"All right . . ."

"Don't be mad. I'm trying to be nice. But it's one or the other. We can't go out with you looking like yourself."

#

Verdow sent Koontz and Berm to check for signs of life around Nicky Bortolotti's house and his body shop. Koontz called Max a few minutes ago saying nothing was happening either place. Max called the crime lab anyway, saying he'd probably need a team to work those locations a little later—to fine-tooth for blood, prints, hair, lipstick on drinking glasses, any sign Bortolotti's had Pam Gramm there—and then got started on an affidavit for search warrants.

He's deep into it when there's a throat-clearing and he looks up and Dana's standing in the doorway. Shook up. "Max . . ."

"Hi. I'm a little busy . . ."

"I'm sorry . . . I'm just . . . I need to talk to you."

"Oh?"

Gonna beg him to forgive her? Ask him to come over tonight so she can make him see stars, make him forget all the rest? His neurotic little thrice-divorced sex machine sensing things are coming apart.

"Close the door and have a seat," he says.

She does. Obedient little hussy now.

"Max . . . I don't know how to . . . what to . . ." Voice trailing off, eyes flitting around.

"Yes?"

"What to say. The position I'm in . . . I mean, whether you'll believe me . . ."

# # #

He doesn't bother walking her down to the elevators afterward.

He doesn't know whether to believe a word of it. More important right now, he's got to write up this affidavit before the judges go home.

He gets it done, gets Mona to type it up, skips downstairs and catches Keys coming out of his chambers at five till five. "Hate to hold you up, Your Honor, but . . ."

Five-thirty by the time Keys reads the thing, asks a few questions and finally notarizes the warrants.

Back upstairs Max reaches Morales, who's been off since three, and asks him to bring Haynes and meet him at Nicky's Body to serve the first warrant. Calls the crime lab asking for a team to meet them there. Leaves the courthouse, gets his car out of the lot on Yamhill and takes off.

His thoughts, as he crosses the river, go back to Dana sitting in his office earlier, finally fessing up. *You've got to believe me, Max, I didn't do anything! I never did what he says he'll tell the police I did!* Admitting Nitzl was an old boyfriend, and they still talked once in a while, and when he gave her grief a while back about dating Roop she wanted to make him feel bad; she told him Roop was at least successful, had more petty cash in his safe than Nitzl probably makes in a year. *It was stupid, Max, telling him Bill had a safe, but I never suggested anything. But he says he'd tell the police I did, and they'll believe it.* She said she stopped at Roop's on her way home from a girlfriend's apartment that Saturday night, forgot her sweater when she left, went back for it and saw them running out of the house, Nitzl and someone else, and Nitzl saw her. *I was so scared when the detectives came to talk to me, I didn't tell them I went back for my sweater, so they didn't know I saw anything and then Jack called and swore he didn't shoot Highwire and it would go away if we stayed quiet—but if I didn't stay quiet, he'd make sure I went down too. I was freaked out, being around you, but I wanted it to work. . . . Oh, Max! Today he called and said he's sure the man that was with him that night is the one that's got the lady from Channel 2, and the police will probably kill him if they find him, or he'll kill himself—but if not, this man will tell on us both. . . .*

I swear, Max, I didn't do anything! Please help me! Please!

# # #

Nicky's Body is a tumbledown place at the end of Johnson Creek Road that should have been condemned ten years ago.

Nobody around.

A loose knob on the door they could probably pull right off, but for fun Morales goes back to the detectives' car for the "key," the ram that opens even a stout door with one whack. Whack! Glass shattering, the door slamming back and wobbling on its hinges as they walk into Nicky Bortolotti's world.

Workbench, tools, motor oil, paint, standard stuff. A few cars at various stages of repair and disrepair.

Bortolotti's clearly not doing much business. From the look of things—the stack of skin magazines next to a broken-down chair in one corner, the two- and three-inch lengths of drinking straws—he mostly sits around snorting crank and jerking off. Sleeps here at least occasionally, on this ratty mattress in the little back room.

They hear the guys from the lab pull up outside. A minute later they're inside, four of them, getting busy.

# # #

"You pouting?" Nicky asks her, careful to keep his voice down.

Across the table—white tablecloth, candles, just like he pictured—she shakes her head no, no, trying to smile. He told her to smile once in a while so they'd look like a real couple.

He gave her the warning out in the parking lot after she was pissy all the way out here. *Be pissy in there and you've got a problem. Just act normal—not too sad, not too happy. Smile once in a while. Don't talk to anybody but me. I'll deal with the waiter and whoever else.*

So far so good.

"You look great, you know it?"

A little sound, like uh-huh.

"It's true."

It's not, but he wants to make her feel better. One reason she's upset is the disguise.

Well, what does she expect? They're talking about her on the news, and even though there's probably not much danger bringing her to Multnomah Falls Lodge, twenty-five miles from Portland, he had to be careful. He thought about cutting her hair but decided to be nice and let her dye it instead. The dye and the oversized glasses he picked up today made her look different enough. She's not his same foxy Pamela anymore, but he had to do it. In the dark later it won't matter.

"You like the food?"

A little nod, not even looking up.

"That's a yes?"

A quick glance and another nod, then she's got her face down toward her surf 'n turf again, even though she's barely touched it.

He leans across and says quietly, "You're getting me mad. Now eat some. Drink some wine. Act right."

Still not looking at him, she picks up her fork. Looking scared. Nicky wondering if anyone notices—twenty people or so in the place—or if he only sees it because he knows she is.

It wasn't supposed to be like this. Hell, now he's not even sure about going to bed when they go back. Well, he is, but the way she's acting . . . First she didn't like dyeing her hair. Then she didn't like the dress he bought, he could tell, even though it was just like the red one that looked so hot on her the day she reported the shootings. Then the shoes didn't fit exactly right. Then, leaving Beaner's, he made her wear the eyeshade and lie down in the back of the rig again until they got a few miles out on 84.

◀

Can't live with 'em, can't live without 'em. Rico didn't mess with women at all, he thought they were trouble, but in real life a guy's gotta get laid, at least.

And he's gonna get laid tonight. Pouting won't get her out of it.

# # #

Max and the detectives pull up the long drive to Bortolotti's house, out in the boonies. A dive, like O'Leary said, peeling paint and all, even an old beater up on cinder blocks on the side.

No sign of anyone around, no response when they knock and call out. Fine. Morales brought the key. Bam! More shattered glass, another door slamming back against the wall, shuddering on the hinges.

Classic doper house. A stink, from some combination of dope, old food, dirty dishes, dirty clothes, unflushed toilets. Foil over the windows to thwart prying eyes. Ratty old furniture—no money wasted on decor—but a PlayStation with dozens of video games stacked alongside and a state-of-the-art sound system with a couple hundred CDs, mostly heavy metal and alternative junk. Posters of some of the bands on the walls: Tool, Anthrax, Doctor Butthead, Weaver Beaver.

A classic three-foot-high bong in Bortolotti's bedroom, taking Max back to college days.

More half-straws lying around. A big-time crankster, Bortolotti.

Magazines: more smut, along with a bunch of *NASCAR Monthly*s and *Four-Wheeler*s.

But no sign Bortolotti's been here lately, much less Pam Gramm.

# # #

They're getting back in the car, summer dusk fading to dark, when Max gets a call. Sheriff Wasco, saying a citizen called in saying she thinks she saw Pamela Gramm having dinner with a guy out at Multnomah Falls Lodge. "Guy named Hector Lopez. That's the name on the credit card he used, anyway. Restaurant manager said they drove off in a green SUV afterward. He didn't get the plate but he's sure it was out-of-state. I just called the card company's eight–hundred number to get an address for Lopez but hit a brick wall, guy explaining the Privacy Act like I never heard of it."

"I'll try 'em. You got that number?"

Max reaches the guy who just talked to Wasco—who says no, he can't give a DA that information either. Until Max pushes, telling him it's possibly a life-and-death situation and if it ends badly the company will be on the hook for a few million in a civil suit and *you, sir, will be out of a job.* The guy stammering, thinking it over, and finally saying that if Max can fax him a subpoena he'll fax the information back. So: a speedy drive back downtown, whip out the subpoena, fax it, wait for the response.

The address that comes back for Hector Lopez a few minutes later isn't out-of-state but out near Gresham off I-84—out near Bortolotti's, for what it's worth. But none of it's necessarily worth much, beginning with the citizen thinking she *might* have seen Pam Gramm. What do you do, call out SERT and then look like fools when it turns out to be a false alarm? Do nothing and look like worse than fools if it ends badly? Max and the detectives decide to drive out and size things up, then reassess.

"The dink couldn't be so stupid," Morales says in the car. "Grab her and then take her out to dinner?"

Of course, they all know hundreds of dumb-criminal stories. Even most smart criminals are stupid, to try to pull something off in the first place.

But Morales is probably right. Is anyone dumb enough to kidnap a newscaster, a recognizable face, and then take her to a restaurant? Even if the restaurant is out at Multnomah Falls, twenty-seven miles from downtown? Portland people go out there all the time. And you wouldn't have to be from Portland to recognize Pam Gramm—Channel 2 reaches most of Oregon and a fair piece of Washington.

Most likely the helpful citizen was mistaken, which is why Sheriff Wasco wasn't more excited and why Max and the detectives aren't calling out a SERT team.

# # #

The house is on a long road at the east end of Randy Bog Valley, a low-rent, semirural area that won't be low-rent or semirural much longer, with developers closing every remaining space between Portland and the surrounding towns. This stretch, in between Portland and Gresham and the cement-truck factory at the east end of an industrial park, is one of the last ones bearing any resemblance to countryside: two- and three-acre plots featuring old rundown houses, clotheslines, vegetable gardens, pickups trucks. Mostly rentals these days, except for the ones belonging to old-timers waiting for the developers to come with the money.

The Lopez place sits back off the road, up on a rise at the end of a long gravel driveway. The gravel will make a racket underneath the wheels. Haynes cruises on by.

There are some woods at the far end of the property, a long wire fence on the other side, then a pond and another acre of ground before the next house.

Haynes turns around and they cruise back, looking up at the Lopez house in the near-darkness. No SUV in sight, no vehicle at all.

But maybe in the garage. There's light at the edges of a couple of windows, as if there are shades or dark curtains in there that don't quite cover.

Fifty yards past the driveway, Haynes pulls over and the three of them look at each other. Well?

Probably nothing to it, they agree. It was probably Lopez and his wife or girlfriend at the lodge, and a do-gooder citizen with a hyperactive imagination. Besides, they can't do much without a warrant.

But then, Pam Gramm might be up in that house with a crankster who's already shot so many people he doesn't have much to lose by shooting one more. Pretty Pam. Pretty, earnest, not-too-bright Pam, who endeared herself to Max by asking if he was satisfied with the 320-year sentence for Harry Wayne Patch. Who still sends him Christmas cards, hoping he'll hand her a scoop someday.

"I'm for parking here and walking up," he says, "see what we see."

# # #

Now that it's finally time, Nicky's not sure he can enjoy it. He's only been up for two days, he's had runs a lot longer, but whether it's the excitement, the drinks at the restaurant, the jumbo line he snorted when they got back, his head's on *fire*. Nothing seems real. He's naked with her—Pamela Gramm!—she's following orders, doing what Candy, that whore, said Pamela Gramm would never do—Pamela Gramm sucking his dong!—but it just feels *weird*, he barely feels it at all somehow; he's in the red zone, green zone, red, green, hardly knows where the hell he's at. . . .

Beeeep!—Beeeep!—Beeeep!—

Mama! Beaner's alarm system! Mama mama mama!

He pulls Pamela off his knob.

Maybe it's Beaner driving up. Maybe he needed something but

couldn't get through because Nicky unplugged the phone yesterday— had to drive over.

No, he would have paged him.

Nicky's up off the bed. Mama, his head!

Pamela's sitting up, wondering what the hell.

"Stay there! Lay there! Down! Lay *down!*"

She does. He grabs his Bermudas off the chair and scrambles into them. Grabs the .38.

Beeeep!—Beeeep!—They're coming!

Pamela's up on her elbows, eyes wide. He sticks the .38 in her face—"Down, I said!"—and she falls back.

He can't leave her loose in here. The window's nailed shut but who knows? The cuffs are still attached to the bedpost. "Gimme your hand!" She whimpers, but he's already grabbing her forearm and slapping the cuff on her wrist like last night. "One sound and you're dead!"

He flies out to the front room, mama mama mama. On the closed-circuit monitor he sees motion, people coming up the driveway. Gotta be Beaner and somebody, right? Except Beaner would drive up to his own house, not walk.

But be cool. It can't be cops. No one knows he's here but Beaner, and Beaner wouldn't tell anybody.

Whoever it is is coming closer. Three people, it looks like. If it's cops, they better not expect him to invite 'em in for tea.

Forget this .38, fucking peashooter. Beaner's serious business is in the closet, the AK-47 with the thirty-round banana clip. You wanna talk, boys?

Shoot first, argue afterwards. No two-bit copper'll ever put any cuffs on RICO!

They're out there talking, not far from the porch.

# # #

It's got to be a marijuana-grow operation, a meth lab, something. That, or Bortolotti's in there with Pam Gramm. Something's going on in there that someone wants to keep secret. Lights are on, but there are blankets or something over the windows.

They could go back downtown, spend hours on an affidavit for a search warrant, wake up a judge for notarization, come back with SERT—and look like fools when Hector Lopez comes to the door, roused out of a sound sleep, asking what the hell, saying the windows are covered because his wife works nights and sleeps during the day.

But Pam Gramm might be in there.

Morales asks Haynes, Should we knock? Haynes shrugs: Why not? They walk up there, Max hanging back.

A dog barking somewhere far off. A car in the distance. The deep quiet reminding Max of summer nights in the eastern Oregon farm country when he was a kid spending a week or two with Uncle Doc and Aunt Nonie. He can almost hear a moo-cow, like he used to hear out there.

The detectives' shadowy forms come into the light from the single naked bulb on the porch. They look at each other, then Haynes taps on the door. Hollow door—no surprise, an old place like this.

No answer. Haynes raps louder. "Hello? Anybody home?"

"Who's there?"

"Portland Police detectives. We'd like to talk to you."

Hesitation. Then the man's again, "Just a minute."

Then the unmistakable, terrifying *clack!* of someone racking a serious weapon. The detectives reach for their nine-millimeters just as the real noise shatters the silence. Semiautomatic fire ripping holes in the door, ripping into a tree behind Max, knocking Joe Morales off the porch. Endless *da-da-da-da-da-da-da* as Haynes rolls off the porch and Max hotfoots out of range.

# # #

The thing goes off, touchy trigger, and somehow Nicky can't stop. Noise, smoke, the door torn apart. When it's suddenly over he drops the thing and stands there wondering what the hell just happened; knowing he's got to *go;* picking up his .38.

A voice outside, one of the pigs.

Go!

No shoes.

Pamela's in the bedroom.

Go!

Gone. Through the kitchen, slamming back the bolt on the door, bursting out. Suddenly out in the night, the old barn to the left and otherwise nothing but open spaces, a slice of silver moon. So quiet. His head whipping this way, that way. Which way?

GO!

Into the little woods down the slope? Mama. Imagines himself lying in dead leaves and whatever, holding his breath as police dogs close in.

Wheels. He needs wheels but his rig's in Beaner's garage, there's no way.

MOVE!

Sprinting down the slope to his right, toward the splintery light on the other side of the trees down there, light from the next house. Down the hill, stumbling on clots of coarse grass and pocks in the earth, twisting his ankle, cutting his bare feet.

Remembering a pond down here somewhere.

Mama, his ankle!

There! The pond, moonlight shining on it.

Gunfire ringing in his head.

Stumbling, staggering, righting himself, stumbling again. Around the pond. There's the house, the window with the light he saw from back there.

Shit!—stepping on a rock or something.

An old pickup there! Is he saved?

No goddamn keys in it! *Get keys!*

Back door of the house there. Stick the gun in somebody's face and get the keys and fly!

Looking through the glass in the door. Kitchen. Placemats on a round table, a plate with a few scraps. Slinging the door open *bang* against a wall, the glass in the upper half shattering and falling.

"Hey!" An old man in the doorway to the next room, pointing a shotgun at him.

saturday, june 9

Max is up all night, trying to turn chaos into some kind of order.

Chaos: Max and Haynes on their knees with Morales in front of the splintered door, trying to slow the bleeding. Pam Gramm screaming inside. Handcuffed to the bed, naked, is how Max found her after he called for help on his cell. Bortolotti gone.

Shots in the distance then, probably someone else hurt.

No. Later the old coot down the hill, Lloyd Fargas, said he heard shooting, what he thought was shooting, and grabbed his shotgun and waited in his living room. When someone smashed his back door he got up and saw a shirtless, barefoot wild man with a pistol; leveled the shotgun, fired, but somehow missed altogether, and the wild man took off. "I don't know, I kinda stumbled, lost my balance, didn't get a good shot." Bortolotti was long gone by the time the Major Crimes Team and the FBI arrived. The dogs tracked him down the path behind Fargas's house to a gully that led to a culvert that ran under the freeway toward the Super Eight Truck Stop, but the trail stopped at the freeway, meaning Bortolotti got a ride and could have been anywhere.

Pam Gramm was hysterical at first but pulled herself together, more resourceful than Max would have ever guessed. Sat with Max and Haynes for two hours downtown, recounting the last two days. Aside from the kidnapping and sex charges, Bortolotti looks good for the robbery at Roop's and probably for the shooting of Highwire Harris, based on his comment to Gramm about "what happened to that nigger basketball jock." And if he was the shooter there, he's probably good for the Ohlander murders.

Max and Haynes and the "up" detective team, Koontz and Berm, drove back out to the house at three in the morning to work the scene with Forensics.

Joe Morales was dead.

Back in his office at 5:30 A.M. Max finds the report from the search of Bortolotti's house last night, what Forensics found after he and Haynes and Morales left. It pretty much confirms that Bortolotti shot Highwire Harris, referring to part of Koontz's original report on the incident at Roop's house *(Roop stated that the shooter wore an oversized black sweatshirt over a blue denim jacket, which Roop identified by the jacket collar showing at the neck of the sweatshirt)* and saying the investigators found a blue denim jacket hanging in Bortolotti's closet with a small patch of blowback on the inside of the right-hand cuff, microscopic blood-spatter that Bortolotti never noticed. They'll get it to the lab to see if the blood was Highwire's or one of the Ohlanders', but it's at least clear that Bortolotti's right hand, at a time when he was wearing the jean jacket, was within a foot of someone spurting blood.

He shot all of them. Max knows.

And knows that *he*, Max, is responsible for the Ohlander murders on some level, and for what happened to Pam Gramm, if he's in any way responsible for Bortolotti staying on the loose after the incident at Roop's—if anything he told Dana went on to Nitzl, who was trying to shield Bortolotti to save his own ass. . . .

Of course it did.

He flashes on the note she left under his pillow . . . so long ago, it seems. *I will stay.* His elation that night, positive his life had changed forever.

Flashes on Merlene chiding him, and him, stars in his eyes, telling her she just didn't understand . . .

It's 5:48, getting light out, as he starts on affidavits for search warrants on Jack Nitzl. *Information received from Dana Marie Waverleigh* . . .

# # #

Nicky's lucky the old geezer couldn't shoot straight, didn't get him any worse than the nick on his wrist. Lucky, then, it was dark and the trucker from Hood River couldn't see how bad he musta looked, and stopped for him. Lucky, then, Tweety was home.

But he's still got big trouble. Gotta go somewhere. Can't stay with Tweety, the pigs'll be talking to everybody and their mother. Can't go home, of course.

Needs cash before he can do anything at all—get some product, get a motel, get outta Dodge.

Jack, the bastard, has cash, or can get some.

Jack, the bastard, probably gave him up. Except how did he know where he was at?

Shoulda put him to sleep a long time ago. And the chick. Donna? *Dana*, the one that told Jack her boyfriend had a safe and then showed up and saw them running out that night. Jack swore he never told her Nicky was his partner but that was just a lie so Nicky wouldn't take her out, Jack's little meat all these years—*sweet piece'a meat,* he used to say.

They're the only ones that know anything. Take 'em out and nobody can prove a thing. Pamela—all right, he snatched her, but he didn't do anything to her.

But what, he's gonna go to Jack's house? That's like Rico going to Joe Massera's place at the end, knowing he had to take out Joe and the blonde. The cops showed up too and that was it.

Is *this* it? The end? He sees Edward G. rolling around on the ground, full of bullets—*Mother of mercy! Is this the end of Rico?*

# # #

Jack, out on the lot with Vinnie a little past nine, knows he's got trouble when two Chevys pull in and Max Travis gets out of the shotgun side of the second one. Three guys with him, cops for sure, two from the first car plus the guy Travis came in with.

Jack heard about the shootout on the radio this morning, then turned on the tube for more. The guy who grabbed Pamela Gramm ("the suspect" was all they called him, but it had to be Nicky) killed a cop last night and got away; he was "still at large, armed and considered extremely dangerous." Jack knew it wasn't out of the realm of possibility the nutcase would come looking for him, wanting help or revenge, either one. He decided the lot was safer than home, not that being out in public would necessarily stop the nutcase from blowing him away. He put the .45 in his briefcase and came to work.

Expecting Nicky to show, maybe, but not Dana's lover boy.

But here's Travis, his hand out like they're buddies. "Nice seeing you again. You're Jack Nitzl, right?"

Jack ignores the jive. "Need some help?"

"You *are* Nitzl, of course. You probably don't remember me, all the business you do here, but we were out here talking Thursday afternoon when a guy showed up, a Mr. Roop, and you took off into your office and never came back. That ring a bell?"

"I remember you. What do you want?"

"We've got a warrant to search your residence and your vehicles."

"Why?"

"You mind?"

"I don't get it, is all."

"Someone's been talking about you. Probably nothing to it, right? . . . So we'll just have a look around, clear it up."

"Who's 'someone'?"

"You wanna come with us, let your salesman take over here? I'll explain."

# # #

"You mind me asking what this is about?"

Jack's standing in his living room with Travis while the detectives look around. He drove his own car over, so he doesn't know any more than Travis told him at the lot.

"Here's the warrant," Travis says, bringing the thing out of his inside jacket pocket. "We're authorized to search the premises and the vehicles listed here for anything pertaining to the robbery last month at this address here"—pointing it out on the first page, Roop's address on Southwest Flower—"or to the shooting of Terence Harris in the course of that robbery."

"Why me?"

"You were there, weren't you?"

"Like hell."

"No? Then you're fine, nothing to worry about."

"So how do you get a warrant to come here?"

"We put our information, which is that you *were* there, into an affidavit, which is a request for a search warrant, and we take it to a Multnomah County Circuit Court judge. If our request seems reasonable, we get a warrant."

"You know what I'm talking about. I mean what *is* your so-called information?"

"That I don't have to tell you. And if you're as squeaky clean as you say, you've got nothing to worry about anyway."

Smug bastard. "I'm clean, I just don't like—"

"Max?" The older detective reappearing from the garage, where he and his buddies went to look around. "You wanna come out here?"

"Sure. Jack, you wanna come?"

"Better believe it. You find anything, it's something you put there."

In the garage the other two cops have the ancient freezer open. Huh? The thing belonged to whoever lived here before, Jack barely uses it. There's elk meat Vinnie gave him last winter, frozen pizzas that probably aren't any good anymore, but nothing else except all that frosty shit that accumulates.

One of the cops sticks his hand in, pointing something out to Travis. "There." Jack steps over and looks.

There's something shiny, half-buried in the frosty stuff, in the back corner where the pizzas were.

# # #

"You have the right to remain silent, Mr. Nitzl. Anything you say from this point forward—"

"*What?*"

"—from this point forward can be used against you in—"

"I'm *under arrest?*"

Travis nods as the older guy goes on, "—in a court of law. You have the right to an attorney. If—"

"Based on *what?* What the hell *is* this? What the—?"

"Based on our information," Travis says, "and the ring."

"I never saw it before!"

"Jack, we got information you were involved in an incident—"

"Information from *who?*"

"—an incident at that Raleigh Hills address I pointed out on the warrant, on Saturday night, May twelfth, or early Sunday, May thirteenth. A robbery, and the shooting of Terence Harris in the course of that robbery, a former pro basketball player—and here we find a 1998 NBA championship ring, and we know Mr. Harris was a member of that championship team. You got an explanation?"

"Someone put it there. It wasn't me, I'm telling you. I don't know what you're talking about."

"Well, you'll have a chance to prove it. Now if you'll let Detective Berm read you your—"

"What the hell *is* this? Where'd you get this *information?*"

They ignore him. "Take him on downtown?" this Berm asks Travis.

"Downtown for *what?*"

"You can call an attorney if you want," Travis says. "Or we'll get you one. If you think you need one."

#

The older cop, at the wheel, follows the other Chevy downtown, Travis up front beside him. Jack in back, behind the metal screen, hands cuffed in front of him. He can't believe it's happening.

Nicky set him up, what else could it be? Took the ring off Harris at some point before he shot him, took the ring off Harris at some point before he shot him, then planted it in Jack's freezer sometime later: when they were at the house afterward, or the day he came over wanting more money, or any day Jack wasn't there—he could have gotten in the garage somehow.

But how about this big "information"? It didn't come from Nicky. Not from Dana, she's scared to death. But it had to be one of them, unless one of them told someone else and that person had to bargain with the cops over some shit of his own. Jack's got no idea.

# # #

In a tight, windowless interrogation room Jack tries once more. "I'm telling you I never saw that ring before."

The detective ignores him, this chump with a combover and a nose like a cauliflower. Turns to Travis: "Wanna tell our friend what we're looking at, Mr. DA?"

"Sure. I'm thinking we can ring him up on burglary, robbery, assault, attempted agg murder. . . . It's a start."

"Which puts him in the neighborhood of . . . ?"

"Well, let's figure . . . this, and this, and this . . . ba-da-bing, ba-da-boom, carry the one—I'd say twelve to eighteen, somewhere in there. At least."

"I didn't shoot the guy! I didn't steal any ring! I wasn't even there!"

They just look at him, the cocky bastards, sort of lean back and scope him out like he's getting in deeper every minute. Is he, somehow?

They just wait.

And damn it, he's ready to change course. No choice. Tell what he thought about telling as soon as he heard Pamela Gramm disappeared.

"All right."

"Yes?"

"I wasn't there, I didn't do a damn thing, but I know who did."

"You don't say." The detective. Thinks he's cute.

"A wacked-out meth freak named Nicky. Bortolotti. You want me to spell it?"

"Later," Travis says. "First tell us *how* you know whatever you claim to know."

Dicey here, but no choice. Good thing he's thought it over. "I know because I told him this Roop had a safe in his house. It sort of came up, we were having a few beers, I didn't mean anything by it—"

"How'd you know Roop had a safe?"

"I knew, all right? I heard."

"From who?"

But Jack will save that piece, thanks. "What's the difference? I heard it and then one night I had a few brews with Bortolotti and it came out. He got all excited and I figured it wasn't such a bad thing. I probably figured he was crazy enough to try something and he'd throw a little dough my way if he scored, I don't remember exactly. I just said it, just talking, and then I forgot about it. Figured he forgot it too, he was so far gone on that meth."

"And?"

But it hits Jack: *Stop. You're making it too easy. They're about to throw away the key on you.*

"And, Jack? Keep working with us here."

"I think I better call my lawyer."

"Oh? You need a lawyer all of a sudden?"

"Well, isn't it dumb of me to give all this away, if you're arresting me? All this stuff you want?"

# # #

Always comical, losers who think they're holding aces.

"The only way you *maybe* get out from under that twelve-to-eighteen we talked about," Max tells him, "is to keep talking. Help us out."

"Without any good faith from you? You think I'm stupid?"

Max lets that go. "I'm just saying the way this works, the only way it can work, is that you tell me what you know, *everything* you know, and I take it to my boss—Mr. Johns, the district attorney—and we decide, *he* decides, whether it's worth dealing for."

Nitzl doesn't respond. Still, amazingly, looking a little cocky.

So, lower the boom. Blindside him. "Otherwise, since we know you were there that night . . ."

"Listen, I told you—"

". . . since we know you were there with Bortolotti that night, wearing your witch mask . . ."

"*Huh?*"

Huh? Playing dumb, trying to, but too late. The giveaway was in the eyes when Max called him on the mask. The overdone *Huh?* was the sad attempt to cover and now, predictably, he's speechless, the wheels spinning frantically in his head.

". . . since you *were* there that night, Jack, you go down with Bortolotti same as if you did the shooting yourself. Doesn't matter who pulled the trigger."

He's still speechless.

Step on him. "So where we are is, you can tell me what you know, every bit, and I go talk to Mr. Johns and he probably tells me to send you home, have you come in Monday to give a formal statement and plead to the lesser charges, do maybe three-to-five . . . or we can have someone take you downstairs and find you a cell right now. I can't tell you who your roommate'll be . . . can you, Detective? Got any friendly folks down there?"

#

The hell with Lover Boy. "I'll give you what I know," Jack tells the cop, "and you get me out from under."

"It's not up to me. Mr. Travis just explained. You tell him, he takes it—"

"Forget it. I said I'll tell *you*. And I won't even tell you anything till he gets outta here."

#

"Not to confuse you boys," Jack says—Travis gone now and Haynes, the older detective, having joined Berm—"but there's more to all this. Who's the radio guy with the voice? Paul Harvey? 'The Rest of the Story'? Well, the rest of *this* story is Mr. Travis's little honey, little piece'a meat by the name of Dana Waverleigh. *My* girl for about the last twenty years. You might want to ask Mr. Big where she fits in."

"What're you talking about, Nitzl?"

"She's the one who knew Roop had this safe, since she was humping him till he dumped her and she started humping Travis. She told me about it, we talked about it. It'd be easy, she said. So, okay, Bortolotti and I went over there. And Harris happened to be there, black guy, and Bortolotti hates blacks and he's tripping and he goes nuts and shoots him. That's it."

"Well, well. And the money?"

"Fair shares. Dana got hers. A few days later she told me she'd gotten scared and told Travis everything, her new man, and he was gonna keep her out of it if she just shut up."

They stare at him. Big-nose Berm finally says, "I'm not buying it. Come on, Nitzl."

Haynes says, "What's going on, Jack? This comes out of left field."

"What's this, good cop/bad cop?"

"No," Berm snaps, "it's two detectives and a loser. You think this is gonna fly?"

"What, you don't wanna hear it? Travis is one of you so he's gotta be pure?"

"He's not exactly one of us, in the first—"

"You're on the same side. Listen, he was in it, like it or not, trying to save his girlfriend. Telling her things that she'd pass on to me. For instance, this woman and her kids that got killed in Dunthorpe? Let me take a wild guess: the bullets that killed them came out of the same gun that Highwire Harris got shot with."

They hear *that*, all right. Looking at each other . . .

"Now, how do you think I know that? Wasn't ever in the paper, was it?"

No answer.

"I know it because Travis was telling her everything and she was telling me. Because she and I couldn't afford to have Bortolotti get caught, and your boy didn't want to lose the best hump he ever had. Now, go suck on that a while."

# # #

When Berm comes out of the interview room after ten minutes, his face tells Max something is very, very wrong.

"So?"

"Hold on," Berm says, breezing past. "I'll be back."

Two minutes later he's back with Verdow—and they breeze past Max with barely a glance, back into the interview room.

Max waits. Fourteen minutes pass before they all come out, Verdow and the detectives and Nitzl. Haynes guides Nitzl toward the elevators. When they turn the corner Verdow says, "A little problem, Max."

"Like what?"

"I've got to take it to the commander."

"Tell me."

"I can't."

"You can't? What do you mean you can't? What'd the asshole say?"

"I'd better hold off."

# # #

Nicky sleeps, finally. After a, what, three-, four-day run? After being wired all night on the ice Tweety kindly provided, after Pamela Gramm and shooting at the cops and the old geezer shooting at *him* . . . Red zone, green zone . . . Sense, nonsense . . .

I gotta crash, Tweety. Gimme something.

It was some kind of downer. Nicky didn't know what, didn't care. Conked out on Tweety's bed with the sun pouring in the window, right in his eyes, but not fazing him a bit. . . .

# # #

Back in his office Max is fading. Up since yesterday morning, warrants and gunfire and naked Pam Gramm cuffed to a bed, Joe Morales bleeding to death . . . warrants, interviews and now this, whatever it is. He's waiting to find out.

Dozing off a few minutes later, head on the desk, when his phone rings. Mike Johns. Telling him to take a few days off.

"*What?* What's up?"

"You didn't hear me? Take some time off. Stay away."

"What's going on? What did that prick say?"

"Don't worry about it."

"Don't worry? Let's see: we're interviewing this prick, suddenly he wants to talk to 'em without me in the room and a few minutes later Verdow's telling me to shuffle off to Buffalo, wait to hear from you and now you tell me to stay away. What the hell did Nitzl say?"

"We'll check it out. You go home. Stay out of the office and away from this case."

"I'm off my own investigation?"

"We'll keep it warm in case things work out. The detectives'll bring McGowan up to speed."

"*In case* things work out? You've got some reason to think they won't?"

Johns stammers, the weasel: Uh, er, ah . . . Not really . . . Just gotta check things out . . . The press, you know, if they hear . . . after last year—

Incredible, the pencilneck bringing up last summer's farce, the outrage about the "out-of-control senior prosecutor" after the Randy Pink wiretap debacle led to then-DA Dan Tower demoting Max to Intake (otherwise known as Siberia) and eventually firing him. Pencilneck conveniently ignores the bottom line: that Max and Paige went on to crack a murder, prove Tower sabotaged Max's wiretap (bringing Tower down and making *Johns* the interim DA) and earn Max not only public apologies from the *Oregonian* and the rest but high, high praise. Which brought Johns to his knees, the wimp. *Come back, Max. I know you've never thought much of me but I need you, the office needs you.* Max so enjoyed making him squirm he stayed away for five months, until Paige convinced him this was where he needed to be.

"Cut the shit," Max snaps at him now. "Forget the press. What're we talking about? How do I wind up in the grease from anything this prick Nitzl said?"

"Conversation's over, Max. Just relax, let us handle it." Click. Leaving Max actually staring at the phone in his hand, incredulous.

The consummate weasel, Johns. *Interim* DA, and he'll do anything to make a run in the next election. Do anything, say anything, at the expense of anyone. Especially Max, whom he's resented forever—Max the golden boy, Max Faxx, all that. Max can still see the gleeful look on the pansy's face last summer when, as Tower's hatchet man, he delivered the news that Max was being demoted pending an investigation of the Pink wiretap.

That didn't work out to his liking, but he obviously thinks he's onto something here.

# # #

Not what Jack expected.

Hell, he didn't know what he expected—it all happened so fast, from the minute they showed up at the lot this morning—but he sure as hell never expected to be in this position. Having to prove something that can't be proved because it never happened. Having to get Dana to admit she started the whole thing, when she didn't.

This hard-looking guy, Norman, the first assistant DA, finally shows up after they leave Jack in the room by himself for an hour and a half. Saturday afternoon, gotta be his day off, but he's wearing a suit and tie, shiny shoes, chest all puffed out, filling the little room. Deep voice: "Nice to meet you, Mr. Nitzl."

He says he's got a deal for him.

Some deal. All right, it was crazy to think they'd guarantee him anything solely on his claim that Dana was the instigator and Travis protected her after things went haywire. But he thought it would get him some kind of promise, something. . . .

"You gotta show me something," Norman says, "or I'll charge

you with attempted agg murder, assault one, burg one, rob one. Your bail'll be about a million dollars, meaning you have to come up with a hundred grand to go home tonight instead of to jail. Now, you think you can show me something? You talked a big game to the detectives."

"I think I can," Jack says, although he doesn't think so at all.

"You think so. All right, I'll tell you what. Instead of a million dollars' bail, maybe we can negotiate. I'll charge you with theft by receiving, say you got Harris's ring from Bortolotti . . . Burglary . . . Probably get bail set at fifty thousand. You pay five and get out on recog. *Except.* You're not *out*. You've got company when you leave, a couple of detectives. And you're working for us, working *with* us, to prove that what you're saying about Miss Waverleigh and Mr. Travis is anything but garbage, anything but a desperate man trying to save his sorry butt. What do you think?"

"What're you talking about?"

"Well, you told the detectives your old flame, Miss Waverleigh, was behind the whole episode at Bill Roop's house. Right? And that *my* old friend, Mr. Travis, the most respected of prosecutors, has known the whole story since he started dating Miss Waverleigh a few days later, and that he knowingly obstructed justice for weeks—"

"Since he started fucking her. You would too."

"—that Travis risked his reputation, his career, everything for this woman he just met. Now, I find this part extremely hard to believe, which makes me wonder about the first part, about everything you say. But as I say, I'm willing to recommend easy bail, let you out in a very—hear me, now—in a *very* tightly monitored situation, in order to find out if any of this is true. Tightly monitored, meaning the detectives will be close enough to smell your BO, so forget about catching a bus to Mexico. What we do then, probably tomorrow, we put a wire on you and you go talk things over with

Miss Waverleigh. Prove to me she had anything to do with anything, much less that Travis did."

# # #

There aren't too many possibilities.

Not five o'clock yet, but as they say, it's five o'clock somewhere, and Max has poured himself some Makers Mark and an ice-water back and come out on the front porch to kick back and think it all through. And sitting in one of the rockers now, considering every possibility, he knows there aren't too many things Nitzl could have said to bring it to this.

That Max *intentionally* told Dana things, is all it can be. Not just stupidly but intentionally.

A slug of Makers Mark warms him up, warms up the sun over downtown in the distance, across the river. Rose Festival Saturday. They had the parade today, as always, even as thousands of people stayed home, subdued by the cold-blooded murder of a Portland police officer. The Fun Center in full swing right now, roller coasters and game booths and food . . . Max recalling the Saturday night years ago when he took his stepkids and their friends to the Fun Center—cotton candy, games, rides, kids laughing, thanking him; Georgia thanking him later, beaming at him . . . One of the high-lights.

What happened?

Here he is, big-time DA (twice divorced, thinning haired, achy kneed) slugging down ninety proof, reflecting on his disaster of a life.

Big-time DA in big trouble, possibly.

# # #

Max calls out of the blue after what, three months?—saying he might be in trouble, might need some help.

He knows she always responds to that. *Paige Prescott, true believer,* he used to say, *champion of the downtrodden and oppressed.*

He said more, of course, when those conversations turned into arguments. *Even if we have to expand the definition of "downtrodden" and "oppressed,"* he'd add, *to include murderers and rapists and all these others you represent, these sociopaths who recognize a bleeding-heart liberal a mile away and take advantage. . . .*

It never fazed her. She is what she is—a public defender and proud of it—and she always felt he respected her in the end. More than once he said she's the best defense attorney in town, PD or otherwise.

Not to mention the best girl, too, he'd say. *Woman.*

"I've got trouble," he's saying now. "Things were coming together—the robbery at Roop's, Highwire Harris getting shot, the Dunthorpe murders, the Pam Gramm kidnapping—all this coming together, and I was smack in the middle. Emphasis on *was,* because all of a sudden I'm out of it and in the grease."

"Out of it?"

"We talked to this prick Nitzl, one of our suspects for what happened at Roop's, and he suddenly says he won't say what he's got to say unless I leave the room. I leave, and next thing I know Johns is pleased to tell me there's a problem, I'm off the case, all these cases, get out, go home. . . . Shit."

"I don't understand."

"That makes two of us."

Max, Max, Max . . . It's always something.

Strange to hear his voice again. Max.

It was his trouble last summer that got them together—the wiretap debacle, his demotion and firing. It was his buddy Mason's trouble that kept them together the first time the road got bumpy. Until . . . what? She still doesn't quite understand. She complained a little after he went back to work and got so wrapped up again, she felt a little neglected, but . . .

"So," she says, "you're calling me why?"

"I said before: I might need help, and who better than you when a guy needs help?"

"That's all?"

"It's enough."

"But it's all?"

Suddenly he realizes what she's asking. "I guess so. I hadn't thought about . . . *You* dumped *me,* after all. Besides, at this point I'm thinking me and the women of the world are better off keeping our distance. This thing I got involved in, this woman I dated a little . . . don't even ask."

"Woman you dated a *little?* The hairstylist?"

"Don't even ask. Although you'll hear all about it if—"

"The one everyone says you're ga-ga about?"

"Yeah, that one. Rub it in, huh?"

# # #

He says he didn't call for anything but help. All right, he never cared for her zealous defense of dirtbags and she considered him *over*zealous in prosecuting some of them, but they came to terms last year (didn't they?) and, bottom line, she's the one defense attorney he completely trusts, and—"Hell, I don't know. I wanted to talk to you, that's all. Figured you'd hang up on me, but what the hell."

"Well, I didn't, did I?"

"You didn't."

Quiet. Her mind's eye flashing back to the Saturday on Mount

Hood last July, the beginning; holding hands in JC-2 during Tower's arraignment, triumphant; the September week in the San Juans; San Francisco; Tommy Mason hugging her in the street after they saved each other. . . .

"So?" she says.

"So, can we get together? Talk? I mean, will you advise me?" he adds quickly, as if to make sure she doesn't misinterpret.

"I've got a date in a little while," she says. Not ready to put herself out there, either.

"Date? Oh. All right"—his tone abruptly changing—"maybe I'll call some other time."

Did his tone change? Did their connection vanish that quickly? And as she pictures herself in another fancy restaurant with the illustrious Dr. Pond, another monologue about his globular-clusters research and his money and how he's the keynote speaker at every conference he's invited to, she hears herself saying "No, we can talk. I can come over."

# # #

Solid, she is.

He'd gone back to thinking of her as Miss Prescott after she dumped him, and even more so after he met Dana (the rare times he thought of her at all after his first taste of Dana). She was chilly, Dana was warm; she was reserved, Dana was out there; in bed she was almost prudish compared to Dana, who bucked and squealed and made you feel like the all-time stud.

But seeing her again . . . yeah, "solid" is the word. Sane, stable, where Dana's neurotic. Accomplished, hardworking, where Dana cuts hair (for a few months now, apparently) and would rather do nothing at all, according to her most recent husband. Intelligence is no contest. Even in bed . . . Paige was slow, sensuous, and finally satisfying in all ways, whereas Max thinks of the raucous sessions with Dana now and remembers something he read once: *Men fall hardest for frigid women—they put on the best show.*

She's real, whatever else she is, and Lord knows Dana's anything but.

Beautiful, she is: getting out of her car now, coming up the steps to the porch. People in the office always said she *would* be beautiful if only she weren't Paige Prescott, but that's crap. She's looked beautiful to Max ever since he cracked the shell last summer and got to the Prescott most people never saw.

"Hi."

"Hi."

"Aha," she says, spotting the glass of bourbon by his chair. "Is that why you called?"

"Nope. Haven't hardly touched it. Have a seat. You want something?"

Two minutes later he's got her set up with a glass of cabernet and she's sitting in the other rocker looking at him, waiting. "Well?"

And he tells her everything: the intersections and overlaps of the home invasion at Roop's, the Ohlander murders and the Pam Gramm kidnapping; Dana's involvement (taking a long slug of bourbon); today's revelations, as far as he knows. Paige is now a supervisor at Metro Public Defenders, not handling cases, so it won't come back to haunt him if he ever ends up in court with any of it.

"Until this afternoon," he says, "I was only concerned about sorting all this out so I could prosecute whoever's got it coming. Now I've got a feeling I'm going to have to defend myself. I said a few things I shouldn't have said to Miss Waverleigh." Can't even bring himself to say "Dana" anymore, not to Paige. "Had no idea I was dealing with the ex of—"

"*Sleeping* with."

"Thank you. All right, no idea I was sleeping with the ex of one of these dirtbags. Yesterday she told me was freaking out the whole time we were together, which tells me she was specifically trying to slicker information out of me, keep tabs—otherwise why keep seeing me, if she was freaked out all the time? All I can figure is Nitzl told 'em I was involved somehow, *knowingly* passing her details of the investigation, and Johns wants to drill me for official misconduct, something like that. Which is why I called the best defense attorney in town."

# # #

Nicky sleeps.

Wakes up, needs to pee, wanders out to Tweety's bathroom. Glimpses Tweety out front on his Hide-A-Bed, looking at a magazine, the *Starlight Parade* on TV. Tweety hears him, Nicky knows, but he doesn't look up.

Eyes himself in the bathroom mirror. Squinty eyed, puffy . . . Well, hey, he needs about another week of sleep.

Pees. A long, long stream.

More sleep. Get yourself together, then go find Jack. Get some money off him, make him take you to the chick, take 'em both out and then get outta Dodge.

# # #

Tomorrow, the cops told Jack. They'll put a wire on him and he gets together with Dana and gets her to say something that proves she was behind the rip-off at Roop's, *like you're claiming she was.*

How's he gonna do that? Call her tonight, tell her she can save them both if she backs up his story and gives them Travis? As if she'll go for that, admit she was involved from the start.

Besides, he's gonna call her? His phone's undoubtedly tapped.

There are two dicks sitting in a tan Chevy out front. Two more, no doubt, in the alley out back. No way out. He's tightly supervised, all right, like that hard-ass Norman said.

Maybe hand her a note when he goes over there tomorrow, when they're listening in but can't *see* what's happening?

But she's not about to admit to anything. For *him?* After all he's done for her? Fat chance.

# # #

"When you gotta be home?" Max asks. "When's your beau picking you up?"

"Seven-thirty."

"Getting close."

"Yes."

But Paige is pretty sure he doesn't want her to go, even though he's told her everything. She's not sure she wants to go.

Max. The superstar prosecutor, local legend (more than local, after the HBO movie last year about the Happy Face Killer case), ladies' man . . . but just Max, to her, big shot who stunned her last summer and through those months together by getting real, getting vulnerable. So that she dropped *her* guard with a man for the first time, and it felt so good.

So, Paige Prescott, you going to hurry home and dress up for Dr. Pond?

# # #

She had to wear her white capri pants, show him the curvaceous calves . . . hardbody. Works out at lunchtime every day, hard, alternating powerwalking and kickboxing and WOW, Women on Weights.

Not that the body is the best of Paige Prescott, far from it.

He'd assumed she was hoity-toity for so long, Bryn Mawr or something, and finally found out she was just a local girl, Wilson High, Oregon State. Attended OSU largely on scholarship money she won for community service during her last three years at Wilson, taking a bus into the 'hood every afternoon and teaching kids to read.

She went to work for the wrong side later, granted—defense, when the DA's office would have snapped her up—but at least stayed at Metro all these years, a public defender, serving people who really needed help when she could have gone private and made big bucks representing *wealthy* psychopaths and perverts.

She looks better today than ever. While Max looks, undoubtedly, like the village idiot.

# # #

"What're you smiling about?"

"Nothing," she lies.

But now Max is smiling, too. Sheepishly. "Ha ha," he says.

The cows. The afternoon last fall on Orcas Island: riding around the island on rented bikes, stopping at a seemingly deserted pasture and walking; stopping, kissing; Max, who'd joked about her being a little bit prim, asking, How 'bout it? Never expecting her to say Why not? and lie down in the high grass and start undressing. She pulled him on top of her and they went at it right there under the big sky until she noticed movement over his shoulder, two cows who'd materialized, chewing their cud, and Max opened his eyes and saw her gawking and looked back. . . . They laughed about it later. *Max! You jumped up like you thought they were going to* charge *or something! God, the sight of you standing there with this look on your face, with your thing sticking out! Grabbing your clothes, "Let's get outta here!"—oh, Lord!*

"Ha ha. Glad you're amused."

Paige believes he really is glad. She believes he's feeling a little like she feels.

# # #

She goes. It had gotten so pleasant he'd started thinking she might blow off her date, but he should have known she wouldn't stand someone up. She says they can talk tomorrow or whenever, she's willing to help if he needs help, but she's got to get home now.

sunday, june 10

Sadness, anger, embarrassment, all the things Max felt as he listened to Barris the other day, Dana's latest husband—it's all back, Sunday morning in Tabor Hill Café, as he listens to her first one.

Brian Maxwell, the one the girls spend half their time with, the guy Emily believes is her father as well as Elizabeth's. He called this morning saying he got Max's message Thursday but he's been busy. He agreed to meet for breakfast after Max said he's a DA and Dana's in some trouble and he, Max, might be, too, thanks to her.

Maxwell's a nice guy, like Barris—with plenty of lingering feelings, like Barris. The floodgates open and it's painful to see the faraway look, the hand-wringing. Which reminds Max how devastated he himself is, no matter how many times he's told himself she's shallow, duplicitous, callous. . . . Paige is forgotten. He's recalling Dana's sweet voice, the sight of her in her granny dress, the blow job the first night, the feel of her flesh, the rises and falls of her body in flickering candlelight . . . *I will stay.* . . .

The most adorable thing he'd ever seen, Maxwell says, when he met her: twenty years old, waitressing in the old Sandy Court Tavern and living in a studio apartment next door. He was a few years older, a promising architect battling bipolar illness. He'd be fine for a few months, then make the mistake most manics do: you think you're fine, you stop taking your Lithium and suddenly you're out of your mind without even knowing it, blowing five thousand dollars on a shopping spree, making calls to the governor, staying up for days on end. . . .

But he was doing okay when they met. Doing well in his career. Dana liked him. And she was irresistible to him, he'd have done anything for her.

Max would have done anything for her, this time last week.

He imagines her at twenty, before divorces and disappointments, bitterness and anger and cynicism. She seemed so sweet and innocent when *he* met her (even after she went down on him the first night), imagine her at twenty.

"She was perfect. Elizabeth came along, I was happy as I could be, but I couldn't hold it together. I'd stay on the meds, level out, be fine, but like I said, you start thinking you're fine, thinking you don't need the meds, and then you start spiraling—up, down, who knows. I was in and out of the hospital. And she was good, she dealt with it for a long time. A good person. But she finally wore out. She left and I couldn't blame her. I've never blamed her."

"For what it's worth," Max says, "she's got nothing but good things to say about you."

"Well, I've been nice to her and the girls. I've always been in love with her, what can I say? I've never stopped believing things could've been different, could still *be* different, because I finally got it through my head to stay on my meds and I've been fine for a long time. But for her it's been over for a long time."

The poor guy. Probably has no idea that that angel blows men on the first night these days, fucks them on front porches and in strangers' bathrooms and God knows where else, deceives boyfriends and even husbands with garbage like Jack Nitzl, lies, manipulates—

"I felt so bad for letting her down that I gave her more-than-generous support for Elizabeth when we split up. I was doing well and she didn't have any worthwhile job experience, so why not? Since then, which is quite a few years now, she's come and stayed with me a few times when things were rough. Separate bedrooms, of course, always. Three years ago, after her second marriage broke up, she and the girls stayed for eleven months. Emily too. I don't know if Dana said anything, but there's this situation, Emily thinking I'm her father."

"She said."

"They were living with me—Emily was three—and Elizabeth called me 'Daddy' and Em picked it up. Dana couldn't tell her I wasn't, didn't want to, and I probably had some crazy idea that she'd decide we should all be together for the girls' sake, something like that. Of course, there was no sign of that. She was frazzled after that marriage, which happened after a brief thing with a druggie who got her pregnant with Em."

Max thinking, *Men. Men. Men.* Recalling Dana's story of the druggie: the guy she saw years later, driving, and she was so shaken she had to pull off the road.

"She married the famous goatman instead. Which is what she and the girls ended up calling him—Goatman. Some guy she met after her parents moved out to the country, this nasty-looking older guy with a ratty ponytail, had a little place out toward Banks with a bunch of goats and chickens. Elizabeth told stories about this horrible little house with critters wandering in and out, Goatman trying to boil chickens he killed. He didn't believe in bathing, he hated the government, all this, like a high-school rebel who never grew up.

Turned out he hated the government because he'd done time for growing marijuana. . . . Just an awful situation. Can you picture Dana living in some shack, trying to live this life? Slogging around in the mud in big rubber boots doing chores? Holding a sheep while this leftover hippie with bugs in his hair sheared it? The guy mistreated her and scared the kids to death. Emily was four, five years old and she'd spill her milk and he'd get angry and hold her upside down by her ankles, threaten to drop her. I've got no idea what it was all about. Dana punishing herself or something, who knows? They moved in with me again when she finally couldn't take it anymore. Separate bedrooms, as always, but I still hoped it might change. Bright, huh? She eventually asked me for a loan to get her own place and go into the program at Beau Monde School of Hair Design, there behind the main library downtown. And I guess she got a job last year."

"At Hair on Burnside, Sixtieth and Burn. She's still there."

"Since they moved that time I only see her when we're picking up and dropping off the girls. She got married again, divorced again. . . . I know she'll never be interested in me. I don't know when we'll ever clear up the fatherhood issue with Emily."

Ouch. The poor guy's pinched look, haunted look—Max wondering how much is the illness and how much his history with Dana, the girl of his lifetime.

The girl of how many men's lifetimes?

He's crushed, himself. To have lost . . . not so much *her,* maybe, but what he wanted her to be. Nonsensical, but . . . to have lost the dream, at this late date. What's left of the dream. He pretty much gave it up a few years back, the vision of a household and a life with a creamy All-American Sally or Cathy or Mary and the kids they'd have together. Then Dana showed up, seemingly the dream come to life, and her beautiful girls. . . .

And now, on the car radio after he thanks Maxwell and says good-bye: . . . *On my own . . . once again. . . .*

# # #

Snap out of it. Rejoin the real world. Remember you've got real-world troubles, such as your career, and forget a neurotic, manipulative, lying slut, no matter how much she turned you on. What was it Merlene said—the intensity is a measure of how wrong two people are for each other?

Back home he grabs the portable, flops on the couch, and calls Paige. Picturing her in the neat little house on Northeast Twenty-seventh, remembering the night there last summer when she first called him Max and he called her Paige after years of chilly "Mr. Travis," "Miss Prescott." She picks up on the second ring.

"Just had breakfast with a guy named Brian Maxwell," Max says. "The first Mr. Dana. Still in love with her. Says he knows it's hopeless, although it's obvious he's still hoping. She probably still sleeps with him once in a while to keep him hoping, which keeps him generous with the child support. Even though Emily, the little one, isn't even his kid."

"I see." Like, *That's not too twisted, is it? What did you get yourself into, Max dear?*

Then again, no, he's probably just sensitive, embarrassed, remembering the beginning with Dana—the whole time, really, until the bottom fell out—when he told himself Paige Prescott could go suck an egg, he'd found someone infinitely better.

She's probably thinking *I'm his attorney now, strangely enough, if it turns out he needs one. We had something for a while and it's over but I'll gladly make sure those Nazis in the DA's office don't railroad him. He's a Nazi too, but not as bad as Johns and Norman and the rest.*

Probably thinking, too, *I'll bet he thinks I want him back, just because I agreed to help him out.* Probably waiting for him to say something that just begs her to kick his teeth in.

Stop. Don't get off on all this, not when you're in danger of getting busted down to traffic court or worse. You had to be a masochist to call her at all, tell her about falling for a flake who might be worse than flaky; no point in being stupid, too. Stick to business.

". . . So she's a loose woman," Paige is saying. "And you fell for her, letting your *thing* do your thinking. And, trying to forge a relationship, you shared a little about your work. Johns'll have a hard time getting an official-misconduct or hindering-prosecution charge out of that. You couldn't have known your girl knew the back side of your investigation."

"Do you have to call her my girl?"

"My apologies."

"It just . . . Forget it. Go ahead."

"I'm just saying Johns can't sink you for this."

"So there's just the fact that I'm responsible for what Bortolotti did to the Ohlanders and Pam Gramm and Joe Morales."

"No, Max."

"Not legally, maybe—"

"Not at all."

"—but morally, yeah. For saying anything that let Bortolotti stay out there. You know what I mean."

"I know what you mean but I know you can't take that on yourself. You didn't mean anything."

"No . . . I was trying to be some kind of new Max, some kind of trusting, sharing, New Age guy."

Nothing from her now, and Max thinks he can read the silence. *Poor boy. Poor messed-up superstar prosecutor. Smart guy in some ways, and not a bad guy, but constantly shooting yourself in the foot.*

"Crazy, huh? Me trying to pull that off."

"Max? You know what? You do have all that in you. I saw it."

"But dumped me anyway."

"I didn't, Max."

#

Two o'clock, Jack finally reaches Dana on her cell phone. "It's me. Where you been?"

"We went to church, the girls and I."

"Church?"

"It can't hurt," she says in a wee little voice. "Jack, I really don't want to talk."

"We've got to. Look, I can help you. You home?"

"No."

"When you gonna be?"

"I don't know."

"I'll meet you there, say, six. If you want outta this."

"Out of it?"

Now he's got her attention. "Six o'clock. We'll have a drink and I'll help you out."

"Jack?"

"Six." And he hangs up. She'll be there.

But then what? They'll have the wire on him, they'll hear everything.

Hand her a note? Saying what? *Your only chance is to give them Travis. I told them he's known everything since his first night with you and he promised to protect you. Give him up and you might have a chance. We both might.*

And she'll think what? That she and Jack can get off free and clear and live happily ever after? She's not that dumb.

What the hell was he thinking, giving the cops that story? They're probably snickering right now over that phone call, the bastards. Thinking, Show us.

#

"You're *hot,* man," Tweety says, all shook up as Nicky wanders into the front room. "They had your picture on TV, driver's-license picture or something. They're after you. You killed a *cop,* man!"

"Did I, now?"

"What're you gonna *do?*"

"Like what? I'm cool right here. You're not saying nothing, are you? Didn't already say something, did you? Not a buncha cops outside, is there?"

"No, I'm just . . . I just . . ."

"'Cause if you say something, that wouldn't be too smart, you know what I mean?"

"I wouldn't. . . ."

"I know you wouldn't. You're not that dumb. Where's the ice?"

Tweety shrugs. "You think you need that right now?"

"Get it. I gotta think."

Tweety's smart enough to go get it. Scared enough to just sit by, quiet, while Nicky fires up.

Good. Yessir. *Yeah.* Things coming into focus. . . .

Fucking Jack comes into focus. Shoulda wasted him and the chick a long time ago. Only ones that can put him at what's-his-name's house the night Highwire Harris got shot, and that shooting's all that connects somebody to the dyke and her kids at the other place. . . .

Except now he killed a cop!

You're hot, man. They're after you. Tweety's standing there looking at him, still thinking it.

Get outta Dodge.

With what? No funds. Tweety's sure as hell got nothing.

Jack. Still owes him plenty.

Well, get it. Then waste him like you should've already, find the chick and do her, catch a bus outta Dodge and you're good.

# # #

Except Jack's not at the lot. His wop assistant, eating Mickey D's like always, says *he's* in charge today, Jack's not coming in.

So, go to his house.

Your old buddy. Guy you thought was so smart, guy pulled the great scam where he rented a house and then rented it to a bunch of other people all at once like he owned it—Nicky recalling that Saturday afternoon at the Hideaway, Jack saying check out the TV, the story about the "flimflam man." Becoming buddies. Jack bringing Nicky in with him and Vlasitch on the cars. Perfect: the Russians doing their thing, Nicky doing his, Jack selling.

Perfect except that Jack was screwing him.

In Tweety's rattletrap van he cruises into Jack's block. Jack's Volvo's in the driveway, a couple other familiar rides in the street.

But what's this? A tan Chevy parked a little ways down, facing Jack's place, two guys in it. A pigmobile, could be.

Ride on by. Look straight ahead, act normal.

Mama, that crystal. Why'd he smoke? Red zone, green zone . . . *You're hot, man. . . . Killed a cop . . .* Jack so cool in the Hideaway that time, *Check out the TV,* the guy on TV talking about the flimflam man that suckered those assholes, Jack cleared fourteen grand. . . .

Shoot him right between the eyes. Get some money first, then put his ass away.

Then the chick. Don't be soft. Look where you're at now, from being soft. Remember when Rico got soft.

# # #

Dana asks if she can leave the girls for the afternoon, pick them up later, she's got some things to do. Amy gives her a look but says sure, she'll take the kids down to the last day of the Fun Center and bring them home afterward, order pizza, Dana can come get them whenever.

At home she bangs a screwdriver and lies down.

Maybe (pray!) it's going to be all right. Jack says there's a way.

Right. You believe Jack now? Trust him?

# # #

Not quite five yet . . . but it's five o'clock somewhere, as they say, and what the hell, it's special circumstances, he's on the verge of losing his job *again*. Johns will do everything he can to make it happen.

Out to the front porch with the Makers Mark again, ice-water back.

Big sky over the river and downtown, the Fun Center roller coaster in the distance. End of Rose Festival Week, last night of the Fun Center. He remembers the night with his stepkids and their friends years ago, another lifetime. . . . Never saw the kids again after the split.

Sun starting to drop, colors in the sky . . . Time passing, life getting away from him. A trail of busted marriages, relationships . . . Nothing constant but the work, and he can't even count on that anymore.

Makers Mark. Ah!—making a face as it goes down, like his dad used to. Chasing it with water, thinking of Paige . . .

Thinking of Dana. *I will stay.*
Like hell.
More booze.

# # #

At five-fifteen there's a knock on Jack's door, as promised. Koontz and Berm with two guys from Vice, as promised, here to wire him up.

"All set, Mr. Nitzl?"

"Set." Yeah, with no clue how to accomplish what he needs to accomplish.

"Take your shirt off, then?"

Go in, hand her the note and pray for a miracle. *The cops are listening in—don't say anything about this note!!!! All right: you don't know it yet but you're in trouble, just like I said you would be. They know I was there that night and they know it was all your idea. But you can save us by giving them Travis. Say you told him everything and he didn't want anything to happen to you, that's why he told you things to keep me and Nicky from getting caught. Talk to me now WHILE THEY'RE LISTENING like that's what happened. Do it or we're both done!*

"Turn around now," Berm says. "Raise your arms."

The box is black, the size of a cigarette pack. Koontz and Berm stand by while the Vice guys attach it to the small of Jack's back, running white adhesive tape over it and around his body a few times. They attach a long wire, twirl it around him twice and secure it just above his heart. Jack feels like a friggin' mummy. It'll be hell getting out of this tape, probably rip out half his chest hair, not that these assholes care.

They attach a microphone the size of a marble to the end of the wire. "There y'are, Mr. Nitzl."

"Now." Big-nose Berm stepping up again. "Our guys in the van will be listening and taping everything. You go ahead and prove what you told us yesterday. Right?"

"Right."

"And we'll get together afterward. Now, my partner and I'll be in our car at one end of the block while you're in there, another team'll be at the other—I mean, in case you don't get what you're after and decide to take off, something like that. But you wouldn't do that, right? And you're pretty sure you'll get what you're after, right?"

"Pretty sure." Uh-huh.

"Great. Now, you're not expecting anyone else to be there?"

"No."

"Don't expect any trouble from Miss Waverleigh?"

"No."

"Good. But let's have a code word anyway, in case anything should arise to put you or anyone else at risk. 'Panama,' 'bluebird,' 'martini,' whatever you think you could work in pretty quick if we need to intervene. You follow me?"

"I get it."

"Great. Let's settle on something, then we'll make sure this contraption's working and then send you on over there. Our chopper'll be straight over your head on the drive over, in case you've got ideas about taking off. Not that you would, since you know you're going to get what you need."

# # #

Max is probably crazy to come over here. It's over, there's nothing to be done, she is what she is and that's punishment enough, right? And there seems to be a possibility, at least, with Paige. . . . But a few slugs of bourbon on top of an nth-degree betrayal, nth-degree heartache, can do things to you, and here he is.

Her crummy little Honda out front. Why didn't she ever get Nitzl, the love of her life, to get her something better? (From *Executive Motors,* for God's sake, with the cheesy plastic pennants flapping in the breeze! Lots of executives buy there, sure!)

He knocks, not knowing what he'll say when he's facing her. Not that it matters.

The knob turns, the door opens, here she is. Startled. "Max. . . ?"

"Hi. Thought I'd drop by."

She doesn't know what to say.

"Well, can I come in? I won't stay long."

She reluctantly moves aside and he steps in. Past her, through the little entryway into the living room. Memories of candlelight, atmosphere, his radiant girl in a T-shirt barely covering her ass . . . All of it gone now. He turns back.

She's staring at him, confused, wishing she hadn't come to the door.

"So," he says.

"So? . . . M-Max? . . . Why're you here?"

"I don't know. Guess I felt like talking. You came to my office Friday when you felt like it. Can we sit down?"

"I came Friday because I wanted to help you and the police."

"You wanted to save your ass."

She just looks at him. Well, what can she say, after all? "Want a drink?" she says finally. "Would it help?"

"A drink, sure. A drink'll make everything peachy."

"Maybe it'll help." She turns into the kitchen.

He's sorry he came. Sorry he ever got involved with her, got blinded by the face, the luminous skin, the body, the blow job, the coo. Embarrassed he was too blind to get a sense of lowlife the first time he came over here. He remembers the first evening, how he was charmed by the "art" taped to the wall here—Emily's full-size drawing of the human body, arrows pointing to "head," "arm," "leg," "foot"—and ignored the battered old particle-board bookshelf with no real books in it, nothing but a few romance novels and some self-help and the cheap old falling-apart photo albums he looked at once and never wanted to see again, fading pictures of her with other guys.

Lowlife. As she mixes drinks in the kitchen he thinks of her refrigerator, always empty except for some bread and bologna and fruit juice, maybe pizzas in the freezer. Not many meals eaten here. *Pop in a pizza, girls, Mommy's going out.*

And that: her so-called parenting. *I've got a date, kids, you're on your own!* Great if you're her date (though Max remembers feeling guilty even then), depressing when you think about the girls. Especially depressing now, knowing she's ditched them countless times for the likes of Nitzl and Goatman and Druggie.

So much he ignored, he was so obsessed with her, so preoccupied with pulling her out of sight and getting a hand under her shirt or down her pants, imagining the next rocket ride.

"Here." She's back, holding out a drink. "Screwdriver."

They've drunk a few of these. Sitting on the love seat in candlelight, Max blissful in the knowledge true love had finally arrived, his rod getting as big as a Louisville Slugger. . . . This time he takes the threadbare armchair.

Sorry he came, suddenly. He didn't need to be reminded of the candlelight, the long T-shirts with nothing underneath, the touching and whispers leading to the mindbending sex, the stretchy legs wrapped around him, the oh-Max-oh-*God!* . . . the coo in his ear afterward, the gazing back and forth, the future they fantasized. . . .

How could she do it to him? "How *could* you?"

"How could I what?" she asks from her spot on the love seat, innocent as a newborn.

Max rolls his eyes. "How could you do it to me?"

"Do what?"

"All of it. You told me you're always honest, straight, no games. I can't believe . . . Man, you're something."

"Can't believe what?"

"That I . . . *fell*, I guess. For your *act*. You—"

"What're you talking about?"

"You were so . . . I was so gone on you. God, it's *embarrassing*."

"What is? That you were so gone on someone like me? A loser?"

"A liar. A deceiver. And it led to killings, kidnappings, a dead police officer. . . . But still, you can sit there so innocent saying 'What do you mean? Huh? Who, me?' It's sickening."

"Listen here, you—"

"I should've known. I couldn't have known you were capable of doing what you did, lying to me from day one, but—"

"I didn't lie to you! Lie about *what?*"

"—but I should've known you weren't what you seemed to be. Three marriages should've told me enough. It couldn't have been their fault every time—not unless you were making some horrible choices, which would also say something. But I've met Barris and Maxwell. They're not bad guys, just a couple of saps who got faked out. Goatman, now, *he* sounds like a mistake. . . ."

She's stunned.

"Yeah, I know a few things. Too late, but people've been filling me in."

"Oh?" Now she's pissed too, eyes bugging out—an expression he's never seen, which reminds him how little they ever got to know each other. "*Oh?* What're you saying, Max, dear?"

"What I said."

"You called me a slut, a liar . . . anything else?"

"Did I say slut?"

"Not the word, but you said it."

"You know better than me what you are."

"You . . . Where do you come off calling me names? So I've been married before—you've got some history too. What's the difference? You're the one that said the past doesn't matter. But now it does?"

"Forget that. What matters is that you had information that would've let the police nail your boyfriend Nitzl and this psycho Bortolotti before anything else happened. You lied to the detectives right at the start by withholding it and you lied to me all along, while Bortolotti's out killing people. Now, what we didn't clear up when you came to the office Friday is, how much information were you sending along to your friends? Everything I said when you'd ask me, oh so casual, how the investigation was going?"

"I—I don't"—stammering—"don't know what you're—"

"What made you think you could pull it off? That I was such a putz, so blind in love? Well, I've been blinded before, for all kinds of reasons, and then woken up and caught on to a thousand assholes who thought they were smarter than me and the cops and everyone else." Flashing on a few he's eviscerated on the stand, cocky lowlifes he figured out and then poleaxed when they least expected it, leaving them stammering in front of judge, jury, their own flabbergasted attorneys—

Brrrrrrrrrinnnnnnggg! Her doorbell.

# # #

Too good to be true, Nicky thinks: Jack leads him right to the chick's place. Two birds with one stone.

He'd been sitting in Tweety's van around the corner from Jack's wondering what to do—wondering if the guys in the Chevy were cops, or nobody—and then here came Jack in his Volvo. Nicky didn't know where he was going but wasn't about to let him get away.

And suddenly, following the Volvo around a curve on Seventy-second Avenue, he realized Jack was going to see his girl. He'd never pressed Jack for her address (soft!), but when he came around the curve and saw the rolling green grass a block ahead, he remembered Jack saying she lived near Rose City Golf Course. This had to be it, this apartment complex on the left.

He circled the block and got back in time to see Jack knocking on a ground-floor door.

# # #

She opens the door looking all stressed. "J-Jack . . ."

He looks past her and sees she's got company.

The fucking DA, Travis! Getting out of the armchair and coming this way. "Nitzl? Well, well. Come on in. I've got a bone to pick with you."

# # #

Nitzl doesn't know what to do. He sure didn't expect to find Max here.

Dana's confused too, coming unglued, looking frantically from one to the other.

Max finds himself smiling. "Is this a little awkward, folks? Come on in, Jack, and let's talk. 'Bout time we all come clean."

"Got nothing to talk to you about, man."

"Oh? You talk *about* me, is all?"

Dana's looking back and forth: *Will someone please tell me what's going on?*

"Your boyfriend," Max tells her, "did some talking about me yesterday, something that got me sent home. Something to put my career up for grabs, which tends to irk me."

"You know what," Nitzl says.

"I've got an idea. I'm not sure."

"Who you kidding, man? We all know the story."

"I don't. It's why I'm here, trying to clear things up. Come on, sit down, help us out."

"I give a rat's ass about helping you out."

"Come on, Jack."

A pause—then suddenly, inexplicably, a change of heart in Nitzl. "All right, you wanna talk? Let's talk. Make me a drink," he tells Dana, coming inside. She goes into the kitchen again, relieved to be out of it. Max follows Nitzl into the living room and takes the armchair again.

Nitzl stays on his feet. "You know what I'm talking about, man. What I told 'em: you knew everything and you were gonna protect Dana. But hey, we'll have a belt and talk about it all." Flashing him a fake smile, then turning toward the kitchen: "Babe? Where's that cocktail? You need help or something?"—

—Max up out of the chair and in the doorway in time to see him pressing something into her hand.

"Whatcha got there, folks?"

# # #

"Nah, can't be," Berm says, sitting with Koontz in the Chevy fifty yards down the street. "Bortolotti?" The guy who came walking up the sidewalk from the other direction just now and turned up the walk toward the apartment.

"Big guy, dark hair, looks like he's been through hell—sounds like him."

"Maybe. Call 'em"—Rubey and Wagner in the van, monitoring the wire—"see what's going on inside. Three's already a crowd in there, four's way too many."

#

Dana didn't know what was going on when Jack came in the kitchen ("Where's that cocktail?"), pulled something out of his pants pocket and stuck it in her hand. A slip of paper folded in quarters. She was looking at him, baffled, as Max appeared behind him, spotted the paper and broke into a smile. *Whatcha got there, folks?*

Whatever it is, Jack grabbed it back and crumpled it up, then changed his mind and started ripping it to pieces.

Max just smiled at him. "Privileged information?"

Brrrrrinnnnng!—the doorbell again, as Jack shoved the shredded paper in his mouth.

"That's a nice look, Jack," Max said, then glanced at Dana, saying, "Someone at your door."

#

She opens it warily—and suddenly it flies back and smacks her in the face, sends her reeling. She lets out a scream as a big guy with a crazed look barrels in. She knows who he is, his picture's been on TV all weekend.

"Hi, y'all!" He's in the kitchen with Jack and Max, whipping a gun from under his dirty T-shirt. "Y'all just be still, now, be *chill*. You, honey, get in here. Get *in* here!"—reaching back and grabbing her arm with his free hand, jerking her into the tiny kitchen with them. "Now, y'all know what they say, right? Happiness is a warm gun? You gimme any kinda reason, I'll warm this sucker up right quick."

#

"Get SERT, fast," Rubey tells Koontz from the van. The Special Emergency Reaction Team.

Koontz relays it to Berm: "SERT. It's *someone* with a gun even if it's not Bortolotti." As Berm grabs the radio Koontz asks Rubey, "What do *we* do, meantime?"

#

"I don't know who the hell you are," Nicky says, pointing the .38 at Travis, "but *you*"—turning it toward Jack—"are a dead man, and you"—Dana—"you're going with him. You shoulda had better sense, you two."

Jack remembers the line from that dumb movie, Edward G. Robinson telling someone he shoulda had better sense.

"This is the DA," Jack hears himself saying. As if it'll matter to a nutcase.

"Really? That supposed to impress me now?" Nicky points the gun at Travis again. "That right? You the DA?"

"I work there, yeah."

"You *did*. I'll cap you, too."

"Be smart, Nicky—"

"*Smart*? You're telling' me. . . ?"

Jack braces for a blast, reminded of Highwire Harris making the mistake of saying something.

"That's right," Travis says, with the .38 pointing right between his eyes. "Any more shooting, you double the trouble you've already got. Sure won't help your case."

# # #

"Won't *help?*" Bortolotti screams back. "My *case?* You think I got a *case?*"

"You can live if you want to, but you make it worse every time you kill."

"Make it *worse?* No fuckin' way I can make it—"

"Listen to me. You want a lethal injection, or you wanna live?"

"Don't pimp me, dude. I'm dead already."

"Probably not," Max says, still looking into the black hole of the gun. "I'm a DA, remember? This is liberal Multnomah County and we can't get a death penalty no matter what someone's done. But you're pushing the envelope."

"Hell. Envelope's *pushed.*" Bortolotti turns the gun toward Nitzl: "Right, Jack?" Nitzl flinches. Bortolotti points it at Dana, who flinches, whimpers.

Back to Max.

Maybe this is how it ends.

But no. "You," Bortolotti says. "Get lost."

# # #

Travis says, "Huh?"

"Get lost, I said. I got nothin' with you, don't even know you. I'm talkin' to these two."

Travis just stands there. Jack wonders what his problem is, the dumb ass.

Nicky can't believe it either. "No?"

"Be smart, Nicky."

How many times is he going to say it? He obviously doesn't know Nicky, to think he might do something smart.

Meanwhile, where's some help? Cops hearing all this, don't they have to they *do* something?

# # #

Koontz tells Berm, "SERT and the negotiators're on the way. Rubey's saying *we* can't do anything. It *is* Bortolotti in there and he's got a gun on 'em."

"What's Max doing?"

"Talking to him—Huh?"—Koontz suddenly getting something on the phone. "Yeah? Well, he probably thinks Bortolotti'll shoot him in the back if he leaves." Turning back to Berm: "Bortolotti told Max to walk out if he wants, it's the other two he's got issues with."

"And?"

"Max keeps trying to talk him down."

# # #

"So you're the hotty," he says, looking Dana up and down.

She couldn't respond if she wanted to. She's going to die. They all are. Right here, Sunday afternoon.

"M-Max . . ."

He ignores her, keeping his eyes on the guy.

"Hotty," Bortolotti says. "Now I see what they're talking about."

She's petrified. The look in his eyes! "Max . . ."

"Easy," Max says. "Everything's fine. Right, Nicky?"

"I said you can get the hell outta here, dude. You got nothing to do with this."

"I'm not going anywhere."

"What if I *say*, dude? Then you will, right?"

"I doubt it."

# # #

"You doubt it, huh?" A spooky grin on Bortolotti, showing some bad teeth.

"That's what I said. So let's work things out."

Might as well die here as anywhere. Hey, it's his fault this guy murdered three Ohlanders, did what he did to Pam Gramm and killed Joe Morales. See it through.

"Work it out, huh? Work it out *shit*. This here'll work things out," Bortolotti says, raising the gun again.

"Be cool, Nicky."

"Oh, I'm cool, dude. You cool?" Points the gun at Nitzl: "You cool, Jackpot?" At Dana: "You, honey?" Now back to Max with it. "Everybody cool, mister. Now, like I said, I got no problem with you, so you might as well roll. Us three'll stick here and talk."

Meaning he kills them, then eats a bullet himself. Maybe kills Nitzl, rapes Dana and *then* kills her, then offs himself.

"Listen, Nicky."

"Listen to what?"

"To me. Look, you don't want to hurt anyone."

"You don't think?"

"No. You don't want to and you don't have to. No one has to get hurt here. No one has to die, for sure." The hostage negotiator's mantra, the mission: *No one dies, not even the asshole.*

"Whatta you think I want, then?"

"Let's sit down and talk about it," Max says. "Right out here." Nodding him toward the living room.

No go. "I told you, dude, these two're who I'm talking to. My man Jackpot. The honey, here . . . Ever notice they always got a honey, these pansies? You seen *Little Caesar*? Rico's friend called the cops on him, Joe Massera—his honey *made* him, this bitch. 'Course Rico figures it out and finds 'em and the guy's wettin' his pants . . . just like *you*, Crackerjack"—turning and tapping Nitzl's forehead with the nose of the gun.

Max thinks he's losing it. "Easy, Nicky. Come on, let's go sit down."

But Bortolotti's snarling at Nitzl: "You bitch! *You* go sit your ass down!" and when Nitzl moves he looks at Max, at Dana, and says "Go sit your ass down, all'a you! I'm calling the shots here!"

# # #

Thank God for Max. Thank God he was here when they showed up, and that he didn't leave when he could have.

Still, she's not sure she'll make it five or six steps to the love seat. He might get shot in the back, in the back of the head . . .

A blast! Jack pitching forward!

She's frozen. But still standing, still alive.

For how long?

Jack on the floor, head up against the love seat, moaning. Bleeding.

# # #

Max holds his hands up, letting Bortolotti know there's no problem, you're the man, don't shoot anyone else. . . .

"Just don't move, dude," Bortolotti says.

"No one's moving. But we've got to do something. He'll die."

"Shit! Do it, then!"

Max kneels beside Nitzl. He's losing blood fast but he still has a pulse. "He needs help."

Dana shrieking at Bortolotti, "Why'd you *do* that?"

"Look, honey—"

Max standing, jumping in: "He needs *help,* Nicky. He's losing a lot of blood. We've got to call—"

"Call *nobody!* You do what *I* say!"

# # #

"He shot Nitzl," Koontz says in the car. "Rubey's pretty sure, anyway. A shot was fired, definitely, and Max is telling Bortolotti they gotta get some help in there. . . ."

"So? We going in?"

Two cars, hopefully SERT, come screeching around the corner at Tillamook as Berm asks the question.

# # #

Nitzl wheezing as Max pushes the bloody shirt up—

A box. They wired him.

". . . You're next, honey," Bortolotti's telling Dana. . . .

Show him. Tell him they're listening, they're right outside, he doesn't have a chance—otherwise he's about to start shooting.

"Nicky. Come here. Look."

"Look at what?"

"Look. He's wearing a wire."

Bortolotti, the cluck, doesn't get it immediately.

"It means the cops are outside, you can't get outta here, so forget that. We just gotta get him some help. He's losing blood, he's going into shock. . . ." Max glances up at Dana. "Get a blanket. We've gotta to keep him warm—"

"You stay right there!"

"He'll bleed to death, Nicky! You don't want a murder here, believe me!"

Bortolotti doesn't hear. He's staring at the gun in his hand like he's seeing it for the first time, like he's understanding what it can do. He turns it at himself for a moment—*Gonna do it?*—but merely turns it that way, nothing more, keeping clear of the trigger. Doesn't have the balls.

"Let her call," Max says. "Trust me, they've heard all this, it's not like she'll be giving anything away. For your own good, let's get this man some help."

"And then what?"

"What can I tell you? Maybe you get points for keeping someone alive. Now, you gonna let her call or aren't you?"

# # #

". . . Even better than what they made at Bodega Bay High School back in my time," Pam says, "which was about as good as shepherd's pie gets."

Her mother-in-law, Judy Gramm, smiles. "Nice to know I measure up to a school cafeteria."

"What can I say? Bodega's was amazing, or seemed so at the time. This is great, is all I'm saying, and I really appreciate the effort you made."

The Gramms, great people, have gone above and beyond the call since her ordeal. Not only taking her and Ken up into the big

West Linn house for as long as *he's* on the loose, Bortolotti, but waiting on her hand and foot.

"Just let me know what else you like," Judy says. "No trouble at all. I love to cook—"

Breaking off when they hear the phone. They've been following the news all weekend, taking all calls, eager for news. Ira gets up, Ken's dad, and hurries to the living room to pick up.

"Hello? . . . Yes . . . Yes . . . Yes, she's here. We're eating dinner, but let me put her on. I'm sure she wants to know." Ira coming this way, handing her the portable. "Carl Click."

Carl. Her fellow weekend anchor, her friend.

"Carl?"

"How you doing?"

"Eating shepherd's—"

"Thought I'd let you know Rudolph just called in"—one of K2's reporters—"saying he heard on the scanner that the cops have Bortolotti in an apartment out by Rose City Golf Course. Someone in there got shot, we don't know who yet. . . . Rudolph's on his way and we're sending the chopper, we'll probably be going live in a few minutes. Thought you'd be interested."

# # #

As Kay Henson sits in the living room at Fresh Start, chilling with Rita, Tad, and Lynnda, KINK interrupts "Mellow Music" with a bulletin that Portland police have located Nicholas Thomas Bortolotti, the man suspected of . . .

Nicky. The monster Kay *knows* killed June and her kids, put Highwire in a coma he might never come out of, and kidnapped and probably raped Pamela Gramm, and murdered the detective.

. . . Tune your television to our sister station, KGW Channel 8 for live coverage. . . .

She'd love to see the monster get what's coming to him, but there's no TV at Fresh Start. KINK goes back to "Mellow Music," the other girls back to their nails.

It's still scary, knowing she partied with a guy who's insane. How close did he come to killing *her*—shooting her, beating her, strangling her with her pantyhose? The night at Ringside she told him she was in love with a woman? The Saturday out at Oceanside when she wouldn't suck him on the beach, not even for a thousand dollars? The day after the murders, when she made the mistake of going to his sleazy hideout to do drugs?

How many others had thought about hurting her? Losers, druggies, crazies.

Thank God she's out of the life now. Nobody's "rump roast" anymore, "choice cut," "USDA prime;" nobody's laughingstock, nobody's potential victim.

On her way to California. *California.* Max Travis said he might need her to testify against Nicky in a year or so . . . but that's in a year or so, if it happens at all, and he said they'd fly her in and put her in a hotel and she'd never have to worry afterward because the monster would never be on the streets again.

And now, maybe they'll kill him. Please!

While the other girls do their nails she pages through *People,* waiting for another bulletin from KINK. She'll never worry about her nails again and she can't focus on the magazine, thinking about it all.

About Nicky. Fiendish, malignant, diabolic, *satanic* Nicky.

Sometimes it helps to know some words. But then, you don't need thesaurus words to describe this monster.

Rapist. Killer. Psycho.

Dead meat, if Kay Henson could get near him with a gun.

# # #

Blood keeps flowing out of Nitzl, soaking the tan carpet, and Max keeps telling Bortolotti his only chance is to end this thing right now, get some help in here.

"*Help?* They'll kill me, you know it, who you kidding?"

"Not if you're unarmed. They will if you're still holding that gun."

Bortolotti looking at the gun in his hand, a .38. His last, his only link to any kind of control.

Lots of control, he's thinking. "*You*, honey," he snaps, abruptly pointing the .38 at Dana on the love seat.

"Nicky! Why make it worse? You do any more shooting, I promise you they'll be in here—"

"Shut up! I'll take you out too, man!"

"Yeah? And they'll take you out. Is that what you want? We all die?"

Making it up as you go along.

"Your buddy's bleeding to death here, Nicky. We don't want that."

"*Whatever,* then! Fuck it!"

"Good." To Dana: "Gimme that phone." Back to Nicky: "You put the gun down, we get some help in here, you've got a chance—"

"No *way!* No one comes in!"

"Then how the hell—?"

"I said no one comes in!"

"Then . . . okay, I'll ask 'em to bring a gurney to the door, we bring it in and—"

"*You* bring it in! I don't go near that door! They'll take me out like a pigeon on a fence post!"

"All right, *I* bring it in, we try to get him on it. . . . But you realize you can kill someone who's in this kind of shape, trying to move him—"

"Tough titty! If he dies he dies, the bastard!"

"I'm calling, all right?" Max reaches for the phone.

# # #

"Please! No!" Bortolotti's got the gun up against the side of her head, she's going to die. "Max!" But he's on the phone, getting help for Jack.

"I *said*, honey, I wanna see those tits, see what the excitement's about."

"Please! Max!"

"Oh, he ain't gonna help"—Bortolotti turning the gun on Max two feet away, still on the phone.

Max looking right at it, but almost like he doesn't see it. "Bring it to the door," he's saying. "Yeah, sixteen-thirty-six. Tell me when and I'll bring it in and we'll try to get Nitzl up. Yeah, it'll be me. He's afraid you'll take him out."

"Ow!" Bortolotti jabbing the point of the gun against the side of her head. "Please!"

The noise will be the last thing she hears in her life. For a split second, before she's dead.

Liz . . . Em . . .

Max finishes his call, turns this way, and tells Bortolotti *"No,"* the gun away from her head. "You wanna start shooting, start shooting, but she's not undressing for you."

"I just wanna see what got y'all so hot. Honey, you just lift up that shirt a minute, I see y'ain't got any bra under—"

"Nicky."

Nicky stops.

"Forget about tits," Max says. "Don't make things worse. Let's all walk outta here."

#

Y'ain't never leaving, 'cept in a pine box. Rico said it to someone. . . .

"They ain't lettin' me walk outta here," Nicky tells him, " 'cept in a pine box."

#

Brrrrrinnnnnng! Max takes the call.

Berm says, "Gurney's at the door, Max. You coming out?"

"Whenever you say."

"Whenever you're ready. There's a nine, under the mattress at the pillow end. Take him out if you have to."

"Thanks. Talk at you later." He clicks off and tosses the phone on the love seat.

Bortolotti's got the gun in Dana's face again. She's sobbing.

"Nicky. Be cool. Five minutes, we can be outta here."

"Yeah? Then what?"

"Just be cool, huh? Let's just make sure we all walk out and we'll talk about the rest later. Let's get your pal on this gurney now. They'll look kindly on you for helping out."

#

Paige has no idea why he's there.

KGW, at the scene, says the police have indicated that Max Travis, senior deputy DA, is inside the northeast Portland apartment with *the gunman*, Nicholas Thomas Bortolotti.

Her apartment. After Paige told him to stay away from her.

KGW's got an aerial shot, another sad attempt to justify its ballyhooed helicopter. You can't see anything, just a short stretch of

Seventy-second Avenue: rooftops, parked cars, what looks like a van or an ambulance, a few antlike figures scurrying around.

The ground shots are better. Ambulance. SERT vans, SERT guys with weapons.

She told him to stay away from her! Stay away, settle things with Johns . . . He said no problem, he didn't want to have anything to do with her, couldn't believe he'd been so dumb. Yet he's in there.

And Paige is crying.

# # #

"Make it snappy," Bortolotti's saying as Max goes to the door. "No cute stuff. I'd just as soon waste you, you and the honey too, 'cause there's a thousand pigs out there and you know they ain't lettin' me walk outta here."

Max says nothing. Bortolotti's losing it; anything might send him off the deep end.

Max opens the door. The gurney's here, and a cast of thousands out there. Gardner, world-class hostage negotiator, in the street behind his car. Patrol cars, SERT vans, ambulance, TV trucks. SERT helmets showing over the tops of parked cars, behind the bushes out front, on the roof across the street. The barrels of their MP-5s.

All of them helpless.

"Get back in here!" Bortolotti. "Do what you're gonna do or I put you *down!*"

"Coming. Coming." Max grabs the sides of the gurney, pulls, bumps the wheels over the threshold . . .

"Shut that door!"

Max slams it and pulls the gurney into the living room. Bortolotti behind him. Dana on the love seat, paralyzed, staring at Nitzl on the floor.

#

Green zone . . . red . . .

No way out. Dude saying they'll look kindly on him—bullshit! "Like hell! Who you think you're talkin' to, man? They'll look kindly on me like *hell!* I oughtta"—sticking the gun in his face—"oughtta— and her too"—turning toward the chick.

"Nicky! Hey!" Dude saying "Help me out here. Let's get your buddy out. You don't want him to die."

"Buddy, shit. Oughtta finish him right now." Finish 'em all, then stick the iron in his mouth. "Finish us all, call it good."

"That's no answer, Nicky."

". . . Start right *here*"—back to the chick—"bitch too good to show me her tits. Listen, honey, you see this?" Her eyes wide as he points the .38. "You *see* it?"

#

Move. He's losing it.

"I'll do it myself, then," Max says.

"Go ahead! Now, honey, I'm not gonna keep talkin'. . . ."

As Bortolotti rants, Max steps around Nitzl to the gurney, get- ting himself between Bortolotti and the pillow end. Glances back, making sure Bortolotti's not paying attention, then slips his hand under the mattress, feeling for the nine-millimeter.

#

"—I said I wanna *see* something!"

He's screaming, pointing the gun right between her eyes, gonna kill her!—

—But suddenly Max, behind him, turns his way . . . with a gun! "Nicky," he says, and Bortolotti turns. . . .

# # #

Bortolotti turns and sees the nine and Max knows this is it, shoot or get shot—

—noise, *thunder,* Dana screaming and scrambling away, Bortolotti wheezing, stunned, the .38 falling *clunk* on the floor—Max thinking how lucky it was point-blank, a long time since Fort Bragg—

"Max!" Dana coming to him as Bortolotti clutches his chest—blood spreading over his T-shirt—and staggers, reels. "Max! Oh!"—grabbing at him, hyperventilating, as Bortolotti reels, reels, and finally drops.

monday, june 11

The Quandary—where else?—at the end of the day.

He was at the apartment till nine-thirty last night with the detectives and forensics team. At Central Precinct till midnight, going over and over things for the detectives, for the record.

Johns reached him late and said take tomorrow off, but even after being up till two Max barely slept and he got up at dawn, made espresso, watched himself on the early news (looking old), went out for a jog, took a long shower—and realized it was still only seven-fifteen. So, gonna sit home spanking off all day? He doesn't have a life, after all, and Johns conceded last night he's off the hook for official misconduct, everything—respectable again—so what the hell, he went in. Handled arraignments for Norman, made two scheduled court appearances, flirted with Kris Brewer in Unit B, allowed Kathy Wilson to sit in his office and flirt with him (as if he'll nominate her for the VCU on the strength of her tits), signed a stack of subpoenas, contemplated the stack of case files on his desk. A little of this, a little of that.

Dana called around three. *Max . . . Max . . . You have no idea how sorry I am. I was just scared, so scared. . . . I would never hurt you. You know that, don't you? . . . I wanted you so much, I wanted us so much. . . .*

I'm sure.

It's true! Please, don't sound like that!

Like what?

Can we talk, Max? I want to talk to you. Please?

Maybe sometime.

Thinking about the harm done. June Ohlander. Andrew Ohlander, five years old. Debra Ohlander, three. Pam Gramm. Joe Morales.

His fault.

He called Paige, finally, whose message had been waiting when he came in. *Hi.*

Hi. Wow. You're the hero.

Right.

You are.

Big hero. Shoot a psycho.

Before he killed someone else. And you could have left before.

Right, and leave two people with him. When I'm responsible for what he's already done.

Max? Give yourself a little *credit, huh?*

You didn't give yourself any for confronting VanKirkman—the episode last winter that put them in the headlines—*even though you knew he might splatter you all over that Starbucks.*

Whatever. We're talking about you.

And nothing here makes me a hero.

All right. I guess. It just makes you Max.

Whatever that means. Whatever it's worth.

Plenty.

You say. You didn't think so a couple months ago.

Max . . . Can we talk? Have a drink later?

I was planning on a drink later. Probably more than one.

The VQ?

So here they are, five-thirty, the Quandary packed with all the usual suspects (except Highwire); Max with a Max Blaster, Paige with her wine; Roop making the rounds as usual, coming this way, natty in white linen slacks and the same Hawaiian shirt he wore to Jack's lot. . . .

"You kids all right?"

"Good. Drinks on the house would be nice, but no, we're good. . . ."

"Drinks're on me, no sweat. You're the man again, it's the least I can do."

"I'm kidding. Hey, I'm still employed."

"No, drinks're covered. Anyway . . . you two're all right?"

"What do I know?" Max nods toward Paige. "She's the one. The Prescott."

Paige chuckles. "Right. Bleeding-heart public defender. 'Champion of the downtrodden and oppressed,' I believe I've been described—"

"Who kicked my teeth in not long ago, reminded me I've got no clue when it comes to women, relationships—"

"I'll leave you kids," Roop says, and slides away.

# # #

"So?" he says.

"So?"

"So . . . where are we?"

"*We?* I think the question is where are you and Miss Waverleigh? Sounds like she was all over you last night . . . her hero. . . ."

"Right. And you're all tied up with Dr. Pond, the superstar of human-genome research."

"Uh-huh. Very funny."

"You're not?"

" 'Tied up' is definitely a stretch."

"All right. And I'm done with Miss Waverleigh. Once you've seen the monster behind the mask, it's pretty hard to forget."

# # #

"So?" This time *she's* asking.

Max shrugs. "Don't ask a putz."

"You're not a putz."

"No?"

"I never thought you were. I never said anything like that."

"Maybe not exactly, but you said plenty. A couple of great speeches about how I need to wake up, all this. Remember?"

"Max . . ." She's smiling, shaking her head, looking at him like she did on his porch Saturday evening. "Max, Max. You're something, you know?"

"I'm sure, but I'm pretty sure I don't want to know what."

"That's not what I mean. I'm not here to tell you anything, make a speech. I'm not in any position to, am I?"

"Except you've always tended to. It's you."

"Maybe I'm coming around, at this late date. I'm not hopeless, you know."

"I never said anything like that."

Smiles.

"You were part of it," she says. "Of *me* waking up. Just by being yourself. Last summer, last fall, when I realized a senior prosecutor could also be all these good things, I had to admit that maybe, just maybe, I might be wrong about a few other things too. All right?"

"So you've found some other things you're wrong about?"

"Heh-heh. Even if I have, I don't know how much I'll admit to."

They josh, but Max is still back there on "all these good things" she'd seen in him. Well, she'd made it easy. She saved him, after all, when Tower tried to flush him down the toilet last summer. Looking at the peerless Prescott face now he sees her appearing through the trees at O'Leary's place on Mount Hood on that sunny Saturday afternoon last July, where he'd gone to feel sorry for himself, no way out of the jam. They'd talked about the jam a few times—he'd gotten into it by doing her a favor, after all—but he never expected to see her that day, on the mountain. But there she was, taking a deep breath and putting herself on the line. Suddenly a woman, suddenly Paige instead of the chilly, snippy Miss Prescott he'd known in court for seven or eight years, the bane of the DA's office, the one everyone said *would* be beautiful if only she weren't Paige Prescott. What a day that was, what a night.

She made it easy to be good.

Summer. Fall. Winter too, until she convinced him to go back to work after New Year's and then got mad when he found himself up to his ass in alligators: the Rockwood Nine, the Larch Mountain thrill killings, a police shooting to investigate. All right, Max Faxx reared his ugly head a little: he was distracted sometimes, he snapped at her once or twice, sometimes he couldn't see her at all for a few days. She wanted plain old Max Travis. He reminded her she'd encouraged him to go back to work, he told her he couldn't guarantee he'd be perfect. They dropped it, made up, and then it came up again. She decided some serious talk was in order. . . .

"Max? You there?"

"Right here. Spacing out a little."

"Thinking about it all? It'll get better. It's been awful but it's over now—"

"Not that."

"Ah."

He's pretty sure she knows.

"Can I tell you something, Max?"

"Tell."

"You know . . . what I meant when I said you're something is . . . as smart as you are, you really are clueless sometimes, aren't you?"

"You have to ask?"

"You didn't get it at all when we talked, when you thought I broke up with you."

"When I *thought* you did? Hold on, now. I'm clueless sometimes, but that was a pretty straightforward dump."

"No. You just didn't get it. We talked about some things that bothered us, both of us, and you got all . . ."

"Yes?"

"I don't know exactly. All I know is I wanted you to get a clue about some things—I didn't mean it had to be the end. But you grabbed that like *you* wanted it to be over."

"I? You're kidding, right?"

"All I said was maybe we needed to back off and think, both of us, and you got all overheated and slammed out and went home. I thought you'd probably call the next day and say 'Maybe you're right, let's back off and talk later,' or 'No, we don't need time, we've got something here, let's just work it out.' Even after a few days I thought, Okay, he's taking some time but he'll figure it out and call. I never thought it was *over*. Because I never said anything like 'It's over.'"

Suddenly she looks like she's going to cry.

"But all of a sudden I heard you were with some floozy hairstylist, some classy-looking airhead. . . ."

"You sent me on my way, I met someone else—I got suckered by a mask, what can I tell you? . . . *Wow*," he says, as it all sinks in.

"What? You're laughing. This is funny?"

"Sorry. I'm not laughing, it's just so bizarre. . . ."

Tears filling her eyes now. "I heard you were with this woman, whoever she was, this airhead—you, the great judge of character—I wondered what it ever meant that you liked me. . . ."

Roop suddenly materializing in full happy-hour mode: "Hey, you kids, how we doing? Another round, some chicken wings maybe? . . . *Oops,* as he realizes they're serious-business."

"Nothing right now," Max says—

—but it's barely out when Paige abruptly grabs her purse, scoots out of the booth and vanishes into the happy-hour crowd, working her way to the door.

Huh?

Roop's as startled as Max. "What'd you *do,* man?"

"Nothing! She was telling me . . . I'm not sure. I think she was trying to say she never broke up with me. Then, I don't know, something about our friend Dana, how *could* I. . . ?"

"Ah. Chick stuff. Comparing herself."

"That's crazy. She knows there's no comparison."

"No she doesn't. They never know. They're never sure, anyway. . . . And what's this, she didn't break up with you?"

"Do I even wanna know?"

"Probably not. She's a woman, and you're you, and we know what that means."

"Not a great combination, right?"

"Not always a great combination," Roop says. "Maybe leave 'em alone a while?"

# # #

Too much. All those nights when he sat at the bar while Roop put her down ("the great Prescott") and reminded him that men and women aren't meant to *stay* together anyway ("You had fun, now have fun with someone else"), all those nights he imagined Paige was happy to be free, looking at more promising options . . . she was waiting for him to get a clue and call?

So here he sits, after Roop continues on his rounds, staring at Paige's half-finished cabernet, at the rest of his Blaster. . . . Another night at the Quandary, all these years later, after yet another disaster.

Monday night, it so happens. Which was when *she* walked in, four weeks ago, and changed his life.

Changed his life! A floozy hairstylist, a classy-looking airhead! Interesting, Max.

Interesting that it wouldn't have happened at all if he hadn't misunderstood Paige (if he actually misunderstood). And three Ohlanders and would probably be alive today; Joe Morales; Pam Gramm would be fine. . . .

All very interesting.

. . . but none of it matters very much.

It's all very interesting, life is, but none of it really matters very much. He and Roop came up with it one night a few years back, boozy philosopher-kings. They still trot it out once in a while, same way Roop trots out *There's a lot to be said for being shallow* and *It's a sin not to sleep with every looker you can, in this brief life.*

Of course it's all bullshit. Who knows? Sometimes you realize the truth is just as likely to be the opposite, the converse, the inverse of whatever you think you know. Nothing matters? Ask the Ohlanders. Ask Joe Morales.

# # #

His phone. Caller ID says it's Dana, on her cell.

"Yeah?"

"Max?"

"Yeah."

"How are you?"

"Excellent."

"Are you . . . Where are you?"

"Having a drink. Figure I deserve one. Or two."

"At the VQ?"

"You bet."

"Can I see you?"

"Why?"

"I love you."

"Good one."

"You saved my life. And I love you. I was stupid, I know. . . . I was scared, I've told you. . . ."

"Not a problem. It's all over."

"I'm outside. I want to come talk to you."

"Outside?"

"On my way in. I thought you'd be here. I . . . Where are you?" Inside now, he can tell, the sounds of the bar crowd coming through.

There: phone to her ear, looking around.

Spotting him. Waving, coming this way, shutting her phone. Looking all . . . sorry? Grateful? Hopeful?

"Hi."

"Hi."

"Mind if I sit down?"

"Sit."

"Can we talk?"

"Talk."

"I just wanted to . . . Well, I said it a minute ago. You probably saved my—"

"Forget it. I'm no lifesaver. I happened to be there. It was—"

"I'll do anything, Max."

"Look—"

"I will. To make up. To be together."

No, no, no, no, no . . . Shaking his head.

"I can be good. I know we make each other feel good, and I can *be* good. I will be."

"I don't see it happening. Sorry."

"Why?"

"You're kidding, right? Do I really have to say?"

"I don't even get an answer?"

"You need one? You don't *get* it?"

"I just know I love you. I'll do anything."

"Look, you're responsible for murders, rapes, grief. . . . You're responsible for *me* being responsible, and that's plenty. I won't even talk about what you do to men. Barris, Maxwell . . . And you did a number on me, too."

"I didn't mean to."

"It doesn't even matter, as long as I don't give you a chance to do any more. Besides, there's the lawyer lady. Remember?"

It startles her. "Yes. . . ?"

"Yes."

"What do you mean? The one you said was so . . . so . . . whatever you said? Uptight? Wrapped up in work? Not a real person?"

"Did I say all that? Not a real person? I don't think I said that. Whatever she is, whatever she isn't, she's real."

"I'm real too."

"Right. That's priceless. You're good-looking, you're sexy, you're sort of pathetic—lots of things, but I'd hardly say *real*. Anything but, I'd say."

She opens her mouth but nothing happens. Max just looks at her, enjoying.

He's still looking when *she* grabs her purse and takes off.

Looking good as she stalks out, he's gotta say, the tight little bottom working overtime. She'll probably get two or three offers before she hits the door.

Poor guys.

# # #

Nothing matters? Maybe not when we're finally six feet under, but things sure as hell matter now. It's your life.

Paige is smart enough to know it.

He flips his cell open and punches in the familiar number, wondering if she'll answer when she sees his number on her caller ID.

Yes. "Yes?"

"It's me."

"I know."

"Where are you?"

"On the bridge. Almost home."

"Come back," he says. "Or I'll come over there, if it's okay."

"Why?"

"Let's have dinner or something."

"Why?"

"You know why. We were talking about it."

"We were talking about two or three months ago. We were talking about you and your airhead. I don't know *what* we were talking about."

"We were talking about now."

"Were we? Why would we?"

"You should know, you're a lot smarter than me."

"Than *I*."

"See?"

"You're flattering me," the Prescott says. "No one's made a movie about *me*."

"Not yet."

Nothing back, nothing but traffic sounds, but he sees her smiling, somewhere on the Morrison Bridge. . . .